NACHO BOYFRIEND

GIGI BLUME

FIRST EDITION

Library of Congress Cataloging-in-Publication Data has been applied for.

ISBN: 979-8-9861828-1-0

Editing by Adagio Scans

Cover design and illustrations by Once Upon a Cover

While I'm dedicating books to pets,
this one's for Orange.
We know you ate the snails…
and probably some of the other fish.

NACHO BOYFRIEND

My weaknesses
have always been
food and men
— in that order.

— Dolly Parton

Chapter One

OLIVE

Donut wall. They have a freaking donut wall.

It's a thing of beauty, really. Heaven splitting open for a choir-of-angels-in-concert kind of beauty.

When I get married, I'm definitely getting one of these. Oh, and they're those gourmet donuts from Sally's Doughnuttery. A magical place I've only dreamed of going, where nothing is under six dollars. Even the donut holes.

But I can't touch these delicacies because I'm not a guest at this fancy wedding. I'm working. If I had an apron, I might get away with *accidentally* dropping one in my pocket, but the stern and moderately curmudgeonly owner of this new catering company I'm working for is adamantly against aprons.

"This isn't a gas station," he'd said when I showed up today. "Lose the apron."

Okay, in what universe do people wear aprons at gas stations? Maybe in the 1950s when they'd do things like check your oil and wash your windshield.

I like my apron. It's a classy one from when I worked at that steakhouse in Jersey. It holds the essentials like my wine key, pens, a cloth napkin for wine service... and donuts. Beautiful round cakes with maple glaze and bacon crumbles, or orange with crème brûlée icing.

I cast a wistful glance at the donut wall, and beyond the Seraphim singing, "Alleluia Blueberrium Glazeoremus'.

I hear my name from far, far away. I'm only jolted back to earth by the red-hot touch of the devil himself. Okay, he's not really a devil. Just scowly and strict in a Gordon Ramsay kind of way. He's all frowns and salty looks. A force to be reckoned with.

I haven't caught his name yet, but in the few hours I've been working for him, I can see that nobody dares utter it—his trembling staff refer to him simply as Chef.

"Yes, Chef. Right away, Chef. Very good, Chef."

He sweeps from station to station, tasting sauces. A

formidable king lording over his lowly minions. It's kind of hot.

And just now, his fiery touch is really just a tap on the shoulder. But I feel it shoot straight to my toes. (probably because I've never had a boss this good looking before and it's throwing me off).

"It is... Olive. Right?"

"Yes. Olive. That's me." I tug at the fabric of my shirt above my breast where a name tag ought to be. But of course, there are no name tags in Hell's Kitchen. Or in this case, Hell's Bougie Country Club.

His eyes glide over my chest and quickly slice back to my face as I yank at my shirt.

"What are you doing?"

Oops. Might as well commit to my brand of awkward.

"Uh, airing out. It's soooo hot."

His lips press together, watching me put on a performance about the heat. I'm flapping my collar, fanning my face like a sinner in shul.

"Whoo. That's better." I dip my chin and blow on my boobs.

"I meant, what are you doing in *here*? Cocktail hour is outside."

Oh. What am I doing? Other than ogling the donut wall. And the boss.

"Presents," I blurt. I don't know why I blurt like I do. I just have an explosive way of talking, I guess. "A guest handed me a couple of presents."

The party is mainly outside, but this room in particular is where everybody is supposed to put the wedding gifts. The woman who shoved two wrapped boxes in my arms couldn't be bothered to do it herself, apparently. So sad for her, she'll never know about this enchanting room of donuts.

My boss, or *Chef* as I should probably call him, squeezes his brows together, forming two deep lines on his forehead. It's quite a becoming forehead, even with the lines.

"Are you done, now?" His voice is like wet sandpaper. Gravelly, yet smooth. And I take note of his attire. He's not dressed like a chef. He's in Armani. Black dress shirt. Charcoal gray tie with just a little bit of shimmer, which matches his slim-fitting slacks and jacket. Somewhere between the time that I arrived this morning and now, he'd changed his clothes. He looks very, very yummy.

Stop looking at Chef like he's part of the menu, Olive.

But I can't help it. I stare at him like it's the twenty-fifth hour of Yom Kippur and he's a bagel. I might even be drooling.

As a kid, and also before graduating from high school, I never knew what I wanted to be when I grew up. I envied those kids who knew exactly where their passions were leading them. But that wasn't me. I was on the undecided list. It's not that I didn't have interests. The problem was, I liked too many things. I'd try something, get bored, then move onto something else. There was a period of about six months where I fancied myself a romance novel cover photographer. I blame my mom's stash of Fabio-emblazoned paperbacks for that particular interest. During that time, I'd people watch. And when a scrumptious specimen of a man would cross my path, I'd picture him on the cover of a racy novel. Or one of those billionaire books. That's kind of how I'm looking at Chef right now. Appreciatively.

Like one would look at Michelangelo's David—if David wore an Armani suit.

Chef grunts like he can't *even* with me. I realize here I'm being completely unprofessional. It's my first day. I need to step up.

"Who hired you?" he questions, all edgy and irritable.

"Um, I submitted my resume to a temp agency."

"Temp agency?"

"Yes, and then I had a Zoom interview with Caleb."

Caleb is another chef. He seems to be second in command to the crabby chef standing before me now. Caleb is considerably less domineering but still incredibly focused and down-to-business.

Chef Crabby Cakes shoves his hands in his pockets and grumbles something imperceptible. Does that anger him somehow? I imagine him as the kind of guy who walks around growling at everything. The kind of guy with a storm cloud following in his wake. One of those lightning storms maybe—but he totally controls it. Like a Latino Thor.

I wouldn't want to get on his bad side.

I plaster on a sunshiny smile and perk up my chest with confidence I'm not really feeling. Fake it till you make it. That's how I got this far. That's how I'm still in Los Angeles.

"Welp," I say, all chipper, shuffling towards the door. "There's a tray of pizza bombs with my name on it."

He scowls at me with those dark gray eyes, sooty eyebrows lurched down so far, it's a wonder he can see anything at all.

"Pizza? Bombs?"

"Just kidding. I'll just go look for the tuna tartare cones or… caviar."

I offer a tiny wave, backing up as I scoot away. It's me belittling myself again. Tiny waves. Backing away from his imposing presence. I'm trying to work on that part of me. Old Olive gave tiny, mousy waves. New Olive makes grand, sweeping exits. Memorable. Jolly. I decide to go for it. Confidence is my middle name. It's how you make it in this town, so I hear.

I suck in a breath, roll back my shoulders, and lift my chin. I'm carefree, Olive, spreading joy to all the realms. With a glowing grin, I salute, spin fabulously, and march purposefully with a brisk stride… straight into the door frame with a *thwonk*. I don't feel any pain at first—the shock is too strong. Then the throbbing in my forehead. And immediately after that, the embarrassment sets in.

The same hand that had tapped me on the shoulder wraps around my arm. The other one branding my cheek as Chef examines my face.

"Are you all right?"

"I'm fine." I laugh it off.

This can not be happening.

"If you're feeling dizzy, take five," he says with just a touch of annoyance. "I can't have you serving like that."

If I tell him I'm dizzy, he'll make me go home. I can't afford not to work.

"I hurt my pride more than anything," I say, waving my hand.

His ashy eyes narrow, and he studies my features for several long moments. I feel so small and mousy in his overbearing presence, and I'm fairly certain I resemble the heart-eyes emoji. I shouldn't be fawning over any man that's not fictional after that disaster of a breakup I recently went through. It was not pretty. My ex-boyfriend made sure I was 'let go' from the marketing firm where we both worked, I found myself with no place to live, and now I'm broke. Which is why I need this job so badly.

"I'm seriously okay. See?" I raise one foot off the floor and balance like a flamingo, touching my fingertip on my nose.

"What are you doing?" he grumbles.

I switch the finger touching my nose from my right hand to my left. "Displaying my excellent balance," I say.

Judging by the enormous frown on his face, he is not impressed.

"Your excellent balance is no replacement for an accident report," he says stiffly. "I'll have one emailed to you by the end of your shift."

With that, he leaves the room, but before I return to my work, I decide I really will feel less dizzy if I take five.

And a donut.

I want someone
who will look at me
the same way
I look at chocolate cake.

– Unknown

Chapter Two

IGNACIO

The problem with owning your own catering business isn't family and friends wanting a dirt-cheap deal on their swanky wedding. No. Au contraire. (Although that does happen from time to time.) The problem lies solely in me and my inability to let a stranger prepare the meal on my brother's special day—not when I can do it better, healthier, and with more discretion.

I tried to stay out of it. I really did. But when I stumbled upon (spied, cough cough) Enrique and January's list of potential caterers, I almost had an aneurysm. One guy was charging four grand a head for (get a load of this) soup! And I heard through the grapevine he cheats with canned broth. Another so-called chef had so much grease on his menu, the paper it was printed on almost clogged my arteries—and not a single mention of vegetables. I couldn't let that happen. My sister's a vegetarian. What would *she* eat?

So here I am, overseeing the reception with my best crew on the job. I promised Enrique I wouldn't do any of the work on the wedding day. And I'm not. Mostly. The thing is, there are a couple of unfamiliar faces on staff. We had to hire some extra servers to account for those of us in the family not on the clock, so we can celebrate with Enrique and January. I made sure we ordered background checks for every single new hire—we don't need any psychopaths at my brother's wedding. A high-profile bride is stressed out enough.

January does look radiant. More than usual, I think. It's the whole wedding day thing, and the way she looks at my brother. Her face lights up like a Christmas tree when he smiles at her which reveals a hidden beauty not naturally present. Don't get me wrong, she's pretty, I guess. I'm not the one married to her, so it doesn't make a difference to me. But my taste in women is a little less blonde and a little less skinny. I like a woman with curves. Something to hold on to. Which is why my gaze keeps skating over the new girl on my staff. Olive.

I'd left the reception earlier, heading into a private room to practice my best man's speech, and that's when

I'd found her there. Eyeballing the donuts. Her face was flush and vibrant, eyes sparkling. Commenting about the heat. Drawing my attention to her hourglass figure. It is a hot day, and the room was pleasantly cool. Still. She needed to get back to our hungry guests. Now she's passing around a tray of appetizers, smiling brightly, although I know how uncomfortable she must be. I know, in part because of the way she blew air down her shirt earlier.

The servers wear black button-ups, but I don't expect them to have the collar closed up to their chins. I'm not a monster. Two buttons undone is modest enough. But that girl... well. Let's just hope the strain doesn't pop a random button into the mascarpone figs. Not that I'm looking or anything.

"You can stop obsessing over every detail now." Mateo, my obnoxious younger brother, shoves a cocktail in my hand. "Relax. The fondue fountain isn't going to blow up if you have some fun."

"I'm not obsessing."

"Oh really? What did Tío Enrique just say before he left us to attack the open bar?"

"I try to avoid anything Tío Enrique says. And did you instruct the bartender not to give him any booze?"

"Of course. And I wasn't listening to anything he said, either. Too many hot girls to watch."

I grunt. Mateo doesn't need any encouragement to pick up women at a wedding. He has a master's degree in the subject.

"Cool your jets and get Mom a bottle of water. I don't want her to dehydrate in this heat."

Mateo turns his head in time to see Mom cooling off her armpits with the ice cubes from Dad's vodka cranberry.

"Good call. Lord knows she'll need it after crying all day." He scoots away and I try to resist going over to check on the cook. It's only cocktail hour, but I'm worried he might not get the entrée right for the sit-down meal. It's a delicate timeline, maintaining temperature without over-cooking the filet. The servers are passing around trays of hors d'oeuvres—seared ahi, Tuscan truffles, coconut shrimp. I take one and pop it in my mouth. Quality check. Could use more orange marmalade sauce. I search through the crowd of wedding guests to flag another server but the only ones I see are at the other end of the garden. And that's when *she* catches my eye again. Olive. But this time it's not her large brown eyes that hold my attention, or the quirky smile she wears when she's offering canapés to a guest. The reason my gaze is fixed on her now, and why my jaw hits the floor, is because she's diving through the air towards Tía Lucy. And Tía Lucy is flying towards the cake.

Strange how something can feel like it's happening in slow motion and still, your body remains frozen. Like my brain is saying, "Don't move," to my feet. Most of the guests are drinking, having too good a time to notice, but those close enough to see the two ladies in flight give a collective gasp. One guy swoops out of the way rather than doing the gentlemanly thing, which would be to catch Tía Lucy before she makes contact with the cake. Not to mention Olive. Her arms are stretched out, hands flipping a full plate of food into Tía Lucy's ample bosom. Varied appe-tizers are airborne, cascading in all directions like a confused water sprinkler.

It's like an Avengers movie without the epic music.

Tía Lucy hits first. Her backside bumping into the cake table. Her shoulders barely tap against one of the layers. The cake might be saved. But less than a second later, Olive crashes into her, both women toppling back, completely annihilating the cake. Now everybody's watching. Tía Lucy looks like she's doing the backstroke in frosting, kicking her legs and flapping her arms. She's stuck, though. Olive is face down on top of her. They look like food wrestlers with globs of cake and icing in their hair and clothes.

I turn my attention briefly to the bride and groom. Enrique's jaw is on the ground, but January is laughing her head off. It's a five-thousand-dollar cake. We don't have a backup. Only donuts. Yet she's laughing so hard, the guests feel encouraged to join in.

By the time I make my way to help Tía Lucy get to her feet, somebody has already removed her from the scene. Her piercing wails can be heard as she's escorted to the ladies' room. Francesca runs after her to help.

I turn my attention to Olive, who's standing in stone silence, her head bowed like a schoolgirl in the headmaster's office. Bits of cake and frosting fall in clumps from her hair to the ground. Her blouse is smudged with tomato and mandarin sauce from the varied appetizers from Tía Lucy's plate. As I step into her circle of shame, her eyes slowly trace from my shoes, up my body, and land solemnly on my face. Her lashes wet with the champagne she'd knocked from Tía Lucy's hand, she regards me from beneath them, feeling every breath of my displeasure.

I cross my arms over my chest and incline my head to the side, and I wonder if she'd hit her head too hard on the doorframe earlier. Because what else can explain why she would feel compelled to leap through the air at a portly, elderly woman... into a wedding cake?

"Am I fired?" she squeaks, shrinking under my stare.

I nod slowly and deliberately. What other outcome could there possibly be?

"You'll still need to fill out that accident report," I say. I hate using the word fired.

She nods contritely and slumps her cake-stained shoulders. Turning away, she shuffles toward the staging area. "I'll just go get my things," she mumbles.

And now, not only do I feel rotten for my brother's ruined cake, but something in my heart tugs for this girl. I only hope she'll get home without another incident.

Not my problem. Not my problem. Not my—oh frickin' A.

"Wait!" I follow her into the staging area, out of sight from the guests. She's wiping her clothes with a kitchen rag.

"Sorry about the towel," she says. "I'll wash it and... return it somehow. I'm also sorry about the cake. And basically ruining the wedding."

"It's just a cake." Why am I even here with her? I should get back to the party. Do some damage control and see if we can replace the cake with something. But no. Dad always taught me to take care of my staff. Even the ones who no longer work for me. "You... shouldn't be driving. Take an Uber."

"No, no. I'm good."

"Are you sure?"

"Mmmm. I'm better than good." She swipes a finger

through the frosting on her temple and dips it into her mouth, sucking it clean with a smack of her lips. "Delicious."

I'm suddenly extremely uncomfortable and itchy in this suit. I need a glass of cold water.

"It's… dulce de leche," I say, my mouth as dry as sand. It's so dang hot.

"Welp. I guess I'll go now. You don't have to pay me for the hours I was here."

"I'll pay you," I snap a little too harshly.

She shrugs and gestures over her clothes. "I figure I'm wearing about fifty dollars' worth of cake."

Fifty dollars' worth of cake. I don't know what she thinks this job pays, but it's a lot more than fifty dollars.

She picks up her bag and that hideous apron she was wearing when she first arrived today. It's green. I'd say she'd be better off working as a barista in that thing, but I wouldn't trust her around hot liquids.

"Goodbye Mr. Chef, sir."

And with a salute from her dulce de leche brow, she walks away—backwards—until she's out of sight.

I really don't think
I need buns of steel.
I'd be happy with
buns of cinnamon.

— Ellen DeGeneres

Chapter Three

OLIVE

I've been in California less than a month and I'm already on my third job. Job one, the marketing firm which my ex decided I was unqualified for. Job two, the catering gig I wish I could blotch from my memory with one of those *Men in Black* flashing wand things. And job three, a server for a Mexican restaurant called Dos Panchos. I can't screw this up. And for the record, I'm not in the habit of getting fired so often, but this town seems to have it in for me. Even so, I'm determined to make this work.

The head server who hired me is amazing, and I can already tell we'll get along swimmingly. I'm all about happy joy-joy vibes. Just smile and be a good listener. That's my motto. Rosa, the aforementioned head server, told me all about the girl I was replacing part time. Bernadette is her name. I'll be taking three of her shifts, and that got Rosa a little emotional. So I listened while she waxed poetic about the many years they'd worked together. Now Bernadette is going back to school. I admire that.

I'd totally go back to school if I could focus on one thing. But I have shiny-object syndrome. So many professions seem like fun. How could I possibly choose?

Anyway, I'm supposed to shadow Bernadette when she gets here for her lunch shift. Until then, Rosa's showing me the ropes—getting me set up on the POS system, providing me with a branded polo shirt and Dos Panchos Mexican Restaurant embroidered apron. They're both black with colorful embellishments stitched in. With big, bouncy girls like mine, I'm grateful for the slimming color.

Once Rosa is satisfied with how I'm catching on to the front of the house operations, she takes me into the back to meet the kitchen staff. Most of them smile politely. The dishwasher is a sweet, chubby man, but the cook kind of grunts at me. I'm sure he's just super busy and focused on his work.

"*Donde esta el jefe?*" Rosa asks one of the guys chopping veggies. I don't speak Spanish, but I'm willing to bet she's looking for the owner, who she promised to introduce me to before we came back here. The man inclines his chin and responds with another Spanish phrase I can only assume means, "Over there."

I follow her over to a door which has a very official sign on it that reads, *Nacho Office, Go Away*. Then there are notes taped randomly below it saying things like, *Do not make eye contact with the gorilla, Reserved parking for the Big Cheese*, and a print-out of Marlon Brando on The Godfather movie poster—but instead it says *El Patron*.

Rosa knocks, ignoring the warning signs. I'm guessing they're all jokes, which just makes me want to meet the boss even more. He must be super fun to work for. I gathered this mostly from my interview when Rosa told me how low their turnover rate is. She's been working here at Dos Panchos for twenty-five years, and Bernadette since she was fifteen.

The occupier of the office (el jefe, el patron, the big cheese), answers Rosa's knock with an indistinct grunt.

I think he says, "Yeah," or "Ewah," or maybe "Pizza." But that seems to be invitation enough for Rosa to crack the door open. She says something to him in Spanish mixed with the errant English words like, "New girl," and "First day."

Am I just a tiny bit nervous? Maybe. But I got the job despite omitting the Wedding of Doom from my resume. The wedding which shall not be named. Except... as Rosa invites me to go inside the office, closing the door behind us, my face gets hot. Then my blood runs cold. I'm hot, I'm cold. I'm cold. I'm hot. At the tender age of twenty-seven, I'm a walking menopause commercial. Because, true to my bad Los Angeles luck, who is sitting behind the boss's desk? Who is this man they call El Jefe, El Patron, the Big Cheese?

The hot chef from Wedd-aggeddon, that's who.

Chef Crabby Cakes.

For one suspended moment, I hope he won't recognize me. That perhaps, I happen to look soooo different in this setting and he'll smile with a welcoming handshake. But the moment his magnificent eyebrows lurch down and his plump lips press into a hard line, my hopes are dashed. Not only does he remember me, he is less than pleased to see me.

"You," he says, all stern and boss-like. He's dressed casually now. Gone is the fancy suit and tie. Gone is the slick hair, combed to perfection. Now the statuesque, airbrushed, GQ model is replaced by a guy in a Dos Panchos polo shirt much like the one I'm wearing, sporting a day-old stubble, and a lazy arm draped over the back of his chair. His dark, wavy locks fall over his forehead as if his styling regime this morning consisted of running his hands through wet hair and letting it dry all higgledy-piggledy. As scrumptious as he looked at the wedding, it's almost unfair how he can pull this look off—the same brand of polo shirt that makes me look like a soft and squishy Build-a-Bear, fits him like a glove, stretching over broad shoulders and hard pecs.

I'm totally getting fired again whilst drooling over the bossman.

I'm just gaping at Chef, jaw slack, eyes round and probably bulging. I should be using my sharp wit to come up with one hundred and one reasons not to fire Olive Isaac, but all I can come up with is, "Yes, me."

Rose points her finger between us. "You know each other?"

I start to laugh nervously as one does when they're about to get canned by the same man twice in one week.

"Well, this is awkward," I say, already untying my apron. In my head, I'm calculating my prorated wages for the fraction of an hour I've worked and wondering if they have to legally pay me at all. Hey, even a couple of bucks will buy a measly lunch. Maybe they'll pay me in tacos.

Like a fool, I blurt, "I like tacos."

Rosa squints at me because she's a sane person who needs actual context in a conversation. "That's... good," she says carefully.

Chef leans forward over his desk, studying me. His eyes remain on my face when he grumbles, "Rosa, will you give us a moment?"

Rosa gives me a stilted smile as she scoots out, keeping the door open. I look out to see half the kitchen staff staring.

Chef is the picture of all that is grumpy and surly. He's all elegance and power while I'm shifting my weight from foot to foot, twisting my apron in my fingers.

I realize this is an opportunity to explain my behavior at the wedding—not that there's any excuse for tackling a woman into a cake. I might have been a tad too enthusiastic at the time.

"There was a bug," I blurt before he can fire me again. At the very least, I could walk out of here with some dignity.

His hard, cool expression morphs into something decidedly less stern. His eyes shift—growing wider and darker.

"What do you mean… a bug? How do you know this?"

His question is clipped with a trace of urgency. I'm pleased to see a restaurant owner so concerned with health regulations. Although the bug at the wedding wasn't a restaurant problem. It was a venue problem. I should assure him it wasn't roaches.

I take a breath, shoulders back, chin up.

"Well…"

"Wait. Don't say anything yet."

He flies from behind his desk to shut the office door, then darts around the office, running his fingers under the desk lamp and stacks of paper.

"Is there a bug in here?" he whispers.

Yikes. Maybe they do have a roach problem.

My eyes scan the room. No signs of insect activity that I can see.

"Not here," I say assuringly. "It was at the wedding."

"The wedding?" Now he's properly alarmed.

"No roach, though," I rush to add.

Chef steps closer to me, crowding my space. He looms over me with his intoxicating presence.

He sparkles with magnetic energy as he says, "Who are you? What are you doing here?"

Is this some sort of test? Maybe he thinks I'm an under-cover health inspector.

"I… I'm Olive Isaac. And I'm here to serve Mexican food to hungry customers."

He steps closer, crossing his impressive arms over his

chest. The polo shirt cuts off right at his biceps, directly at my eye level.

"Try again," he says. "Who *are* you? FBI? Or did Churro send you?"

"I'm Olive Isaac. From New Jersey."

He snorts. "What kind of fake name is Olive Isaac? What do you know about Francisco Ortega?"

He's practically on top of me now. I can feel the warmth of his breath on my neck. A single strand of hair falls over his eye—but he doesn't sweep it into place. He just stares past it with a menacing glare—like a hunky pirate. He's frighteningly beautiful, and despite how odd this feels, what with talk of the FBI and whoever this Churro fellow is, my instinct to run for the hills has escaped me. I root my feet in place—and the sensation of my body gravitating toward this man instead of away from him is breaking all sorts of physics laws and feminist ideals.

Do I *really* need this job that badly?

Then reality sets in. I do. I really, really do. Sure, I could crawl back to New Jersey with my tail between my legs, proving to my dad this move was a mistake. I could let myself wallow in self-pity while my ex-boyfriend lives the dream. New job, new woman, new life. Olive, who supported him, dropped everything for him, and schlepped my things across the country for him, is nothing but an inconvenient memory. I can't let him win.

I gulp audibly and channel my best inner Lady Gaga.

"I'm not from the Health Department, if that's your concern. I only want to explain what happened at the wedding. That's all."

"Listen, if you have information, you need to tell me."

"It wasn't anyone's fault. Bugs land on food. That's the risk you take at an outdoor venue."

"Listen, like I told Churro's guys—" He stops mid-sentence and studies me more closely. "Wait. What do you mean by *'bugs land on food'*?"

"Bugs land on food. I wanted to tell you at the wedding, but I didn't think it would have made a difference. And I promise I wouldn't have applied for a job here if I'd known you're the owner. I mean, what are the odds? It must be serendipity. I have to admit, I lost a little bit of sleep over it, and I felt really bad. Wow. It's so weird, though. Is the catering a side gig, or…?"

"Will you get on with it, please?"

"Right. Well, that woman. You know." I gesture a falling back motion.

"My aunt. Lucy."

"Aunt Lucy. Got it. Anyway, she was about to take a bite, but a bug landed on her food. It was hitching a ride into her mouth like a grimy little hitchhiker. So I panicked."

I shrug. He knows the rest. He saw me diving for his aunt and the cake disaster that followed. And then the look on his face as he towered over me, blocking the sun, so the intense frown he wore was all shrouded in shadow. It wasn't my finest moment.

His eye twitches and I can't tell if he believes me or not.

"So… when you say bug… you mean… insect?"

"Well, yeah. What other kind of bug is there?"

Other than the way my ex used to say I bugged him all the time while he was trying to concentrate—distracting him from his 'genius'. Whatever.

"It's actually kind of funny," I add, hoping he actually

does believe me. And let's face it—the whole story is wild and a little bonkers. And if I'm being honest, I probably could have handled it better. Maybe by tapping her on the shoulder or something.

Boss man is just standing in front of me with those inky eyebrows so low over his eyes, they're practically covering his entire face.

"There was a bug," he says with a thousand degrees of displeasure. "An insect. In her food."

"Crazy, right?" I force a laugh. So far he hasn't brought up my ninja moves—AKA tackling a geriatric aunt.

"Was it a fly or...?"

"I really couldn't say." The more I think about it, the more outrageous it seems. Chef grumbles something under his breath, then goes back behind his desk, sinking into his chair. He seems so distraught. With a tremendous sigh, he presses his elbows on the desk and lets his forehead fall onto his steepled fingers.

"Are you all right, sir?" Surely, my insect story couldn't be the source of his apparent distress.

"Yes," he replies curtly.

He doesn't fool me, but I won't push it. If I knew him better, I'd get him to sing something happy with me. Maybe 'Let the Sun Shine In' or 'Tomorrow' from *Annie*. Singing a happy song always helps me when I'm feeling blue. Or whistling. Whistling is good, too.

As if by their own volition, my lips pucker and I blow a faint tune. I don't even realize I'm doing it until he says, "What are you doing?"

He seems to ask me that a lot. At least I'm not devising ways to sneak a donut this time. I smack my palm over my mouth. I am not doing anything at all. Nope.

"Uh… I just wanted to explain what happened at the wedding before you fire me again. So, now that you know…" I plop my apron on his desk. "Here. The shirt is probably sweaty by now, but I can bring it back after I wash it—along with the towel I took from the wedding."

"I'm not going to fire you," he says laconically.

My tummy flip flops, but I'm not sure if it's from the relief or hunger.

"Are you sure? You don't have to pay me for…" I check my Fit Bit. "The hour and fifteen minutes I've been here. Or you can pay me in tacos if you want."

"Do you *want* me to pay you in tacos?" he bites.

I shrug. "I mean… I'm not picky."

He lifts his eyes to look at me. *Really* look at me for the first time. Something sparks behind his eyes.

"I'll tell you what. Keep the shirt and the apron—and the towel. Go out there and finish your shift. Then come back tomorrow and do the same thing. And if you don't ruin any more cakes, you can come back the day after that. And I'll pay you legally with taxes taken out and every-thing. Sound good?"

"Yes. Yes, thank you."

I scoop up my apron and cling to it like it's a lifeline.

"Now go," he growls. He's so commanding, it makes my skin tingle. So stern and… crabby.

I crack open the door, but before I can get out of here, he says, "Oh and Olive?"

"Yes Chef?"

"Tacos are free during your workday."

Free tacos! Oh my goodness. That's the best thing I've heard all day. Well, except that I'm not fired.

"Thank you, Chef. Uh, do you want the door closed?"

He nods, dismissing me with a wave of his hand, getting back to his work. And before I shut the door, his sooty eyes slice to meet mine and I have a sudden craving for crab cakes.

Ice cream
is exquisite.
What a pity
it isn't illegal.

— *Voltaire*

Chapter Four

IGNACIO

"Dude. She's a real chick-magnet."

"Shut up," I say, practically growling at my brother, Nate.

We're in Laguna Beach, where he has his insurance office next to the downtown art galleries, pubs, and boutiques. We're strolling the boardwalk on Main Beach and the chick-magnet he's referring to is my sister-in-law's dog—a ridiculously tiny Yorkshire terrier named Brownie.

January's assistant, Cher, dropped Brownie off at my house this morning after dog-sitting all week while my brother Enrique and his wife are on their honeymoon. Now it's my turn for dog duty, I guess. Something about Cher's contractual days off. It's all good, except for the explosion of pink all over this poor animal. Today it's a pink tartan dress with a matching pink bow perched on her head. A baby pink collar with a matching pink leash complete the ensemble. Along with the dog, special food, toys, and treats, Cher dropped off a whole Louis Vuitton suitcase stuffed with Brownie's frilly clothes.

"I dunno if it's *chicks* we're attracting," I say.

Nate dips his head to scan his outfit—ivory, snug-fitting slacks that taper to just above the ankle, a canary yellow button-down dress shirt (also form-fitting), tan Rothy's without socks, and designer sunglasses. He's impeccably dressed since it's a workday for him, but walking next to him with this prancing dog fashion show is projecting more of a 'couples' vibe than 'two brothers hanging out' vibe.

As if on cue, two bikini-clad women intersect our path on the boardwalk, having come straight from the sand.

"Awww! Can we pet your dog?"

"Sure," I say, dropping my voice to the lowest possible register. "It's not my dog, though."

The women are so enthralled by Brownie, they probably didn't note the last thing I said or the manly timbre of my voice. I suppose I don't really care.

"She's so precious," one of them says, letting Brownie lick her face. It's kind of disgusting. This dog might eat her own poop for all she knows.

"I just love her little outfit," says the other, crouched so low, her bikini top is revealing more than what's prudent. I just want to move along, but Nate's enjoying himself immensely.

"Are you girls local?" he asks, trying to lay on the suave guy act.

"Yeah," one of the girls answers. "Emerald Bay."

"Some nice homes up there," says Nate, all smooth talker.

The girls glance at us and shrug. The one who let Brownie lick her face tosses her hair over her shoulder.

"Thanks for letting us pet your dog," she says, waving as she and her friend walk away. "Happy Pride."

Nate opens his mouth and snaps it shut. I laugh, pointing a finger up from his shoes to his snug, yellow shirt. "This is a good look for you… honey."

I snap my fingers in a Z formation.

"What? I…" He calls after the girls. "I'm not… he's my BROTHER!"

But they're long out of earshot and I nudge Nate to cross Pacific Coast Highway with me, since we've reached the corner just as the crossing light turned green.

"Let it go, brother. You won't get any phone numbers with a dog in a pink dress."

Spotting an ice cream shop, Nate makes a beeline for it. "Fine. But I'm starved."

"Didn't you just finish your lunch?"

"That was a half hour ago, Nacho."

He orders a single scoop, offering to treat me to a cone, but I decline. My body is a temple and ice cream is structural damage.

"You know I don't eat sugar," I say.

"Oh. Then you can ignore the candy bar I slipped in your lunch box."

"You mean the insulated bag I keep in my car for my juice cleanse?"

He shrugs. "Like I said. Ignore it. Anyway... I'm guessing you didn't come all the way down here to watch me eat ice cream," he says.

"As lovely as this is, no. I need some insurance advice."

"And you couldn't have just called?"

"It's a... sensitive matter. Has to be in person."

One brow hitches up with interest. "Were you involved in a hit and run? Because if you were—"

"No. Nothing like that. It's for the business."

"Oh. Well, I think there's two million liability coverage on each restaurant."

Since my dad retired, he left me with all eight locations of the Mexican restaurant chain he built out of nothing. He'd intended one restaurant for each of his children, but my siblings each chose their own careers, and so we worked out a plan that's fair for everyone. They each get a monthly stipend, and I get all the restaurants.

"I'd like to know specifically, if that covers... embezzlement."

"Does this have to do with Pancho Two? I thought you worked that out with the vendors."

"I did. But there's more."

Pancho Two is my dad's old business partner. We call him Pancho Two because he was dad's second in command —and they share the same name. The nicknames of Pancho One and Pancho Two caught on so well, they named the restaurant Dos Panchos.

The concept was all Dad's, but since Pancho Two was good with paperwork and real estate, Dad offered him a small percentage of the restaurant. Seven more locations and decades later, Pancho Two had exceeded his original contract. Dad, being generous, gave him an excellent parting bonus. But that wasn't good enough for Pancho Two. Instead of bowing out gracefully, he stole goods and sold them on the black market, right before he disappeared with his new wife to Costa Rica.

My whole family knows this part of the story. What they don't know is that Pancho Two had been laundering money for an organized surfer gang called The Point Break Posse for several years.

"They came looking for him a few months after he left the country," I say, offering every detail I can remember. Maybe Nate knows how I can take legal action and maybe recoup some money in a claim.

"Only Dad and Enrique know this."

Nate, who's been silent as I recounted the events of two Christmases ago, how two guys named Churro and Roach came into the restaurant, demanding I get Dad on the phone. How they made threats if they didn't get the money. How Dad filled a duffel bag full of cash and paid what the surfers demanded.

"We thought we'd seen the last of The Point Break Posse that day," I say.

"Wait," Nate says, thinking intently. "Was that when Dad was rushed to the hospital? He thought it was a heart attack, but it was only *really* bad gas."

"Yep."

I don't need reminding of the fart jokes that ensued after

that.

"Woah. Only Enrique knew? Why didn't you tell the rest of us?"

"The only reason Enrique knows is because he was helping me reshape the business after Pancho Two left a colossal mess behind. And we chose not to tell any of you so you'd have plausible deniability."

"So why tell me now?" He throws his unfinished ice cream cone in the trash—a very uncharacteristic action for Nate.

"Because they're back," I say. "I need to know if insurance would cover... if we can prove a former partner embezzled money."

"How the blazes would that help you against a guy named Roach and the..." here he whispers harshly, "Point Break Pasta?"

"The Point Break Posse," I correct.

"I prefer Pasta."

I press my fingers into my forehead. It doesn't help against the splitting headache I've had for weeks.

"I'm just at my wit's end right now, and I don't want to upset Dad again."

"You have to go to the police, Nacho."

"What? Just stroll into the LAPD and say, "Hey guess what? My restaurant has been laundering money for years. Funny story, actually."

"I don't know. Maybe FBI? CIA? NATO? You can't take these guys on by yourself."

"If I go to the authorities before I know our family is safe, the gang will go after Mom and Dad and every single one of us. They probably have corrupt law enforcement on their payroll. Haven't you seen *Narcos*?"

"No. I can't watch that stuff."

"Are you going to help me or not?"

He sighs. "I'll look into your policy. No promises."

On our way back to his agency, we pass by a vacant commercial space. Out of habit, I cup my hands around my eyes and peek inside the darkened window. I can't see much, but it's spacious. I'd love to open a restaurant in downtown Laguna, but the rent must be astronomical.

"Thinking of bringing Dos Panchos to South OC?" asks Nate. He's seen me peek inside enough windows to know what I'm looking for.

"Something like that," I say.

This isn't the market for Dos Panchos, but I don't feel like explaining that to Nate. But the concept I'm working on with my friend Caleb would fit right in here. The demographics in this area are just what we're going for.

Thinking of Caleb reminds me I haven't asked him if he has info on Olive I need to know. He wouldn't hire anyone who didn't pass the background check with flying colors, but I'm curious. She went on and on about a bug. I assumed she meant a wiretap and almost lost my cool. But she continued with this crazy story about keeping Tía Lucy from eating an insect, of all things. Was she being serious? There's something different about that girl, like she doesn't think before speaking. Normally I'd find that incredibly annoying, but she seems to pull it off somehow. Like she's a clumsy sprite with a penchant for technicolor word vomit. And the way she asked to be paid in tacos. Who does she think I am?

There's a special place in hell for someone who fires the same person twice in one week. I wouldn't do that unless I'm absolutely sure she's a mole.

Olive is still at the restaurant when I return from visiting Nate. Her shift is ending, and Bernadette is showing her how to make her bank drop into the floor safe. I watch with interest as she slips the envelope in the slot. If she's gleaning information about where we keep our money, she's good at hiding it.

When she's finished with that, Josh, our bartender, calls her over with a flight of tequila on the bar. I check the time. He's early today, which is a shocker. Josh has perfected the art of arriving fashionably late, but since he's fast at setting up the bar and doesn't need much prep time, we let it slide.

Right this second, he's leaning over the bar, smiling at Olive the way I see him smile at pretty girls for tips. Olive is sitting on a barstool, enthralled by whatever Josh is saying. Girls love bartenders like Josh. I have no idea why. Yeah, there's the dazzlingly white teeth and sculpted haircut. He looks perfectly put together in the black-on-black vest and dress shirt he wears. In reality, he's just a dude who spends all his money at concert festivals and complains he's always broke. His proficiency in mixology and flirting with the female clientele keeps him well stocked in butt-hugging jeans and hair gel, and that seems to be enough for him. I don't have any issues with the guy. But right now, I don't like the way he's looking at Olive.

"What's going on, Josh?" I slap my hand on the bar casually. Just the boss joining the powwow.

"He's giving me a tequila lesson," says Olive, cheeks

bright and perky, like crabapples perched on either end of her smile.

I raise my brows at Josh. "Are you now?"

Educating our servers on the spirits we sell isn't strictly prohibited, but I don't remember Josh offering this level of training to the barback we hired last summer. The guy didn't last through August, but that's not the point. Josh is giving Olive the *special* treatment.

He shrugs nonchalantly. "She didn't know the difference between añejo and reposado."

"That's great. You know what, though? A shipment came in this morning, and I need you to take inventory. I'll take it from here."

"Oh…" He scratches the back of his neck. "Ooh-kay."

Giving Olive a little wave, he goes into the back, leaving me alone with the new girl and a flight of tequila. I take Josh's place behind the bar and lean on the speed rack, fixing my gaze on Olive, studying her tells. She looks back at me wide-eyed. This girl is no mole. I'm just paranoid and haven't slept enough.

"What is it you'd like to know about tequila?" I ask, frowning at the way she beams at me. She's like a chipmunk with that smile.

"Well, I'd like to know what's good in a margarita," she says. "Rosa tells me I should upsell whenever possible."

"Okay, that's a start." I slide the flight of tequila directly in front of her. "At a glance, what's the difference between these samples?"

She squints her nose. "Uh, color?"

"Exactly. And what gives tequila color?"

"The different varietals." She seems proud of her

answer. But she's wrong.

"You're thinking about wine, which comes from several types of grapes. All tequila comes from blue agave."

"Ooooh. Is that like a fruit?"

"It's a plant. Like a cactus."

"Is it really blue?"

"No. Can we focus, please?"

"Okay. I'm just trying to be thorough in case a customer asks."

"No customer is going to ask if the plant is blue," I snap.

She throws up her palms in surrender. "You got it, Chef Cra—" She catches herself here, mixing my name up with another chef, maybe. An old boss in New Jersey, perhaps?

"Nobody calls me Chef here," I say, circling my index finger around, indicating the restaurant. "Here, I'm Ignacio."

Her eyes twinkle. "Ignacio. Got it."

"Back to the tequila," I say, strangely only slightly annoyed. This feeling—it's more like annoyed adjacent. "It's the aging process that gives it color… usually."

"What do you mean by usually?"

"Some brands add food coloring and sugar. It's an abomination. But we don't carry any of those brands here."

"That would be a travesty."

I can't tell if she's serious or making fun. I don't really have the patience to find out.

"Moving on." I pick up one of the shot glasses from the flight. "Silver tequila is not aged. It's the purest a tequila can be after it's been distilled."

"Does that make it the best?"

"It depends. I prefer silver tequila in margaritas. Take a

sip."

She pulls a face. "I'm not great with hard liquor."

I can appreciate that. I don't partake all that much myself.

"Then just pass it under your nose. What do you smell?"

Olive lifts the glass to her nose and takes a sniff. "It just smells like alcohol."

"Okay. Try the next one. That's called a reposado. Aged about six months."

She takes the reposado in hand and takes a shallow whiff. "Smells the same to me."

"No, you need to really take it in your senses. Appreciate the notes. Hang on a sec."

Leaving my spot behind the bar, I circle around to stand next to where she's sitting—to help her experience the aroma and culture of the beverage.

"Close your eyes," I say. "Let go of everything you think you know about liquor."

Her eyes flutter shut, long, dark lashes fanned along her cheeks. And there's a witchy smile on her lips as if poised to crack a joke.

"Something strike you as funny?" I lower my voice to a whisper—a little too close to her ear. At this distance, I can smell her shampoo. Something overly sweet and fruity, like strawberry.

Her eyes are still closed, but her mouth hooks up in one corner, like she's fighting a smile.

"No," she says impishly. "I'm just… waiting to appreciate the notes."

"We can conclude our lesson for today."

"No." Her eyes flash open to meet mine, and her little

hand flies to catch my forearm. Something strange stirs in my belly. "I want to learn."

"Then close your eyes."

She lowers her lids again, and I try not to notice the contrast of our skin temperatures as her fingers rest on my left arm. With my right hand, I lift the reposado to her nose, passing it back and forth.

"Now concentrate. What do you smell?"

She takes a deep breath through her nose, taking in the aroma, her little fingers giving me a slight squeeze.

"Vanilla?"

"Good. What else?"

She sniffs again. "Maybe a little cinnamon?"

"Not bad."

She grins. "Okay, next."

"Hang on. Open your eyes." I slip my arm out of her soft hold and lean back a little. "You need to cleanse your olfactory palate."

"How do I do that?"

"Well, you're supposed to take a whiff of the crook of your elbow."

"Ah, like when you're candle shopping."

"I guess. But your skin probably smells like tortilla chips after working all day."

"It's a good thing I like tortilla chips," she quips.

"Here." I roll up my shirtsleeve, folding over the fabric of my cuffs until my elbow is exposed. Olive's pretty pink lips part ever so slightly. I'll never understand women's fascination with shirtsleeves. "Use my elbow. I haven't been here all day and don't smell like tacos."

If I smell like anything, it would be Yorkie. That little rat dog better not be making a mess in my office.

Olive's eyes dart from my arm to my face. "You want me to sniff your elbow?"

"To reset your nose, yes."

A flush creeps up her face even as she rolls her eyes. "Okay… weirdo."

I ignore the weirdo comment and lift my arm to meet her nose. She takes in a long pull of breath, touching her nose to the crook of my elbow. I hadn't realized until this moment how sensitive the skin is there. How the sensation of another person's touch—even a nose—can send ticklish reflexes up my arm.

I shake it off and tell her to close her eyes again. She shuts them like shutters, sitting up straight.

"Nose palate successfully cleansed," she says brightly.

"Alright. Tell me what you think of this one."

I pass a glass of añejo tequila under her nose. "What flavors can you detect?"

She sniffs it in, taking a moment to give it some thought.

"Caramel, apricot… and maybe pecan." Another sniff and her face illuminates. "Chocolate!"

I test it for myself, inhaling the notes and sipping a drop on my tongue. Wow. She's good. I would have guessed walnut, but I think she's right about the pecan.

"You have a nose for this," I say, surprised at how impressed I am.

She opens her eyes a sliver, squinting up at me. "You really think so?"

"So far." Unless it's a fluke.

"This is fun." She dives in for another whiff of my arm, but I yank that bad boy back real quick.

"I think we're done for the day."

"But what about the one that looks like a cup of honey?"

"That's an extra añejo, which means it's expensive." I guzzle it down in one shot and slam the glass on the bar. Juice cleanse be damned.

Her heart-shaped lips part in surprise, but I can't think about that at all—or the tickle still lingering on the skin of my inner elbow.

"Time to clock out, Olive."

I head directly to my office, waving off the cooks and their filthy joke of the day. I barge in, feeling all the weight of the financial mess Pancho Two left behind, the pressure from the Posse, and now the jumbled twisting in my chest from one touch on the inside of my elbow.

I need a vacation.

As the door flies open, I'm met with a trembling dog—round, black eyes staring up at me nestled in a face full of fur. Her pointy ears are tucked behind her head. I must have startled her when I stormed in, having forgotten she was here.

I feel bad—until I take one step inside and narrowly miss a puddle. She literally just did her business in the parking lot behind the restaurant. How does *that* much pee come out of such a tiny dog?

I scoop her up so she doesn't accidentally walk through the puddle and set her on my desk chair while I clean the mess.

Cochina perra.

"I don't care about that suitcase full of pink dresses," I say, playfully scolding. "As long as I have to take care of you, you're going naked."

Give me
liberty or …
a jelly donut!

– Homer Simpson

Chapter Five

OLIVE

Maybe my calling is to be a Spanish teacher. I'd have to learn the language first, of course, and I could never teach adults—but children aren't quite so intimidating. I could teach Spanish to children. Small ones, like toddlers.

After working two weeks at Dos Panchos, I've already picked up some phrases from the cooks. In my enthusiasm to learn, I repeat everything they say to me. Then they laugh. It's so cute.

Now, they call me into the kitchen every day and gather around me, teaching me a fun, new phrase which I write on my notepad. I make flashcards when I get home.

Today we're having a slow morning, so I'm in the back, taking my notes. Alfonso is especially committed to teaching me the correct pronunciations. The guys are all so impressed by my quick study, they're cheering me on.

Until the bossman shows up.

Ignacio barks something to them in Spanish, and they scatter like a flock of pigeons. He's behind me, towering over me both in height and in lofty presence.

I spin on my heel and find myself face to face with his chest. It is quite the impressive chest. Tilting my chin, I gaze up at his stormy expression and clutch my notebook in the small space between us, pen poised to write.

"Um… can you repeat that, please? All I got was *hijos de pu*—"

"Don't you dare repeat it." He turns to go, but stops to say, "And I don't want you learning Spanish from those guys."

Ugh. The nerve.

"Why not?"

He comes in closer to me, leaning down so there's only an inch or two between our noses.

"Because you're a good girl," he grumbles. "Aren't you, Olive?"

Gulp.

"I uh… just want to learn some phrases…"

"Then get an app."

He saunters away toward his office, and when he glances back over his shoulder and sees me rooted in place, he curls his index finger, signaling for me to follow him.

"Olive," he beckons, his voice stern yet somehow velvety smooth. This silly crush I have on my boss is getting to be a problem.

My traitorous feet carry me like a lamb to the slaughter, stopping right outside his office.

Ignacio does a once-over of my form. "What are you wearing?"

"Uh, my Dos Panchos polo shirt, my apron, and leggings."

"Leggings? Is that what you're calling them?"

"Yes, because that's what they're called."

He twists his lips and scowls at them. "There are candy canes all over them."

"I know, right? Aren't they the best?"

I have two pairs of leggings with candy canes but these ones aren't faded. And they're black, so they're slimming.

"It's like Christmas threw up all over your legs."

I squint at him. "Are you one of those guys who barely tolerates the holidays?"

"No. I love Christmas. But it's the middle of June."

"Well… the customers love them."

"I'll bet. Especially the male customers. They're skintight."

"That's because they're *leggings*." Sheesh. Has he really not seen leggings before? "Rosa said to wear black pants."

He crosses his arms and glowers at me, but I swear there's a tiny crack of a smile in the corner of his mouth if you look reeaally hard. With a microscope.

"Next time, wear plain black. Jeans are fine."

With that, he slips into his office and shuts the door. In my face. And so, I knock.

"What?"

I crack the door open. "Um, I'll have to wait to get paid. I don't have plain black pants. Or jeans."

"What happened to the slacks you wore at the wedding?"

The wedding which shall not be named. And boy, this is embarrassing to admit.

"They ripped."

He doesn't have to know they ripped when I fell into the cake. And he certainly doesn't have to know they ripped right in the butt crack.

He scrapes a hand down his face, dragging skin from below his eyes into his cheeks. Then he unlocks his desk drawer, pulls out a few twenty-dollar bills, and shoves them in my direction.

"Come."

He's just waving the bills at me like he's bored—like I better get my butt in the office and take it before he falls asleep. But I hesitate, lingering in the doorway, not wanting a hand-out from him or anyone.

"I… I don't want to take your money."

"It's for your uniform. I can pay for your uniform."

"Oh that's okay. I can go shopping this weekend."

"Oh for heaven's sake, will you get in here and take the money?" He waves his hand around more wildly, flapping the bills back and forth like little flags.

At this point, it would be an insult to refuse, I suppose, so I do his bidding with gusto, hopping in front of his desk to accept the money.

"Eighty? I can get a pair for twenty." I try to give three of the bills back to him but he doesn't allow it.

"Then buy four pairs of pants. Buy a few gallons of gas. Heck, buy yourself some real candy canes and sing ho ho ho. Just don't wear those leggings to work."

I can only stand before him, blinking lamely. My mouth might be ajar.

"Are you sure you're not a humbug?"

He points to the door. "Get to work."

"Roger that." I salute him and scoot back into the dining room where I find more customers have arrived for the lunch crowd.

Today's my first day without Bernadette here. I've grown accustomed to asking her a million questions, so suffice to say I'm a little nervous. But Rosa assures me I'm ready, and now that Bernadette is taking her summer classes, she'll only be here twice a week. Depending on how busy the restaurant is, I might be able to get more hours, even when Bernadette's here. I might even get a chance to fill in for servers at other Dos Panchos locations. I put my name in the hat for those shifts, too.

I make it through the lunch rush, only messing up once. Rosa's quick to fix my mistake and the customer is none the wiser. Oh wait. Make that two mistakes. But the second one wasn't entirely my fault. There was this scary, burly, bald guy. He had tattoos all over his face and neck and wore a permanent scowl. *He* didn't care for my candy cane leggings, so take *that* as a sign of his character. Before I could even bring his beer from the bar, he'd devoured all his chips and salsa. He called me over, waving the chip basket in the air.

"*Mas pan*," he'd growled.

Pan? I had no idea what *pan* was. But being the gung-ho student of Spanish I am, I asked Alfonso, the cook. *Pan*, so it seems, means bread. Bread. Okaaay. This is a *Mexican* restaurant, not a bakery. But who was I to argue with tattooed Lux Luther on steroids? If that frightening man wanted *pan*, I was going to give it to him. Lucky for me, I found some rolls in the kitchen—probably used for employee lunches or something on the breakfast menu. I replaced the greasy tissue paper in the chip basket with a clean one, filled it with rolls, and brought it to the customer.

He was *not* pleased. Actually, he was quite livid, shouting at me in Spanish—which I didn't understand except one word—the *one word* Ignacio specifically warned me not to repeat.

I'm beginning to see the wisdom in that.

Rosa calmed the man down and took over the table for me. All in all, not a bad day.

I think the tips were pretty good. I'll have to wait until the end of my shift when I balance my book. But I'm hopeful. Most of the customers gave me a little extra just for spreading joy with candy canes on my leggings.

It's quiet now. There are a few stragglers that will take me until my shift ends. The side work helps me pass time. I think about Ignacio, the way he practically threw the cash at me. My tips are probably enough to buy a pair of pants once I pay my rent. I'm two weeks overdue. It's a miracle my landlord hasn't evicted me. But he's a sweet, old guy despite how hard he tries to hide it. I think he has a soft spot for me, being from Jersey himself.

"Can you take another table?" Rosa asks me, finding me in the server station, doing my roll-ups. Fifty roll-ups per server—that's the rule. I usually end up doing seventy-five because I'm a can-do kind of girl.

"Sure, I don't mind," I say. Technically, I should be done taking new tables for the day. But I need the money, and Rosa knows it. She's giving this one up for me.

"They have menus," she says, pouring two Cokes. "And I took their drink order. Here. Table thirteen."

I smile gratefully and take the drinks from her, heading to table thirteen with a bounce in my step. I could really get the hang of this, and hopefully I'll be able to make rent on time next month.

But my happy steps slow down and become dreadful slogs when I come upon the two people sitting at table thirteen, waiting for their Cokes. My ex-boyfriend, Aaron, and the blonde hussy he left me for. The one with cheap perfume and too much eyebrow liner. The one who has the gall to smile at me while Aaron just stares, slack-jaw, his face the color of paper.

"O-Olive." He gulps. "What are you doing here?"

"I'm still holding the Cokes, two feet from the table. My stomach completely bottoms out, seeing them together like this, all smushed side by side on the same seat of the booth. Yuck. She's practically on his lap.

"Hi, Olive," she says with her slimy voice. "Are you going to give us our drinks?"

I'm frozen solid, unable to form a syllable. Oh, there are so many things I'd just love to say to them. Things I may have rehearsed. Witty, salty things. But in my mind, I'd always thought I'd be super successful at something, like maybe I'd be meeting a super important client for my super important corporate job. I'd be like, "Oh, hey. Starbucks on me." And then we'd glide out the door of the Starbucks, expensive coffees in hand, and there I'd run into Aaron and Eyebrows. In this scenario, they'd be begging for coins with a dirty, used coffee cup they'd found in the trash.

"Alms for the poor," they'd say, or something pathetic like that. And I'd toss them a quarter with pity on my face and Aaron would see how successful I'd become without him. And he'd beg me to take him back, groveling at my feet.

Sometimes I'd toss them a hundred-dollar bill, saying how I just don't have anything smaller. But then I rewind my daydream and make it a penny because they don't deserve a hundred-dollar bill from me. Not after I walked in on them doing the deed—on TOP of my favorite quilt. No. They don't even deserve the penny. They owe me a new quilt, dagnabbit.

"Olive?" Aaron shifts his eyes from the Cokes in my hands to the table. Like now he's instructing me how to do my waitressing job? "Are those our drinks?"

And something in me just goes pop. A tiny water balloon in my head. Pop. This isn't Starbucks. I'm not a successful business lady. Aaron and Eyebrows aren't begging for coins, and these two drinks in my hands are not fancy coffee drinks.

Don't do it, Olive. Don't even think about it.

The little voice in my head is a wise sage. But she's not the one holding two tall glasses of cola.

I'm at war—like a force outside my body is holding me in place while I struggle to break through so I can douse Aaron in Coca-Cola.

"Wow, Olive," says Aaron, clearly noticing my eye twitch. It's one of my tells. "You got yourself a service job. Good for you."

It's the "Good for you." that does it. So condescending. So smug. So... Aaron.

"Good for you," is what he said when I tried to learn Ukulele and sucked at it. Or when I took that karate class. It's what he always says to remind me I'm not good enough. That no matter what I do, I'll fail. I try and try and try, but at the end of the day, I'm just spinning my wheels. I'm not like Aaron... everything comes easy for Aaron Lipshitz. Especially blondes, apparently.

My hands make their move, going for that 'ol *splash-his-face-with-water* schtick, like in the movies. Except it's not water. And so, that force outside me, which was holding me back completely before, decided in that moment to only hold me back... partially.

I must pause here to say I'm not one of those vindictive people. I could never understand women who slashed their cheating boyfriends' tires or even slapped them. I always admired the women in films who, instead of resorting to rash actions, would have a smart and witty one-liner to really put the guy in his place—or a power speech. But I'm not clever enough for that, always coming up with something to say hours after any confrontation. When I caught Aaron cheating, I didn't say a word. I didn't cry. I didn't break anything. I held up my chin, grabbed a random house plant, and left without letting them see how much I was shaking. I left that horrific scene with dignity.

But right this second, well, my dignity can just shove it.

Just a little splash. Maybe it will look like an accident. Then I see Ignacio in the corner of my eye, chatting with a customer at a nearby booth. And that's when it all falls apart. Not only do I not want to get fired, I don't want to disappoint this man who'd given me a second chance. He may be a curmudgeon, but he's a fair curmudgeon.

Much like the wedding cake fiasco, my brain is too slow to stop action already in motion, and instead of a triumphant spectacular splash in the face, my hands clonk the glasses on the table, letting them tumble over, spilling sticky cola onto the laps of both Aaron and his horrified trollop.

She screams, of course, turning heads all over the restaurant. Thank goodness it's not very busy this time of day. I lock eyes with Ignacio, watching the familiar look on his face. It's the cake all over again. Somewhere behind me, I hear Aaron barking at me as if he's far away.

"What the heck, Olive!"

There's movement at the table, probably Aaron and Eyebrows scrambling for napkins. But all I see is Ignacio, and my throat burns. I feel the sting of tears behind my eyes, and my nose is getting all tingly. I can't cry. Not here. Not in front of Aaron. Not in front of all these customers. So I run. I bolt right out of the dining room, through the kitchen, and out the back door, letting the ugly cry explode out of me next to the big, smelly dumpsters outside.

I'm not a crier, usually. But here I am, bawling my eyes out—at work, of all places. I don't even know if I'm more upset about Aaron or my money problems, or that I'm about to get fired again. I guess it's everything combined.

Not thirty seconds later, Ignacio is next to me, finding me in a pathetic heap of tears. I try to wipe my face, but I'm too snotty and wet.

"Olive?" His voice is softer than I would expect for someone about to fire my stoopid butt for the second time. I'm hunched over, hiding my blotchy, red face from him, but he comes around to stand right in front of me, tilting my chin up with his finger. I can hardly see his expression through puffy eyes and a deluge of tears flooding my vision. Thank goodness I don't have to see the disappointment on his face when he tells me to hit the road. But he doesn't say a thing. Instead, he disappears back into the restaurant, leaving me alone at my dumpster pity party. He's probably getting my bag and car keys to get me out of here without a scene. Too late. I'm positive I've already accomplished that.

He returns a minute later with a whole roll of toilet paper and gently places it in my hands. I wipe my eyes and blow my nose, which is the most unattractive thing a lady can do in front of a man. Except maybe barf—which I very well might do out of sheer embarrassment. Once I've dried my nose out and maybe stopped crying, I toss the tissues into the trash bin. Ignacio takes the toilet paper roll from me and replaces it with a damp towel.

"This will make you feel better," he says. "Would you like a glass of water?"

I rub the towel over my face, smudging what's left of my make-up. It does feel nice. I'm grateful for this even though I don't understand.

"Why are you being so nice to me?" I ask, willing myself not to cry again. I know what I look like when I cry, and it's not pretty.

"You're my employee. I take care of my staff."

"But…" Is he just going to wait to fire me when I'm not so sobby?

"Who were those people?" he asks. "Do you know them?"

"You're not going to ask about the Cokes?"

He lets out a half laugh. "If there's one thing I've learned—especially with you—is that there's usually more to the story than meets the eye."

I can't help but crack a small smile. One of the dishwashers comes out the door, ready to take his break. Ignacio says something in Spanish with a tone of irritability and shoves the toilet paper and towel into his chest. Then he softly places a hand at the small of my back, guiding me around the corner, away from the busybody kitchen staff.

"You don't have to tell me if you don't want to," he says.

But I *do* have to tell him. I made a scene in his restaurant.

"He's my ex," I say with a sigh. "And the girl he was with…"

He blows out a hard breath. "Let me guess. He was two-timing you. With her."

"Bingo."

"Wow." He shakes his head. "You know you didn't have to take that table. I wouldn't have minded if you'd turned him away."

"I didn't know until I was right there, delivering their drinks."

"I'm guessing that spill wasn't such an accident after all?"

Heat rushes to my cheeks. I'm so busted.

"It's okay," he says. "Maybe next time you won't miss."

"Whaaa?"

"Come on." He leads me to a silver SUV, and clicks a key fob, opening the hatch. "It's been a heck of a day for both of us."

He sighs and opens a small lunch box. Inside, there's some healthy-looking green drinks in bottles kept cold by an ice pack, but inside one pocket, there's a Snickers bar.

"For emergencies," he says, ripping it open and handing it to me.

He invites me to sit on the tailgate, helping me hop up. His legs are so long, all he has to do is lean to sit inside the hatchback. For several lengthy minutes, I nosh on the candy and my *Schande* almost melts away. There must be something magical in chocolate. I feel remarkably better.

Ignacio downs one of his green drinks and then takes a long, deep breath through his nose and lets it out through his lips, cleansing whatever bad mojo mucked up his day. I wonder what that must be.

"Better?"

He's watching me expectantly, sharing more than a candy bar—he's sharing a moment of camaraderie.

"Yeah, actually," I say, smiling into his gloriously handsome face. "Thank you."

Oy gevalt. His beauty is almost blinding. "Do you always keep chocolate bars in your little lunch box? For, you know, emergencies?"

He snorts. "No. I never eat sugar."

"So you had a pretty bad day, too?" I ask.

He slides off the tailgate, wiping his palms on his thighs. "Shall we?"

It's not lost on me how he's completely dodging my question. Not that it's any of my business, but he *did* just share his emergency candy bar.

He helps me down from the tailgate and closes the hatch. "Rosa will close your last two tables. You can wait in my office until the ex is gone."

I'm a little disappointed our little tailgate party is over so soon, although I will admit to being surprised it happened in the first place. My grumpy boss does have his moments. And I am more than curious about his bad day— I find I'm a little concerned for him.

Then I see Aaron and Eyebrows walking through the parking lot.

"That won't be necessary," I say, jerking my head in Aaron's direction.

I will not cry again.

Ignacio growls—he's actually baring his teeth. Then he scoops my hand in his, drawing close enough that I can feel the heat of his body.

"Do you trust me?" he asks.

Gulp.

"You just fed me chocolate. Of course I do."

"Good." He gently but firmly pushes me until my back hits the SUV. The tips of his shoes tap against mine and he leans in extremely close, still holding onto my hand. "Is he looking this way?"

My eyes shift over Ignacio's shoulder. Aaron's steps

have slowed almost to a stop, and he's definitely looking at us.

"Yes," I say, shifting my gaze up at Ignacio's ash-gray eyes. "He's watching with great interest."

Ignacio leans in closer, his nose a half-inch from mine, and his eyes dance over me.

"Play along with me," he says, right before his lips fall onto mine.

Ask not what
you can do
for your country.
Ask what's for lunch.

— Orson Welles

Chapter Six

IGNACIO

I'm going to hell for this—or at least a thousand years in purgatory. She's my employee. This is wrong on every level imaginable. But her lips are soft and warm. My own lips are locked shut, though, and I'm keeping things friendly by keeping it shut, talking to her against her mouth. This is just for show.

"Ith he still wooking?" I mumble into the very closed-mouth, very *fake* kiss. I'd make a terrible ventriloquist.

I shift my body an inch or two so she can get a good view behind me. She glances over, wide-eyed and blushing fiercely.

"Mmmhmm."

"Err woo nokay? Em e mecken woo contonton?"

She giggles into my lips. "What?"

I open my lips, just enough to speak, but still brushing against hers—for authenticity purposes, of course.

"I said, are you okay? Am I making you uncomfortable?"

Her cheeks burn red, and her eyes flash bright. "Oh. No, not at all. I uh, appreciate the gesture."

Reaching up with my free hand, I glide my palm under her jaw, the tips of my fingers dipping into her downy-soft hair.

"What's he doing now?" I ask, secretly hoping he's still watching us so we can keep up this ruse. How pathetic am I that a fake kiss is the only action I've gotten in over four years?

"He's uh…" her eyes dart over my shoulder and back again. "Standing next to his car. Arguing, it looks like."

"And is he still looking this way?"

"Yes," she says, her voice a little shaky. "They both keep glancing over here."

"It's working, then."

"What's working?"

"Making him jealous. Making *her* jealous is just a bonus."

"Is this how you take care of all your employees?"

"Only the ones wearing candy cane leggings."

I hear the swish of footsteps dragging along the gravel

of the parking lot. A cheating d-bag *would* be the type of guy to drag his feet when he walks.

The blonde he's with calls to him, "Where are you going?"

"He's coming over here. Why is he coming over here?"

"Don't you worry about that," I say. "Ready to put on a show?"

"A show? Aren't we already putting on a show?"

"Just play along." I crane her neck up, pressing her further against the car until her back arches and her hair spreads out on the window. I capture her lips, more convincing this time, angling my face so anyone within viewing distance would be extremely uncomfortable to see how my mouth moves over hers, how with every pass over her lips, I'm claiming her.

"Call out my name or something," I say, trailing my lips down to her jaw. "Pretend you're into it."

"Oh, okay." She watches the progression of my mouth.

"And close your eyes."

She squeezes her eyelids shut and cries out, almost robotically, "Oh my! Ignacio. You are an excellent kisser. I am so amazingly aroused. Wow! I hope no one is watching."

"Maybe tone it down a few notches," I say, burrowing my face in her neck.

"Uh..." Her hands fly around my back, clawing at my shirt. "Like this?"

"That's a start."

I take her mouth again, skating my hand down to the waistband of her ridiculous candy cane leggings. Seriously, doesn't she know how much they accentuate her figure?

She meets me in the kiss, responding with keen spirit. I growl into her because, holy cow, she tastes of chocolate. I can't remember the last time I had chocolate.

She makes a sound in the back of her throat, which sparks a long-lost feeling deep behind my navel. It's been so long since I've touched a woman like this.

That's the only reason I can think of that explains why I'm here right now, basically making out with Olive pressed against my car. I am so flippin' deprived of romance in my life; I conjured up an excuse to kiss her. Sure, when I learned what that a-hole did to her, something inside me kicked into action. Making him jealous was the first thing that sprang to mind. Yeah, I know with a clearer head, I could think of several other things that would work better. But I don't have a clear head at all. I haven't had a clear head since the day Pancho Two swindled all that money and took off to Costa Rica. And now, with the surfer gang, I'm a walking pressure cooker.

Seriously, anything I could have done to Olive's ex would have been a better option than kissing her. Punching him in the face and getting charged with assault would have been a wiser course of action. But here I am, choice made, and my body is suffering the consequences. I'm a little kid, scooting my socks on the carpet, and she's a balloon, setting my hair on end with her wackadoo static electricity.

This is what happens when you work too hard. *Any* touch can set you up in flames.

Somehow, it registers that the footsteps have stopped. That Olive's ex-boyfriend not only got discouraged from interrupting us, but is gone altogether.

"Olive?" I whisper. "I think he's gone."

"Huh?" She slowly opens her eyes, blinking as if just coming to. "Oh."

"I don't want to make it obvious by turning around. Can you just check real quick?"

She shifts her gaze to where she'd looked before.

"His car is gone," she says.

Something in my chest dissolves—ice cream melted on a sidewalk sort of disappointment. I shouldn't have kissed her in the first place, let alone wish for an excuse to continue.

"I guess that did the trick," I say thickly, even as I remain pinned against her like wet toilet paper on a stucco wall. If I peel myself away now, I'll rip into shreds.

"Yeah," she says with a heavy breath. "I guess it did."

I swallow hard, and I kinda, sorta hate myself right now. I'm her boss, for crying out loud. How many Hail Marys will it take to scrub *this* from my permanent record?

"Olive, I…"

"You don't have to say a thing," she says quickly. "You really did me a solid. Thank you for your… convincing performance."

"Right." Wow, do I feel like an ass right now. I step away from her and really do feel like soggy, ripped toilet paper. "Well, I think we can safely say he won't be coming back."

Olive clears her throat, adjusting her polo shirt which had slipped out from under her apron.

"I think maybe I'll… do my close out now."

She's spooked. I spooked her. Tomorrow she'll slap me with a huge harassment lawsuit.

"Can you come in a little early tomorrow?" I ask,

because all I need right now is a disgruntled employee. We need to have a talk, but first, I need to make sure she comes in. "I've been meaning to go over your schedule. See if you can fit in a taco Tuesday."

Her eyes brighten. "Taco Tuesday? Are you sure? Because, like I said—"

"Naaaaacho!"

Crap. I turn to see my dad storming toward me from his parked car, Mom and Abuela trailing from behind. How much did they see?

"Go ahead inside," I say to Olive. "See you in a bit."

"Nacho?" she questions. "As in delectable processed cheese drizzled over corn chips?"

"It's my family's nickname for me. But I have a feeling my dad's going to start calling me a whole lot of other names you won't want to hear. Go inside. I'll catch you later."

With a suspicious squint, Olive heads to the back entrance of the restaurant, but not before waving enthusiastically with a bright smile in her voice. "Hi, Mr. Precio."

She skips away and as soon as Dad reaches me, he starts to tear me a new one.

"*Que la madre*, Nacho. What the *diablo* are you doing?"

"Just talking, Dad."

"Just talking! Your grandmother saw you *'just talking'* while we were parking the car. I didn't pass these restaurants down to you *para que puedes fregar* the waitresses."

"It's not what you think," I say. There's no talking to him when he's worked up like this. I turn to my mom, who's finally caught up to Dad, right behind Abuela. My grandmother is a spry lady for her age, and the only reason she didn't reach me first is probably because Dad jumped out of the car while it was still rolling.

"You tell me what I *think*, Nacho," says Dad, crossing his arms. "Since you're so smart."

"Francisco, remember what the doctor said about you getting worked up." Mom, always the peacemaker, raises a brow at Dad, then comes in for a hug. "How's my baby boy?"

I hug her back, taking refuge in the extra-long embrace. "I'm good, Mom."

"Good?" repeats Abuela with a thick accent. "*Estás haciendo muy 'GOOD', muchacho. Muy bien para ti, fallando las damas en la calle. Qué desgraciada!*"

"I wasn't... can somebody please tell grandma I wasn't doing anything vulgar?"

"Tell her yourself," says Dad.

Good grief!

"*Abuela... tienes falta.*"

"Some respect will serve you well, Nacho," warns Mom.

I try again with a hard sigh. "*Abue, lo siento. Pero estás equivocada.*"

Really, how many ways are there to tell someone they're mistaken? And why is one way better than the other?

"*No tienes que saltar a conclusiones,*" I continue. "I was just... comforting her. *Consolándola.*"

She scoffs. "*Consolándola. Estoy segura que si.* To think I live to see the day... *mi hijo crió niños que son mujeriegos.*"

"I'm not a womanizer. Grandma, please."

"Spanish," warns Dad.

"*Por favor, Abuela. No soy...*" I can hardly get out the word. "Mom, tell her I'm not like that."

Mom rests her palm on Abuela's arm. *"Te lo juro,"* she says, *"Ignacio es un buen chico que va a la iglesia todos los domingos."*

"That's right. I *do* go to church every single Sunday," I say in agreement.

"Nunca se aprovecha de las mujeres," she continues.

This seems to soften Abuela's resolve to cut off my *huevos,* so Mom wags a brow at her and nods slowly, saying, *"Y es virgen."*

Oh, for goodness sake.

"MOM!"

Seize the moment.
Remember all those
women on the 'Titanic'
who waved off
the dessert cart.
— Erma Bombeck

Chapter Seven

OLIVE

"Mr. Precio, I am very much obliged and embarrassed. You've shown me a great kindness yesterday and I…"

No, too formal.

"Thank you for fake kissing me yesterday. And for the chocolate."

Eeuck. Too desperate.

I'm waiting for Ignacio in his office as instructed when

I arrived at work early. I'm told he's running a few minutes late, so I'm taking the opportunity to practice what I'll say to him so he doesn't think I'm a psycho nymph.

After the fake kiss yesterday, all I wanted was to curl into a ball of shame and never show my face to the male population ever again. Boy, did I ever screw up.

It's like I'm doing everything in my power to get fired from all the jobs in Los Angeles at record-breaking levels of chaos.

Note to self: tip the busboy a little extra for the soda pop clean up on table thirteen. Ugh!

And then Ignacio did me a favor, making it extremely clear it was all for show. And what did I do? Cling to him like a spider monkey.

Way to play it cool, Olive.

"Thank you for your kindness yesterday. I'd like to offer my appreciation."

I repeat that one a few times—let my mouth get used to the words.

"…offer my appreciation for… sticking it to my ex? Not firing me? Chocolate smooches?"

I'm roused by the opening of the door, and there's Ignacio, looking fresh with his hair perfectly tousled. He halts in the doorway, gaping at me like he'd forgotten about our meeting. His eyes fix on mine, and I feel all the effects of his overbearing presence. I stare right back, my throat so dry it's almost painful. And my gaze dips to his mouth for one second—the tiny scar on his lower lip reminding me of the feel of him.

"Thank you for your appreciation," I blurt.

His aforementioned lips tug at the corner and for a minuscule moment, he lets his gaze rake over my form.

"You're welcome," he says.

"I mean… thank you for your kindness. I appreciate it."

Gah!

A shadow passes over his features and he shifts his eyes to the floor.

"Is it okay if I close the door?" he asks.

Yes. You may absolutely close us in this office alone where I will definitely not maul you.

"Sure," I say, hoping to God Almighty, I did not let the 'maul you' part slip out.

Instead of taking his usual place behind the desk, Ignacio leans against the wall and crosses his arms.

"I want to assure you there will be no repeat of yesterday's… overtures," he says.

My heart drops. Why does this feel like someone's breaking up with me? Stupid heart.

"Of course," I reply. "I… couldn't agree more. That was a one-off. Noooo more overtures. That's exactly what I was about to say." I chuckle nervously. "You beat me to it, boss."

Would it be awkward to give him a friendly slug in the arm? I think probably yes.

"The thing is, Olive, I'm in a position of authority over you and I overstepped a line. For that I'm sorry."

"No need to apologize. I apologize for making you feel like you need to apologize. And I apologize for using the word apologize too many times."

Can somebody please stop me?

"Good. I'm glad we cleared the air. Now about your schedule…"

"Did your dad say anything to you? Those nicknames you didn't think I should be around to hear?"

He sighs and shakes his head. "It was more my grandma. She's not afraid to speak her mind."

"Oh! So... how much exactly did they see?"

My face is on fire right now. It's one thing to put on a show for my horrible ex and his hussy, it's quite another to scandalize one's grandma.

"Let's just say I got a mouthful. But she's fine now. Don't worry."

"I'm too curious. You have to tell me one little, juicy tidbit. What did she say?"

"Just some choice words in Spanish. You don't want to know."

"Oh, but I do. How am I supposed to learn Spanish if no one tells me the bad words?"

"I'm not going to teach you any bad words." He circles around behind his desk and sits, firing up his computer. "So we have you for three shifts a week at this location..."

"I'd like to meet your grandma," I say cheerily. "My *bubbe*, rest her soul, was a lot like yours. If she didn't like something, she'd let you know it. 'Olive, don't eat so much, you're getting a muffin top. Olive, your hair looks like a bird's nest. Olive, why do you have to go out with that goy'?"

"Goy?"

"It just means non-Jew."

He blinks. "You're... Jewish?"

"Of course I'm Jewish. My last name is Isaac. What did you think?"

"Right. I just… never mind," he grumbles. And then, "Is your ex-boyfriend—the guy from yesterday a… goy?"

I snort. "Aaron Lipshitz is definitely not a goy. He still brags about his accomplishments in Hebrew school."

"Well, I suppose if it got him into a good college…" says Ignacio, rubbing the back of his neck.

"He was twelve."

"Oh."

There's an awkward silence between us, neither of us knowing where to look. I guess talking about an ex can be a real downer.

Then, like every cliche in every rom-com ever, we speak at the same time.

"I think—"

"It's getting—"

I laugh stiffly, and motion for him to go on. "Sorry."

"No, no. What were you going to say?"

What I was *going* to say was how I was done with Jewish boys and would very much prefer a Spanish guy. But that would be super cringe to the power of ten.

"I… forgot," I say. "Go ahead."

Ignacio's eyes glide over my features, snagging on the area of my mouth for a split second while he bites his top lip. I basically turn into matzoh ball soup with just that one look.

"You need to get to work now," he says, putting back on that gruff disposition. I could be wrong, but I think underneath that crusty exterior of his, there's a creamy center. And I'm determined to get to it. He will likely resist, but I'm anything but a quitter.

"Okey dokey, boss." I open the door, shooting him finger guns. "Can't wait to meet your grandma."

"Not gonna happen."

I close the door behind me and wave at the guys in the kitchen. Every single one of them is looking at me funny. The dishwasher is wagging his brows and flashing a grin so wide I can see the space in his back teeth.

I jump right into the lunch rush, hoping to get a moment to talk to Bernadette about community college. I'm thinking of taking some classes. But every time she passes me, she gives me a little wink. At one point in the day, I run into the kitchen for a brand new bottle of Tapatio for a picky customer, and Ignacio's there in the dry storage area—so he pulls the box of hot sauce from the shelf for me and offers to carry it to the server station. The cooks whistle and hoot as we walk back to the front of house together, and Ignacio barks something at them in Spanish, which makes them shut up real quick.

Finally, at the end of the rush, I have time to chat with Bernadette while we do our side work. I'm so inspired by her going back to school at twenty-seven and want to get some advice. I ask her how it's going, and she tells me about her math classes. Plural. Now I regret asking because… math. Snore.

She grins and offers me a sideways glance.

"So… when were you going to tell me about you and my cousin?"

"Your… cousin?"

"Nacho."

"Right. I just forgot he was your cousin for a minute there." And that little detail about dating, apparently.

Kissing maybe, but that's confidential, or at least I'd thought.

"It's fine. We don't look related."

"Must be your fabulous nose ring and sparkling personality," I say.

She bursts into peals of laughter. "He is a grumpy old man, isn't he? But love is blind, am I right?"

I nod dramatically, with my eyes big and round. What is she even going on about?

"I had no idea he even had a girlfriend."

"I'm sorry. What?" Girlfriend?

She elbows me and drops her voice to a whisper. "It's okay. My grandma told me."

Of course she did. Now I *really* want to meet this grandma of theirs.

"What exactly did she tell you?" I ask. I know how meddling grandmothers can be. Mine was a real *Yente*.

"We didn't talk about it for long," she says. "She only mentioned how relieved she was that Ignacio has a serious girlfriend after all these years."

Whoa there. That's a lot of stuff to pack on. My imagined involvement with Ignacio went from kissing to dating to serious girlfriend faster than latkes and applesauce disappear at Hanukkah dinner.

I hear a throat clearing behind us and there's Ignacio, looking stern as ever. He jerks his head and walks into the back, clearly expecting me to just follow him without uttering a word.

"I guess that's my cue," I say with a shrug. I can't say I'm thrilled to be summoned like this, but I'm insanely curious now.

I trail ten steps behind Ignacio only to end up, once again, in his office. I close the door as I step inside, slightly apprehensive about the whole no-making-out rule, especially since I've been upgraded to serious girlfriend.

Ignacio clears his throat and signals me to sit down in the seat opposite his desk. He remains standing, though, leaning his hip on the desk. He studies me for a full thirty seconds before uttering a word.

Then, with casual indifference, he says, "There's been a small misunderstanding."

And, kind of annoyed, but mostly amused, I say, "Small misunderstanding? I think it's a doozy."

"Damn Bernadette. Did she tell you? I'm gonna douse her car with Axe spray."

"It's not her fault. How did your grandma get the idea in her head in the first place? It's not like *you'd* tell her I was your girlfriend."

I'm pretty much joking, but Ignacio's jaw twitches and he stares intently at the wall. There's nothing interesting on the wall except a tax schedule poster.

"Or did you?" I accuse. He runs long, thick fingers through his mess of hair. I gasp like a Southern Belle. "You did. Mr. Precio, I'm all astonishment. And after such a short courtship."

"I'll take care of it," he says, not amused in the slightest. "I'll tell them we broke up."

I snort. "Well, I think you should probably take me to dinner first."

"It's not funny. My family's weird about these things. Especially my grandma."

"I think I love your grandma."

For someone who's the last to know she's dating the boss, I think I'm being pretty chill about this whole deception. Ignacio is the opposite of chill right now. There's a vein popping out of his neck. I want to smooth it over with my fingers—kiss it away.

"I didn't expect the news to make its way around the rumor mill. My dad must have told one of the staff. And those guys are bigger gossips than Mexican women in a telenovela."

So that's why they were wagging their brows at me.

"I'm sorry, Olive. When my grandma started on me yesterday, I panicked. She might be sturdy, but she's ancient. Also, she knows how to intimidate people."

"So, how serious are we talking about here? Two, three weeks?"

"Six."

"Oh." I blink at him. "Six weeks is before the wedding."

"Six months."

Six months!

"Wow. That's something, since I've only been in California for three months."

He grunts and busies himself with stacks of mail on his desk. "It doesn't matter because I'm ending it."

"Ouch."

"You know what I mean. The lie. I'm ending the lie."

"I certainly hope it's not a reflection of my performance as a girlfriend, because I am an amazing cuddler."

"I'm sure you are."

"Also, not to brag or anything, but I'm really good at spooning. The small spoon, of course."

"Isn't that the same as cuddling?"

"No. Quite different."

His nostrils flare and he's just staring at me like I'm completely nuts. I flash him my cheeriest grin.

"That's all very fascinating, Olive, but I think we're done here. I wanted you to hear it from me, but I guess it's too late for that. I'm just sorry I had to drag you into this."

"I'll do it." I shoot up from my chair, extending my hand to him to shake on it. His eyes bounce from my hand to me, from me to my hand, and back again.

"Do what?"

"I'll be your fake girlfriend." I stretch my hand out with more determination.

"I didn't ask you to be my fake girlfriend. I told you I'll take care of it."

I tap my chin. "We'll need to come up with a meet-cute," I say.

"A *what*?" he snaps.

"A meet-cute. We locked eyes across a crowded room and knew we were fated mates, or we were strangers on a train and wound up talking for hours and walking the streets of Austria all night, only to meet six months later in the exact same spot. Or… oh!" I frame a shot with my hands. "We reached for the same pair of black cashmere gloves at a department store and it was the last one, so we tried to decide who got to keep them by spending an enchanting evening having coffee, ice skating, and writing our phone numbers in classic novels."

"That seems oddly specific and asinine."

Hmmm. What else?

"We could go for the classic Holiday trope. Me and another troubled woman, sad and disenchanted with our lives, decided to swap houses during Christmas. You, her handsome brother, came to visit her quintessential English country cottage. But you're surprised to see *me* there. Then I realized you're the guy for me because you made me cry for the first time ever."

"Not only does that sound horrific, it's incredibly unbelievable."

"I suppose time travel is out of the question?"

"The whole idea is out of the question."

"At least we got the first kiss out of the way. That one's always a doozy in the fake-dating trope."

"There will be no fake dating or cute meets—"

"Meet-cutes," I correct.

He covers his entire face with his gloriously large hands and breathes in and out. In and out. Then uses those same hands to pull fistfuls of his hair.

"It'll be okay," I assure him. "Turn that frown upside down."

He slams his hands on the desk and grits his teeth. Did someone say his name three times to summon Chef Crabby Cakes?

"I'll think of something on my own. A break-up story. I don't need you to play-act a part."

"Listen." I stuff my hands in my apron pocket. "I know how this goes down. You told the whole *mishpocha* you have a long-term girlfriend. They lose their minds over it, calling all the relatives and neighbors. Then all of a sudden you and your mystery girlfriend suspiciously break up? One, your family won't believe you ever really had a girlfriend, or two, they'll burn you at the stake."

"Not if we break things off amicably," he says through his teeth. I can tell he's trying so hard to keep his cool.

"Meanwhile, I still work here."

He shrugs. "So?"

"It would be awkward."

Ignacio lifts one brow and watches me for a long moment. His gaze is charged—or maybe it's just my imagination. But there's something behind those steel-gray eyes that shoot right to my feels. Like he's downloading a shmexy virus in my system. Beep boop beep.

"And how long would we have to keep up this ruse? Until you don't work here anymore?"

The computer chip, or whatever thing is buried in my body, swoops down and crashes behind my ribs. I don't want to think about not working here. Not while I'm still figuring out what I want to do with my life.

But I shrug, like I'm all casual about it. "Until it's not awkward anymore."

He grunts. "Thanks, but no." He goes back to whatever work he has on his desk. "Keep the door open on your way out."

Okay, he's not going for my offer. And if I'm honest, it is kind of ridiculous. But he can't just dismiss me this way.

"What about my schedule? You said—"

"Rosa can go over that with you."

He shoos me off with a wave of his hand, not bothering to look up. Just as well. His whole face is a weakness of mine, and I better get my act together before I embarrass myself again.

With a sigh dramatic enough to make my disappointment clear, I shuffle to the door and sweep it open. My heart almost leaps to my throat when I come face to face with none other than the senior Mr. Precio. He stares at me, a little intimidating, but only a shadow of the man Ignacio is. And I can see how he must have once been a towering presence of a man, foreboding and stern—just like his son.

"You must be Olive," he says, kind of grumbly—and I'm not sure if he considers meeting me a good thing, or if he's seriously displeased to see me. I nod, smiling in the warm way I decided a long time ago would be my signature. There's a lot of sadness and ickiness in the world, but a smile can change someone's day around.

"I sure am," I say, and I decide to go in for a hug. I've found that either you're a hugger or not. Mr. Precio is clearly in the 'not' camp. His arms stiffen at his sides, and although he's not made of marble like Ignacio, his reaction is indication enough to keep the hug under one second.

"Take a seat," he says, and I do, lowering myself into the same chair as before.

Mr. Precio is not one to close doors. He also has a booming voice, loud enough for the kitchen staff to hear him say, "So you're the girlfriend."

Ignacio pinches the bridge of his nose. "Dad, this is Olive. She's kind of in a hurry to get home, though. She… has a sick goldfish."

Oh, brother. Ignacio keeps getting deeper and deeper.

"It's actually my neighbor's goldfish," I say. "Little Orangie can wait."

"But didn't you promise to take Orangie to the vet?" Ignacio's flashing his eyes at me, ticking his head to the door.

Mr. Precio raises a brow. "You're taking a goldfish to the vet? I've never heard of such a thing."

"He's a very spoiled fish," I say solemnly. "And frankly, I think he's just faking it to get attention."

"What's wrong with him?"

"He's... turning white," says Ignacio. "And the vet closes soon, so..."

Mr. Precio pulls a face. "Sounds like someone cleaned the tank with bleach."

I shrug and cross my legs, leaning back in the chair. "Oh well. There's no hope for Orangie now. I might as well stay a while."

Ignacio palms his forehead and takes a seat behind the desk.

"Dad, you were just here yesterday. You should be home resting."

Mr. Precio swats at nothing in particular. "I can't rest with those two ladies bickering, *que la fregada*."

"What two ladies? Mom and Abuela?"

"*Tu sabes*, Nacho. Your mother can't take a joke, and Abuela can't keep her mouth shut."

"What did Abuela say now?"

"She makes fun of her Spanish, that's all."

I throw a quizzical look at Ignacio.

"My mom came to the U.S. when she was eleven, so her Spanish isn't perfect," he says to me. "But neither is mine and I get by."

His dad snorts. "Abuela *especially* makes fun of you and your brothers."

"I mixed up my pronouns ONE time!"

Mr. Precio laughs and laughs. "Whatever you say… *La Ignacio.*"

He's giggling at his own joke so hard, he starts coughing.

"Are you okay?" I offer. "Can I get you a water?"

"He's fine," says Ignacio. "And he's not as funny as he thinks."

Mr. Precio taps my knee. "I'm okay. Thank you."

"Alright, well this has been fun," says Ignacio, getting up from his chair to shoo us out. "But I have piles of work."

"I can tell when I'm being kicked out." Mr. Precio flicks his hand at Ignacio, then turns to me. "This used to be my office, you know," he says, as though I'm his new confidant.

"Really?" Of course I knew that already.

"Would you like to have a *cerveza* with me?"

Aww. He seems so sweet. I'd be a monster to refuse.

"No beer for you, Dad. And nothing with sugar." Ignacio scowls at me behind his dad's back, slicing his hand across his own throat. Okay, okay. I can take a hint.

Looping my arm through Mr. Precio's elbow, I walk out of the office with him, heading to the front of the house.

"I would love to have a drink with you sometime," I say as sweetly as possible. "But I suppose I really do need to check on that goldfish. Can I take a raincheck?"

The old man covers my hand with his, squeezing me in tighter by his side.

"What are you doing Sunday?"

"Laundry, probably."

Ignacio, who's following behind us, clears his throat in an extremely obvious way.

"Then I expect you for dinner," says Mr. Precio with a

wry smile, the old bugger. "My house. Good food. *Buen vino*. Do you like ribs?"

"I love ribs," I say.

We're at the bar now, and Ignacio clears his throat again.

"Olive, may I have a quick word?"

"Pork or beef?"

"Dad, she's Jewish. She doesn't eat pork."

I toss up a hand and blow a raspberry. "I'm not Kosher. Pork is fine."

"Olive?" Ignacio warns.

I give Mr. Precio another hug, which he reciprocates this time. "It was nice to meet you, Mr. Precio. I'll see you Sunday."

"Call me Francisco. And come casual. We're not fancy, unlike my son. *Pretencioso*."

"Casual is my middle name," I chirp, even as Ignacio squeezes between me and his father to get the bartender's attention.

"No sugar for my dad," he orders, tapping the bar.

Josh, the bartender, gives him a nod and then greets Mr. Precio with a familiar smile. The old man says something under his breath and Josh laughs, both of them glancing over at Ignacio.

"What do you think you're doing?" Ignacio hisses as he leads me by the elbow to the busser station.

"What? Nothing."

"You can't just come over on Sunday."

"Why not?"

He presses his fingers on his temples. "Because you're not really my girlfriend."

"Okay, fine. But I was going to bring the Manischewitz."

"Well, now you don't have to go through the trouble. What is Manischewitz anyhow?"

"It's kind of a sweet wine. It's not very good, but it's cheap, so…"

Ignacio lets out a sigh and scrubs his hands over his eyes. Now that I have a closer look, he seems tired and stressed. The delicate skin under his eyes has a slight yellowish purple tint. And that tousled hair? It's poking in every possible direction.

"Are you alright?" I perch my fists on my hips, inclining my head to the side. "Do you need emergency chocolate?"

He breathes a half-hearted laugh. "No. But thank you."

I squint one eye at him. "Are you sure?"

"Very."

"Okay, well… I guess I won't see you Sunday."

He offers a closed-lip smile, and for a moment, there's a small twinkle in his weary eyes.

"I guess you won't. Goodnight, Olive."

With a cheeky wink, I nod and head over to clock out.

"And Olive?"

"Yeah?"

He waves in my general direction. "Thanks for adhering to the dress code."

"Anytime, boss."

After a good dinner,
one can
forgive anybody,
even one's own relations.

— Oscar Wilde

Chapter Eight

IGNACIO

I lean in to whisper in Olive's ear. "How do you know all the responses and gestures?"

"I'm a quick study," she whispers back. "Also, YouTube."

Of all the whacky situations I could have imagined myself in, kneeling in the pews next to my Jewish fake girlfriend at Sunday Mass would never have crossed my mind.

Yes, yes. I know. I was very much against bringing Olive

to the Sunday-with-the-fam thing. Turns out I'm easy to bribe. All it took was Mom and Dad agreeing to keep that pink-dress-wearing dog for the rest of the summer while Enrique and January are on their ludicrously long honeymoon. I have a feeling my parents would have taken Brownie anyway since they have a Yorkie of their own from the same litter. It's not a big ask. But here I am, victim of my own botched negotiation. I was never good at making deals outside of a restaurant. It's why Enrique always beat me at Monopoly.

And apparently, I can't even talk my fake girlfriend into waiting until *after* church to meet me at my parents' house for dinner. She insisted we ride together. "For appearance's sake," she'd said, and then met me at the restaurant after I was done with the Sunday brunch crowd.

"Are you sure you're not uncomfortable?" I ask. It's time for us to go up for communion, and I'm not so sure she knows to stay in her seat.

"Don't worry," she assures me, scrunching her adorable little nose in a way that spreads warm sparks through my chest. "I'm aware of the rules."

This was a horrible idea—simply because, after that kiss, I can't seem to look at Olive the same way. Her rosy cheeks. Her soft, pink lips. Her—

Stop it, man. You're in church.

I look over at my sister Francesca, singing up there with her guitar, beautiful as ever. And then my gaze drifts to that boyfriend of hers on piano. I don't know what she sees in the guy. He spends half his time in New York. I'm not on board with that for my sister. And I just can't trust a guy named Edmund—I read too much Narnia as a kid.

After Mass, we walk back to the house. I usually rush ahead of my Mom and siblings to get dinner started, but Dad's cooking tonight—his self-proclaimed famous pork ribs he's been slow cooking in his new smoker. Francesca, of course, will have tofu, and my Jewish fake girlfriend—well, I guess if she's okay with pork, I'll go along with it.

"You have a lot of siblings," Olive says as we leave the church. "We took up an entire row."

"Yeah, well. Not all of my brothers are here."

"The one on his honeymoon?"

"Him, yes. And my brother Guillermo. We call him Memo for short. He couldn't get away tonight."

She grins, taking my hand for show. "Cool beans."

I'll take that a sign of her approval—not that I'm seeking it. I've decided to end our charade when Abuela goes back to Mexico. I just haven't told Olive yet.

The smell of the meat reaches my senses before we even reach the house. I find Dad in the backyard sipping on Trader Joe's beer, listening to Carlos Santana on a Bluetooth speaker while watching soccer on the big screen T.V. he installed under the patio covering. The volume is turned up full blast on both devices.

The two Yorkies sit expectantly at his feet, going crazy over the aroma of the meat. Brownie's in a sparkly pink T-shirt today, but Mom's dog, Lulu, isn't even wearing a collar. I have a feeling the state of Lulu's nakedness has something to do with how Dad has absolutely claimed the dog as his own, even though January and Enrique adopted her for Mom. There's no way he'd allow any dog of his to wear pink. According to Francesca, Dad is smitten with that tiny dog—carrying her everywhere he goes and speaking baby talk as he feeds her treats. I don't think he was this enamored with his own children when we were babies.

"Awww," coos, Olive. "Puppers."

Olive is committed to playing her part well—clinging to my arm like a doting girlfriend who can't keep her hands off me for one second. If I did have an actual girlfriend, I wouldn't need her so frickin' close all the time. I don't do PDA nor would any woman I date. But somehow, it doesn't bother me with Olive as it would with other girls. I suppose it's because I know she won't expect anything when I take her home tonight. No expectations. No complications. Just how I like my life.

Then a miracle happens and Dad turns off the game when he sees Olive. This must be an alternate universe. Dad turns off his game for *no one*.

Olive hugs him (as she did with Mom and every single one of my siblings earlier), and—wonder of wonders—he hugs her in return.

"How's Orangie?" he asks her.

She ticks her head in confusion. "Orangie?"

"Your neighbor's fish."

Oh boy.

"Great," she says, brightening. "He made a full recovery."

This woman. Even her made up stories have a happy ending.

Dad smiles—as much of a smile I've ever seen on him—and clasps a hand over Olive's.

"Glad to hear it," he says. "Beer?"

"Ah, gevalt," she says, snapping her fingers. "I left the

Manischewitz in the car. We parked and went straight into temple—I mean church."

Yeah, I was hoping she'd forget about that bottle of wine.

With a sigh, I offer, "I'll go grab it. I have to park the car closer to the house anyway."

Finding it faster to go through the side gate, I head through the rose garden, fishing the keys out of my pocket. I get as far as the Saint Francis statue Mom placed at the edge of the garden, when I hear the banshee shriek of Tía Lucy.

Rushing back in two seconds flat, I come upon the scene —Tía Lucy, recently arrived with her purse still slung over her shoulder, pointing an accusing finger at Olive.

"You!" she cries, really putting the back of her throat into it. She's gearing up to light a torch and lead a mob with pitchforks.

Somebody please tell Tía Lucy this isn't the Salem Witch Trials, nor are we at an eighteenth-century hanging.

Olive points at her own chest, backing up slightly, and as Tía Lucy prowls toward her (in her portly Tía Lucy way), awareness dawns on Olive's features. And I realize I didn't prepare my family for this. Of course, at the wedding, my parents were too far away to see, and the crowd was too thick, the chaos too wild for my siblings to get a good look. But Tía Lucy never forgets a face. What's worse, she's a grudge holder to the tenth degree. And right now, there's murder in her eyes. Murder with four layers of fondant fresh in her memory.

Hobbling after Olive, she charges, and Olive—not knowing where to go—dodges behind the long, rustic farmhouse table we sit at for Sunday dinners. It's a bespoke piece crafted by an old Peruvian woodworker Dad had traded favors with back in the day. We have a lot of memories with this table. But right now, it's acting as a barricade for the woman who wronged Tía Lucy and a five-thousand-dollar wedding cake.

For a full minute, Tía Lucy chases Olive around the table, stopping to change direction and back again. Lucy's shouting something imperceptible as Olive squeals, interjecting apologies while circling the table. At one point, she kicks off her shoes, which Lucy almost trips over. Dad finds this whole show quite entertaining, sipping his beer, bobbing his head to "Oye Como Va" by Santana.

Meanwhile, a crowd has formed—Mom, Abuela, my tíos; Enrique, Pedro, and Borris, and of course, my siblings.

It only takes Tía Lucy to run out of breath before the chase is over, at which point, Dad starts a round of applause, his brothers joining in.

"*Échale vampiro*," shouts Tío Pedro. I have no clue what he means by that, but Tío Pedro rarely makes any sense at the best of times.

Some of Olive's hair has fallen loose from the two clips she had above her temples. She's like a disheveled sprite. Tía Lucy doesn't look quite as fresh. Her face has turned Day-Glo pink, and she's panting as though she'd just come from the Pamplona bull run. Sebastian fetches her a glass of water, and, seeing as there's nothing else to see, my uncles join Dad for a beverage and turn the game back on.

"Tía?" I say, approaching her tentatively. "I see you've met my… girlfriend?" Probably not the best thing to say under the circumstances.

Her head slowly turns like a Chuckie doll to glare at Olive. If she wasn't so winded, she'd have a few choice words, none of which are proper to repeat.

"Why don't you sit down, okay?" I guide her to a chair and she flops on it, leaning an elbow on the farm table. Once she takes a few swigs of water and catches her breath, she croaks out, "Am I living in a nightmare? Oh, my head."

Any minute now, she'll be asking for smelling salts.

Abuela, who has very little patience for her son's crazy sister-in-law, swats her hand and goes back inside the house. Mom comes over to comfort her sister but has a tick of a grin on her face. It's been a while since she's had any form of entertainment, apparently. Well, not since the wedding. Leave it to my Olive to spice things up.

She's not *your* Olive, idiot.

"Tell me what *she's* doing here," Tía Lucy demands.

"That's Olive, *hermana*," says Mom. "Nacho's girlfriend."

Olive is still on the other end of the table, guarding herself behind one of the heavy wooden chairs. I extend my hand, inviting her to come. She shuffles over, gliding under my arm. She fits perfectly at my side. So pillowy soft.

"Tía, when you hear what we have to say, you're going to love Olive just as much as I do."

Olive shifts under my arm. Why did I have to bring up the L word? As far as anyone is concerned, we've been together for six months. That seems like a reasonable amount of time to tell your girlfriend you love her. Right?

If it bothers Olive, she doesn't show it other than a slight twitch. She goes on to tell the same story she told me. How there was a bug on Lucy's food. How she had to act fast, or

Lucy would have had a creepy crawly in her mouth. Olive actually says the words 'creepy crawly' to dramatize her point.

I see a transformation come over Tía Lucy's face. She's not completely appeased, but her skin is returning to a normal color, at least.

Mom is trying her best to hold back a laugh, but my brothers—who frankly I'd forgotten about—are busting up.

"You know, I thought you looked familiar," says Nate.

Mateo shakes his head. "Not me. I had a front-row seat when you flew into the cake, and I didn't recognize you at all today."

"It's the catering uniform," says Olive. "No one looks at your face while you're serving."

"But then you just left the reception," says Mom. "Cake or no cake, you're Ignacio's girlfriend. You should have stuck around."

"She was too embarrassed, Mom," I say.

And Olive adds, "I didn't have a change of clothes."

"*You* didn't have a change of clothes?" cries Tía Lucy. "What about me? Francesca had to clean me up in the restroom. My new dress was damp and crusty the rest of the day."

"I'm sorry," says Olive. "Truly."

Tía Lucy pulls a face as though she's considering if she wants to forgive Olive just yet. Olive opens both arms.

"Wanna hug it out?"

Tía narrows her eyes at her. "What I want is to lie down."

Sebastian escorts Tía Lucy into a spare bedroom and

Olive mouths the words *"I'm sorry"* to me. Mom notices this and pulls her into a hug.

"Happens to the best of us, *cariño.*"

She hooks arms with her and leads her off toward the garden. Olive winks at me over her shoulder as they retreat. Something squeezes inside my chest—a feeling I don't care for. I've gone down this road before and it wasn't pretty. I decide to busy myself with the only thing that settles me. Cooking.

"What are you doing for vegetables, Dad?"

He's too engrossed in the soccer game to hear me, not to mention how Tío Enrique shouts over me.

"Que animal. ¡Metela, boludo!"

Borris and Pedro join him with groans of disappointment.

"Dad?"

"Hijole chambón," Tío Borris grunts.

"Padre mio," I yell.

All three uncles turn their heads. Well, that seemed to work. Dad raises his eyebrows at me as if to let me know I have two seconds of his attention or else wait for the commercial.

"Veggies? What's for dinner besides ribs?"

"No te preocupes, Nacho. Aye elotes y papas."

I roll my eyes. "Corn and potatoes aren't vegetables."

I go into the kitchen, where Nate is making himself a peanut butter and jelly sandwich.

"Nate, can't you wait twenty minutes?"

"Nope."

This guy. He's never without food in his mouth for more

than a half-hour at a time. Good thing he burns it all off by surfing.

Opening the fridge, I rummage through the disaster of uncovered food containers of cooked meat, mystery salsas, and jars of every condiment imaginable to get to the box of spring mix. I find broccoli and carrots in the crisper and start a pot of water to boil so I can blanch them. I know my way around this kitchen like the back of my hand, but that doesn't help much when Dad's always moving things around. He's the worst person I know at organizing. After opening a few cabinets, I finally find the olive oil, honey, and balsamic vinegar, then get right into preparing the salad dressing.

Nate watches me move about the kitchen, leaning against the counter. He's left the peanut butter and jelly out, not at all bothered by the crumbs and drippings of jam on the countertop.

"So…" he starts, mouth full of sandwich. "Your *girl-friend* seems nice."

He accentuates the word girlfriend just to irk me.

"Yep. She's nice," I say, pouring the oil into a bowl.

"I'm just like, surprised, you know?" He takes another bite, gulping half the sandwich into his mouth. Seriously, can't he eat like a human person instead of a Rottweiler? I don't think he even tastes it.

"We were… keeping it secret." I point to the fridge. "Pass me the Dijon. It's in the door."

"Why?"

"Because the recipe calls for it. You're right there, Nate."

He sighs and retrieves the Dijon mustard from the

refrigerator door, passing it to me by stretching his arm as far as he can without moving his feet.

"I mean, why the secrecy? Six months is a long time to keep a secret from this family."

"Ah, this family." I shake my head, mixing the ingredients together with a whisk. "This family is the whole reason I haven't brought her around. You're all nuts."

He holds up his hands in surrender. "Okay, okay. I was just wondering if it was because—"

"Don't you dare say it." I point the whisk at him, droplets of dressing flinging in his direction.

"I wasn't going to bring up the 'S' word."

My brothers know better than to bring up *that* four-letter word around me, but sometimes I hear them use it as a substitute for another 'S' word when they don't realize I can hear them.

S-H-A-Y. After four-and-a-half years, I still can't stand to hear *her* name.

They'll casually say things like, "What a load of bull-shay." or "That movie was total shay."

Dante's personal favorite is, "This car is a piece of shay."

I suppose using my ex's name as a curse word is my brothers' unconventional way of standing in solidarity with me.

"Just don't scare Olive away," I say, turning on the faucet to wash the broccoli. As I toss the broccoli in the colander, I mentally slap myself. Why should I care if my crazy family scares off my fake girlfriend? That might even be a good excuse to break up.

I don't notice Nate has moved to my side until he pats his hand on my shoulder.

"Popeye, if we didn't scare off Enrique's fancy heiress, I think your Olive Oyl is safe."

"Har, har."

He sneaks a piece of broccoli and uses it to point to the spring mix.

"Don't forget the spinach." He dips the broccoli into the dressing and pops it in his mouth. "Needs salt."

"That's it." I scoop up a damp kitchen towel and spin it from the corners, making a whip. Nate runs, flying out of the kitchen, but I'm just fast enough to snap the towel at his retreating ass.

Oh man, that whip crack is a satisfying sound—almost as satisfying as Nate screaming like a little girl, followed by the laughter of my other brothers.

"I think the Duke did love Gilda, in his own way," says Francesca.

"What? No." Mateo pulls a face. "He was a horrible person."

Now that everyone's done chasing each other, and the Precio family 'normal meter' has once again gauged up a few decibels, we're enjoying a ceasefire at the grand farm table on the patio deck. Tía Lucy, ever so dramatic, has declared she's too faint to dine with the rest of us, and is still resting. Between the way my brothers are inhaling the ribs, Dad sneaking scraps under the table for Brownie and Lulu, and Tío Pedro serving himself an obscene amount as an excuse to take leftovers home, I doubt there will be much food for Tía Lucy when she decides to emerge.

"All I'm saying," says Francesca, "is Rigoletto was so obsessed with revenge, he didn't listen to his daughter when she said she loved the Duke. He basically called her a silly woman. If he hadn't been so blind with hate, she wouldn't have died."

"No, no no. Gilda died from her own stupidity," cries Mateo.

Olive asks me, "What are they talking about? Bridgerton?"

"An Italian opera. They'll be at it all night." I chuckle to myself, watching her trying to listen intently to my siblings. "Clearly, you've never seen Bridgerton."

She blushes. "Oh, heavens, no. Have you?"

"Heck no. But I'm pretty sure the girl doesn't die."

Sebastian waves his baked potato, having just taken a bite. "Isn't that the one where the guy's in a bar and the whore has a knife under the bed?"

"Language, Sebastian," Mom cries. I didn't even think she was paying attention to the conversation. "And use your fork."

"We're eating ribs, Ma."

"You can use your hands for the ribs, but your fork for the potato."

"I'll just get the fork full of barbecue sauce," he argues.

"That's what napkins are for."

I lean over to conspire with Olive. "Just watch. Now we'll have a whole etiquette conversation on top of the opera conversation."

"Oh, the irony." She nudges me with her elbow—even that benign touch sends my heart racing.

"Do you see now why I was trying to spare you from my family dinner?"

She shrugs and beams at me with that million-watt smile. "I don't mind."

"'La Donna è Mobile' is all about how the Duke was heartbroken when she left," continues Francesca.

Mateo practically chokes on his corn on the cob. "You're kidding, right? He's a complete rake."

"Yes, he's a cad, but he was willing to change for Gilda. That line where he says how he could become a faithful man for her because she's so pure…" Francesca clutches her heart. "It's the classic bad-boy trope."

"You're too romantic and trusting for your own good," says Nate. He's referring to that movie star Francesca brought over for dinner two Christmases ago—who happened to be… wait for it… a rake. They were engaged for a hot minute—until Edmund decided he (cue the puking) suddenly liked my sister after *all these years of being just friends*. Jealousy works like that for fickle guys like Edmund. And Francesca wonders why my brothers and I don't trust him. Still, she did dodge a bullet. Her movie star fiancé was outed by the 'Me Too' movement not long after she broke off their engagement. Some actress claimed he was her baby daddy, and then all sorts of women came out of the woodwork with their own stories. Francesca swears he never touched her, but if I would have been able to find him, there wouldn't be much left of his face.

"Nothing wrong with being romantic," says Edmund, giving my sister googly eyes. I notice just then how my other brother, Dante, hardens his stare at Edmund.

"Trusting is another matter altogether," he grunts, taking a vicious bite of ribs, eyes pinned on Edmund.

Mom calls to him from the other end of the table. "Dante, there are no vegetables on your plate."

It's true. Dante's plate is piled high with barbecue ribs and nothing else. Not even a baked potato.

"What happens to the Duke?" Olive asks Francesca. "Is he sad when the girl dies?"

"We never find out," says Francesca. "The play just ends when she dies."

"He doesn't give a flying fig if she dies," cries Mateo. "The Duke's too busy doing it with the assassin's sister."

"Mateo!" cries Mom.

Dad barks at Dante, also from all the way across the table. "*Come un poco de ensalada.*"

"*Tu eres uno para hablar,*" chirps Abuela, sitting next to Dad. "*Nunca comiste tus verduras.*"

"This is why he has health problems," says Mom, agreeing with Abuela that Dad should have eaten his veggies as a child. This, Abuela considers an invitation to slip some underhanded jokes about Mom's horrible cooking and poor domestic skills. She's loud and works the room for laughs among her sons, clueless to the cultural differences in social etiquette. Or maybe that's just Abuela's way. Mom chooses to ignore her, draining her wine glass.

At the opposite end of the table, Sebastian chimes in about the assassin's sister from the opera, mouth full of meat. Francesca is certifiably grossed out by this, being a vegetarian, which prompts Mom to scold Sebastian for speaking with food in his mouth.

Everyone's talking at once now—which is normal for a

Precio family dinner. We kind of have our own opera—a quartet of melodies all at once. Dante and Nate are grilling Edmund about what exactly his views are on trust and forgiveness.

Abuela, Dad, and my three tíos are now making plans for another shopping trip, as if Abuela hasn't been shopping almost every single day since she arrived in California.

Olive is having a robust conversation with Mateo, Sebastian, and Francesca about redemption arcs for fictional characters. And I'm just watching her, astounded by the way she slides into the family dynamic with ease, laughing and shining her light. She has a full, hearty laugh, and her whole face illuminates with true joy. She's not a demure girl by any means—but she's every bit a woman, so carefree and breezy.

And those leggings. This time they're blue with skiing penguins in red and green-striped scarves. She's a walking ABC Christmas special.

To complete the ensemble, her orange T-shirt entirely clashes with the color scheme of the leggings, but somehow on her, it just works. The shirt is cut off at the waist, exposing the tiniest sliver of skin when she leans across the table for more sour cream, and I have the feeling it's a half size too small—the way it stretches over her chest, rendering the words 'Camp Half Blood' almost unreadable.

My fingers itch to tug at the hem of her shirt so nobody but me will catch a glimpse of the ivory skin above the waistband of her ridiculous leggings. I've never met anyone so open and artless yet remain a complete enigma. How everyone seems to love her—through her unbridled sincerity, her impetuous zeal for life. How she makes people laugh and smile—men and women enamored by her, even as she reverts all the attention away from herself. It's fascinating to watch.

Eventually, Dante and Nate abandon their interrogation of Edmund to listen to Olive tell the story of how she accidentally entered the Sonic drive-through going the wrong way. Somehow, she convinced the cashier to take her order anyway, then proceeded to the pick-up window with her car in reverse. The folksy, spontaneous way she tells the story, unashamed to make fun of herself, has Edmund and my siblings rolling, practically falling off their chairs.

Dad, completely clueless that he's interrupting, shouts across the table.

"Olive, show my mother your shoes."

"My shoes? Right now?"

Before my dad was born, when God was passing out manners to new souls awaiting their assignments, Dad must have stepped out of line while tact was being passed out. Apparently, he doesn't see the hillbilly factor with showing one's feet at the dinner table.

"Yes, yes," he says. "Just let us see them."

"Dad," Francesca warns through gritted teeth, shaking her head at him. "Why?"

Tío Borris (who I thought was the cool uncle when I was a child but now realize he's the stuck-in-the-80s uncle) throws up his hands.

"I bought my mom a pair of shoes and they're too big," he says, shrugging.

"*No me gustan,*" says Abuela with a scowl.

Dad points his fork at Tío Borris. "Maybe let her pick out her own shoes next time, *burro.*"

"I wanted her to have nice shoes!" Borris responds.

Abuela pulls a face. "*¿Por qué querría unos zapatos tan feos?*"

"I don't think they're ugly," he protests.

Tío Enrique decides to add his two cents because he just can't help it. Never mind that his mouth is full of meat. "*Ni siquiera sabes su talla, carnal.*"

Then he kind of grunts and swats his hand at Tío Borris. Tío Pedro is finding this whole thing amusing, quietly laughing in his corner seat. Somebody better remove all beverages from his vicinity. He already spilled beer down his front while cheering for the soccer game earlier. Now his clothes smell like the floor of a sports bar.

"*Madre, deberías comprar zapatos como Olive. Son muy bonitos.*"

"Okay, I heard my name in that sentence," Olive whispers to me. What are they saying?"

"My uncle bought my grandma some shoes that she basically hates, and Dad's trying to convince her to buy a pair like you're wearing."

"Oh." She scrunches her nose the way she does when she's a little confused. "My Crocs?"

I can only roll my eyes and shrug.

"Now I'm curious," says Mom. "I hadn't paid attention to her shoes."

"Show us your shoes, Olive," says Dad.

Borris agrees. "Yes, show us your shoes."

Oh, good grief.

Dad won't give up until he gets his way, and now my whole family wants to see her Crocs. So my easygoing fake girlfriend, instead of getting up to walk around the table like a normal person, scoots her chair back and kicks up her leg—right next to my face. My jaw hits the floor. Abuela applauds. Dad gloats as if he's the grandmaster of fashion.

"You see? Those are some nice shoes."

Olive, casually sitting with her leg stretched straight in the air, looks up at her foot, rotating her ankle side to side. "They're just your average classic clog."

"*A mi me gusta*," says Abuela, nodding approvingly.

Francesca gapes at Olive. "How are you so flexible?"

"Karate."

"You can put your foot down now," I say.

Olive lowers her leg and scoots her chair in.

My brothers glance between themselves and then over to me. Mateo wags his brows suggestively. I glower at him.

"*No las he visto en el* T.J. Maxx," Abuela says dismally.

"*Regresamos al* T.J. Maxx tomorrow," says Borris. "There's another one on Martin Luther King Boulevard."

Abuela nods. "Martin Luther King. *Buen tipo ese hombre.*"

Dad groans. "*Todos los días*, T.J. Maxx. Why don't you take her to the beach or a museum?"

"I don't have time for that," says Borris. "I have to work."

Dad slams his fist on the table. "*Aye que la fregada.*"

"Where did you get your shoes, Olive?" Mom asks.

Olive, who has been trying to keep up with the Spanish but is left with a baffled expression simply responds by saying, "Jersey."

Tío Enrique scoots his chair back and rubs his belly, clearly uninterested in where Abuela might find a pair of Crocs. "*Estoy lleno, mi chavo. Pero que rico los* ribs."

"Six hours in the smoker," says Dad.

As if on cue, Tío Pedro sneaks another serving of ribs and a baked potato, taking his plate into the kitchen where he'd left his to-go containers.

"I'll bet we can find Crocs at the fashion district," says Mom.

"*Ese lugar me pone feo,*" says Dad.

Mom frowns. "What do you mean you don't like it? You love the fashion district."

"I only like the soccer store." He waves his hand dismissively. "You can go if you want to. Just the women."

"Me alone with your mom? In downtown L.A.?"

"Take Francesca with you."

"No thanks," says Francesca. "Last time I went there I stepped in feces. And I'm pretty sure it wasn't from a dog."

Sebastian nods. "The sidewalks do smell like urine."

"Olive, would you like to go?" Mom looks at Olive with pleading eyes. "Ignacio can drive us."

"ME?"

Dad throws me a hard glare. "Nacho, Abuela wants new shoes. Don't make your mother take her alone."

Francesca shakes her head slowly at Olive, with her eyes big and wide. "Don't do it," she whispers.

Olive glances between Francesca and Edmund, knowing they've spent time in New York. "Is it as bad as the Bronx?"

Edmund just laughs. "It's nothing like the Bronx."

"We tow cars from there all the time," says Dante. "I've never stepped in feces."

"So I'm the only one," Francesca deadpans. "Lucky me."

Dad claps his hands together. "It's settled. Nacho, you'll

take your mom and Abuela downtown, and then you can buy your girlfriend something nice."

"You do realize I have restaurants to run, right?"

"Do you ever take a day off?"

"Yes. I take Sundays off," I say.

"Going in for five hours doesn't count as a day off. Find a day this week when the restaurant might not fall apart without you there, and take your women shopping. Olive, what would you like to shop for?"

"Um, I don't know. What kinds of things do they sell?" she asks innocently.

"If you like low-waisted jeans and satin quinceañera gowns, you'll be in heaven," I say.

Olive twists her lips, thinking about it for a second, then hitches one shoulder. "Sounds fun. I'll just watch where I step—just in case."

"I remember that day," says Sebastian. "Francesca almost threw up and mom had to buy her a new pair of shoes."

Francesca tosses her hands up. "Okay, enough of that. We're eating. Someone please change the subject."

"You brought it up," says Sebastian.

"So, Olive," says Edmund. "You never told us how you and Ignacio met?"

Francesca claps her hands together. "Yes, please. I live for a good meet cute story."

What is it with meet cutes all of a sudden? I thought Olive made up that term.

Olive's delicate little mouth curls crookedly, and she glances at me briefly with that impish grin.

"Well, then. Have I got a story for you."

Food is not rational.
Food is culture,
habit, craving
and identity.

– Jonathan Safran Foer

Chapter Nine

OLIVE

My last customer of the day is quickly becoming one of my favorites. He comes in for a late lunch almost daily, and even though his check doesn't come out to much, he always tips well. Like, *really* well. But that's not the reason I like him.

Tom is in his late sixties maybe, and always has a crazy story dating back to his hippie days in the 1970s, living in his van. He's never worked a steady job in his life, surviving from selling his handcrafted jewelry while on the road following the Grateful Dead, or finding valuables on the beach with his metal detector. Nowadays he shops yard sales for antiques and resells them on eBay. I guess he does pretty well.

Today, when he first came in, he had a gift for me. A box full of garden gnomes.

"I knew you were a collector of sorts," he said. "I don't think you could sell them on eBay for a profit, but if they put a smile on your face, they're worth more than money."

"I love them," I said, picking up the big one. "Wow. It's super heavy,"

"I think maybe he's made of concrete," Tom replied. "For durability, I suppose."

"Well, thank you. I shall cherish them always and think of you."

"Oh, and I almost forgot to show you this."

He reaches into his pocket and pulls out a purple Beanie Baby.

"Mint condition," he said, then shoved it back in his pants pocket. "I'll just keep it in my pocket for safekeeping. Don't want to get salsa all over it."

I've never understood the fascination with Beanie Babies myself, but if there are people out there who like them as much as I like gnomes, then I approve wholeheartedly.

Tom ordered his food—his usual chicken tacos and a side salad, and after he's done with his meal, I have his check ready, waiting for him to return from a bathroom run. It's a whole routine. He eats his tacos, goes to the men's room, then comes back to his table to pay for his meal, ready to tell me a story from his life that is too amazing to be true.

But today, when he reaches for his wallet, a string of curse words comes out of his mouth that would make a sailor blush and, jumping up, he runs back to the bathroom like his pants are on fire.

He returns a few minutes later looking all worked up. I'm thinking he had some bad reaction to the beans or something, but when I ask if he's okay, he rolls his eyes and tosses his palm on his forehead.

"I'm fine. But I can't say the same about the other guy."

"What other guy?"

"When I went to the bathroom—the first time—my bear must have fallen out of my pocket.

"And… you noticed it was gone when you went for your wallet?"

"That's why I ran back like a bat outta hell."

"You sure did."

He wipes his brow. "When I got there, the stall was occupied, so I kicked down the door."

"No way. Was it locked?"

"Well, yes."

"You must have strong feet."

"Those stalls are flimsy."

"So, was the bear still in there?"

"There was this young guy sitting on the toilet—with his pants down."

I cover my mouth, holding in a laugh. "Are you serious?"

"He was just sitting there, looking like a dumbass—

excuse my French—cradling the Beanie Baby in his hands. His face turned white when he saw me."

"Oh, my word." I'm cracking up now. "What did you do?"

"I yanked it from his hands and stormed out."

"Wow. He'll have a story to tell."

"All I can say is it's a good thing his pants were already down, or he'd have to change his briefs."

Tom laughs and digs for his wallet, handing me his credit card. "I almost lost five hundred big ones."

"Five hundred dollars? I didn't know they were worth that much."

"Five hundred *thousand*," he elaborates. "It's extremely rare."

"What are you carrying it around in your pocket for?"

It's no secret Tom is a little odd, but you'd have to have a few screws loose to carry a five hundred-thousand-dollar stuffed bear in your pocket—into the bathroom!

"I came straight here from the auction. You want me to leave it in my car to get stolen?"

I shrug. "You have a point, there."

To be honest, I'm still stuck on the fact he kicked down a bathroom stall door wearing flip-flops.

When I return with his receipt, he's shaking his head.

"Man, I feel bad for the guy. Can you go check to see if he's okay?"

"Um… can you point him out to me?"

He scans the room and finally spots him, pointing to a guy sitting in a booth with a young woman who I assume is his wife or girlfriend. I wonder if he's telling her the story of the maniac who kicked down the bathroom stall door while he was pooping.

"Offer my apologies and let him know I'll pay for his meal. It's the least I can do."

He signs the bill but leaves his credit card for me to open another tab. Even before the Beanie Baby, Tom has always thrown cash around like a gangsta rapper.

"You know what?" he amends. "Let him order anything he wants. What's your best tequila?"

Oooh. I know this one.

"Don Julio 1942. One hundred percent blue agave with notes of floral, caramel, and spice." (Although I'll forever associate it with the spicy scent of Ignacio's inner elbow). "It's forty-five bucks a shot."

"Send him two. And one for me. Lord knows I need it."

"Right away, my friend."

I pop on over to Bathroom Stall Guy (as I now call him) and introduce myself. This is Rosa's table, so I think it's only polite.

"Hi, I'm Olive, and my customer over there…" I motion to the other side of the restaurant where Tom is sitting. "He'd like to apologize for… well, we don't have to get into details."

He and his girlfriend glance at each other, then up at me.

"It's okay," says the guy. "No worries."

"Order anything you want on the menu. It's taken care of."

"Well… I don't know."

His girlfriend kicks him under the table. "Get the fried ice cream."

He sighs and holds up one finger. "One fried ice cream."

"One fried ice cream coming right up. And I'll send over a flan, too. It's made in house and soooo amazing."

"Okay. Fine."

"Also, I think you'll love the Don Julio 1942. It's our best extra añejo tequila—aged three years."

The guy slices his hand across the table. "No, that's okay."

"Are you sure? My very wealthy friend over there is buying. For your troubles."

"For your troubles, Mike." His girlfriend knows a good deal when she sees it.

Mike sighs. "Okay. Sure. Tell him… thanks."

"You got it."

If I had to guess, the guy is mortified about the bathroom situation, while his girlfriend has been scolding him for letting the Beanie Baby go.

I put the order in on the POS system, then go over to find Rosa to tell her what's going on. She doesn't look as surprised as I thought she would. She just raises an eyebrow.

"Never a dull day at Dos Panchos," she says. "I'll get the desserts. *You* bring the tequila."

When I get to the bar, Josh has the three shots ready in adorable snifter glasses and is totally impressed. "Nice upsell," he says. "How did you manage that?"

I shrug. "I know a thing or two about tequila."

Loading the snifters on my tray, I drop two off for Mike and his girlfriend, and then take the other to Tom. He invites me to sit with him for a minute, and as I lower myself on the booth seat across from him, he lifts his glass to toast Mike across the room. I turn around to see Mike raise his glass back at Tom and takes a sip.

"That was generous of you to pay for his meal," I say. "The tequila was a nice touch, but I think he would have been happy with just the food."

"Yeah, well… I scared the you-know-what out of him. He needs the drink more than me."

"You're probably right. Chocolate cake is my comfort food, but I can see how one little shot of tequila would calm someone's nerves."

"It more than calms your nerves. This is the best tequila I've ever had. It's almost like bourbon."

"It's aged in oak whisky barrels," I say, so proud of my new knowledge of the aging process. If only Ignacio could see me now.

"So I have a question," he says, swirling the liquid around in his snifter. "Is blue agave really blue?"

"You know what, Tom? That is an excellent question."

I can't wait to tell Ignacio.

At the end of my shift, I'm finishing my close-out at one of the corner booths, setting aside the tip-out money for Roberto, my favorite busboy.

He's a rail-thin man in his mid-thirties with the most gigantic smile I've ever seen. And he's insane-level fast. Every time I turn around, he's there, swooping in to clear plates, wipe tables, refill drinks, you name it. He's constantly cracking jokes, making everybody laugh, and he just makes the day go by quicker.

I portion a few extra bucks for him, not only because he's an amazing busser, but because his wife just had a baby. Rosa tells me as soon as Roberto leaves his shift at Dos Panchos, he rides his bike to the Sizzler to work a night shift. I only wish I could give him more.

I clip all my piles of receipts separately and stuff them in my server book. I'm deciding between trying the enchiladas or quesadilla today for my one free meal when Ignacio slides into the booth with two plates. He sets one of them in front of me, sets down two silverware settings, and does his sign of the cross thing. I watch as he mumbles a prayer followed by another cross gesture. When he opens his eyes, he catches me just staring at him.

"What?"

I smile. "You brought me food."

"Yeah." He grumbles. "If we're going to keep up this ruse, we should be seen eating together."

"Thank you." I look at my plate. It doesn't look like anything on the menu. "What is this?"

"Filet *en nogada*."

"Say what now?"

He sighs. Sighing is Ignacio's reset button, I've learned.

"It's a grass-fed filet mignon medallion topped with a whole roasted poblano chili pepper, bathed in a walnut cream sauce, and finished with a sprinkling of pomegranates."

"Oooh, fancy."

"Not fancy. Just healthy."

I poke at the chili pepper with my fork. "Looks fancy to me. It's not spicy, is it?"

He shakes his head, all gruff and stern. "No."

I dip a finger in the sauce. As soon as it enters my mouth, I'm thrown into a food rapture. My eyes roll to the back of my head. I think I levitated a little.

"Oh, my word!" I say. "I just died and went to heaven."

I take a bite, cutting off a slice of meat and pepper this time, and I can't help but groan a little too loud. A few people turn their heads.

"Let's not recreate that scene from *When Harry Met Sally*, okay? Just eat."

"But it's… soooo gooood," I tease.

"Stop it."

I laugh. "I thought we were trying to keep up the ruse."

"Don't make me regret this. I'm already peeved about getting suckered into shopping downtown on Wednesday."

"Well, hopefully it won't take too long."

He snorts out a half-laugh. "You don't know my grandma very well. When she comes to visit, she spends ninety percent of her time at the store. Usually T.J. Maxx. She never has room in her luggage for all her new stuff—or over packs beyond the weight limit. And then the scale comes out, Dad weighing himself without the suitcase, then weighing himself again *with* the suitcase and subtracting the difference. Every. Single. Time."

"How much longer is she staying?" I ask.

"Another couple of weeks, I guess."

"And she lives by herself? In Mexico City?"

"No. Her brother lives with her. And my grandpa, half of the year."

"Your grandpa? I shouldn't have assumed, since he wasn't at dinner…"

"That he was no longer with us?"

I grimace, feeling foolish. "Yeah."

Ignacio spots Roberto and flags him down. "Oye, Beto." He motions a sign for water and holds two fingers up. Roberto salutes Ignacio, points at me questioningly. I nod, and he gives me a thumbs up. He knows my poison.

"My grandpa came to the wedding but went back home the next day. He doesn't like city life—which includes Los Angeles. My grandma doesn't like country life. So they have their own houses, and split their time between Mexico City and Abuelo's farm in Arizona. Abuela will go to Arizona for a couple months, and Abuelo will spend a couple months in Mexico City. The rest of the time, they live separately."

"Hmm. Isn't that hard for your grandma? Only having her husband for a few months out of the year?"

He snickers. "I think they prefer each other in small doses."

I stuff another bite in my mouth and hum. "Mmmm. If my husband cooked like this, I'd never let him out of my sight for a minute, let alone half a year."

"My grandpa's actually an excellent cook," he says. "He taught me how to make this sauce."

"Really? I can't place the flavor. What's in it?"

"Walnuts, cream, sugar, and brandy."

"No wonder it's so good. Sugar is my love language."

A small smile cracks on his face. "I'm glad you like it."

"Like it? I want to marry it."

Just then, Roberto shows up with our drinks. Water for Ignacio and horchata for me.

"*Algo dulce para la mas dulce güeda de Dos Panchos,*" he says with his goofy smile.

I shake my finger. "I know *dulce* means sweet and that's all that matters."

Ignacio gives him a sideways glare. "*Gracias, mi chavo.*"

"Oh!" I open my billfold to get Roberto's tips. "Here you go."

He bows to me, then bows to Ignacio. I bow back—as well as I can sitting in a booth. Ignacio swats him away jokingly. Roberto wanders off.

"This is amazing," I say, taking another bite. "So different from what you serve here. Is this from your catering menu?"

"Yes and no," he says. "The catering business is… just a side gig. A test kitchen."

"What do you mean by that?"

"I have this friend. Caleb."

I nod because I know this guy. "He hired me for the wedding."

"Right. He's a chef I know from culinary school." He sighs. "I don't know why I'm telling you this. I haven't told anyone. Not even my brothers."

I cross my heart. "Keeping secrets is my jam. I once had to hold on to a *Stranger Things* spoiler because of a leaked script Aaron got from the marketing firm. It was a dark six months of silence."

He regards me for a moment and shakes his head.

"Okay, here goes. I want to open a new concept restaurant. Something of my own. So I reached out to Caleb to work through some recipes. We needed to test them out with little investment, so we started catering. It's extremely low risk. No overhead, almost no capital needed. And we only do six or seven gigs a year. Caleb has a full-time job at the Four Seasons, so he's not available very often."

"What about your brother's wedding? Were you testing those recipes?"

"Yeah, sort of. I do a lot of planning and always offer tastings. It's not like I'm experimenting on the day of an important event."

"Well, if it was an experiment, it was a yummy one," I say.

He tosses me a confused look. "Did you... taste the food? Besides the cake."

"No." I shrug. "But it smelled divine." I sip my horchata. Yum. Roberto added the perfect amount of ice. "So, are you thinking of adding those new recipes to the menu here?"

He laughs. "Oh heck, no. It's not on brand. My new concept is a mix of tastes and cultures. It would have a rotating menu—dishes inspired by seasons and mixed societies."

"Hmmm. I don't know what that is, but it sounds delicious."

Ignacio slides his plate aside and skates his eyes over the table, looking for something. He dumps the sugars out of the ramekin, tossing the artificial sweeteners to the side.

"I'll be right back."

He disappears behind the bar, gathering stuff in his arms. He returns with an empty glass, some bar fruit, and a bottle of something.

"There's not one type of cuisine you can say is pure," he says, dropping limes and lemons inside the glass.

"Everything is a mixture."

He produces a tiny baseball bat looking thing and begins to smash the citrus to a pulp.

"Marco Polo brought pasta to Italy from China. Sugar..." He opens a packet of Sugar in the Raw, pouring it on top of the fruit, "was originally cultivated in New Guinea."

He pops in a couple of maraschino cherries and mint, smashing that, too, because why not?

"Tomatoes are from the Americas, yet you think of marinara as an Italian sauce."

Here he throws in all the bar fruit. Pineapple, strawberries, oranges. Is he making some kind of strange smoothie?

"You think of potatoes as Irish or German. But they're native to Peru."

I understand the point he's trying to make, but that weird witch's brew is starting to look a little questionable.

"You're kind of making a mess there," I say with a grimace.

"Exactly. This is what it means to be human. We're all a mess of DNA soup."

"Well, there's probably an indigenous tribe somewhere..."

He tops the mixture with the contents of the bottle, which I now see is club soda. With a spoon, he scoops out ice from my horchata and drops it in the glass. Then he guzzles his water in one long gulp, covers the empty cup over the other glass, and shakes the thing like a martini.

"I'm getting a whole Tom Cruise vibe from you right now," I say. "Please tell me you're going to flip the bottle behind your back and catch it without looking."

He cracks a smile and sets the concoction in front of me with a flourish.

"The best way to experience a culture is with your mouth."

I squint at him. "I think maybe you should rephrase that slogan if you plan to put it on your website. Just sayin'."

"Okay. How's this? You don't learn culture. You eat it."

"Better. But this is a drink."

"For Pete's sake, just taste it."

"For realzies? You want me to actually drink this?"

"Yes, I do."

"Ohhh-kay. Because I thought you were just demonstrating the DNA soup thing with a bunch of random ingredients and fanfare."

He shrugs. "Maybe I was."

I grimace, slowly lifting the glass to my lips. "I might regret this, but here goes."

I pinch my nose as if that will help and take a sip. Then I take a bigger sip.

"What is this wizardry?" I say, astonished. I saw how much sugar he used. One package of Sugar in the Raw. I mean, who likes that stuff? But this is scrummy.

"It's just an example of how good it can be when cultures mix."

"Like a Mexican and a Jew," I say cheekily.

His beautiful lips part, and for a second, I think I feel a real connection. Then he cracks a joke.

"If this is your way to get me to set you up with one of my brothers, it's not gonna happen."

I slide my plate over so I can reach across the table and take both his hands in mine.

"Come on."

His hands swallow mine, thumbs tracing circles over my knuckles.

"Part of the ruse?" he questions.

"No. You said a prayer over your food earlier. This is mine. A mixture of cultures."

I close my eyes and feel his fingers press into my palm as I whisper the prayer.

"Baruch atah Adonai, Eloheinu melech haolam, hamotzi lechem min ha-aretz."

When I open my eyes again, he's watching me curiously.

"Amen," I conclude.

He smiles softly, just watching me.

"What? Do I have something on my face?"

He does not confirm or deny messiness on my person.

He just says, "Aaron's a real *schmuck*."

"Look at you, learning some Yiddish."

"I'm serious. You're… a nice person. I don't understand how a guy can do what he did."

I sigh, because Aaron is just a lot. It's not a new thing. I feel like I've been making excuses for him for a long time.

"Aaron's the type of guy who's always been a big dreamer. Always reaching for the next thing. The better thing."

"Overcompensating, if you ask me."

"When he landed a job at that big marketing firm in Hollywood, I stupidly followed him here."

"I'm not on board with you putting yourself down, Olive. It wasn't stupid."

"Well, I didn't think so at the time, obviously. I got a

menial job at the same firm, coffee runs, making copies, that sort of thing. Then Pamela caught his eye. She's a 'project coordinator'—such a big shot."

"Pamela?"

"Eyebrows."

"Ooooh. Got it."

I cringe at the memory—how she was always super sweet, yet condescending to me. Passive aggressive. I just thought it was an LA thing, but I guess it's more of a *claws-in-your-boyfriend* thing.

"Anyway, Aaron moved on to something new but forgot to send me the memo. And that's when I walked in on them —ruining my favorite quilt."

I realize we're still holding hands. Ignacio lowers his head and kisses my knuckles, then turns my hands over and kisses my palms. It's strangely the most intimate thing anyone has ever done to me.

Then he looks up at me and blinks, tenderness in those ashy eyes.

"You're a human being. Not a career, or an object. There's no… better thing. That woman isn't better than you. And Aaron is certainly not better than you. As a matter of fact, he traded down, if you want my opinion."

A grateful smile forms on my face. "I value your opinion very much."

"Good. Now I'd like to hear how you managed to sell three shots of 1942 on a Monday afternoon."

Cooking is like love.
It should be entered into
with abandon
or not at all.

— Harriet van Horne

Chapter Ten

IGNACIO

Olive's apartment is an insanely small upstairs studio unit in West Hollywood. The house seems to be almost a century old, built originally as a single-family home, divided into a fourplex at one point. It's old but quaint, I suppose. The landscaping is well maintained, and a spiral staircase leads upstairs to Olive's sunny front patio. Her landing, about three square feet, is covered in flower-pots and colorful fairy gardens. There are at least five plaster gnomes of different sizes keeping guard, and two on either side of the door. It's absolutely cluttered and hodge-podge to the point where there's hardly a path to walk. But it's cheery and bright… and *so* Olive.

She answers the door in a frantic rush, her hair in a bun poking upward in the shape of a cone from on top of her head.

"Ack. You're early."

I check my smartwatch. "Only five minutes."

"Come in, I'll just be a sec."

I step inside. The place is small, but clean. It's basically a single room with an Ikea cube shelf unit to separate the living area from the sleeping area. The kitchen comprises a tiny electric stove and a one-basin sink, all tucked in one corner.

Olive shrugs with that adorable smile-grimace of hers. "It's not much, but it's mine. Well, not *mine*, mine. I don't own it. I rent from a sweet old man who's just the best. He's a veteran and has five grandchildren. But he doesn't see them all that often. So I bake him banana bread or cookies and told him he can visit for coffee when he comes to collect the rent. He hasn't taken me up on that yet. He tells me the hardwood floors are new because of a pipe leak last year, so that's good. And it came fully furnished. The shelf and everything."

"That's all very fascinating, but weren't you…"

I wave my hand in her general direction. I'm guessing she was about to style her hair—or whatever women do to get ready. Will she wear her Crocs today?

"Oh, yeah. I just need to slip outta my pajamas."

Her *pajamas* have the pattern of little dogs in Santa hats

adorned all over the pants and cami tank top. Conscious of my gaze on her, she crosses her arms over her chest.

"I forgot I'm not wearing a bra. I'll be right back."

Heaven help me.

She disappears into the bathroom—the only private space inside this apartment. Finding myself uncommonly fidgety, I pace through the apartment, examining the almost non-existent kitchen and her poor excuse for cooking utensils. Then over to the cube shelf, where she has small plants, books, and... a LOT of gnomes.

"You know, I'm actually really excited for today," she says through the paper-thin bathroom door. "I'm not really into shopping, but I haven't seen much of L.A. since I moved here."

"Oh, really?" I say absently, because I'm taken aback by the amount of Christmas decorations she has. Mostly gnome statues, their creepy, jolly faces smiling into the middle distance. The plush gnomes, which are slightly larger, don't have visible faces—just enormous hats tucked down over their eyes right above large, round noses, where white Gandalf beards take over the rest of the face and body. Some gnomes have hats with holly. Others have hats with stripes... or red plaid. Some have hats that look like ugly Christmas sweaters. And she doesn't just have Christmas gnomes. Oh no. There are gnomes for every occasion.

Looking around the room, I notice the throw pillows, the string lights hanging over the window, the actual plastic Christmas tree, all eighteen inches of it on top of a side table. I'm a little bit horrified and slightly amused.

"I'm ready."

Olive emerges, wearing the same exact clothes. The only difference is her hair, which cascades over her shoulders in rich, brown waves. And she's wearing her Crocs.

I blink a few times and can't help but ask, "Didn't you say those were… pajamas?"

He glances down over her body. "No, silly. My pajamas had beagles in Santa hats. These…" she slaps her thigh, "are corgis."

"Olive, there is absolutely no difference between your pajamas and your street clothes. Long, cotton *Christmas* pants and a tank top." I realize here that the tank top is solid white, not patterned with dogs. But it's still basically the same outfit. At least she's wearing a bra now.

"It's very different," she says. "The pajama pants are softer and thicker."

"And what about all this?" I say, gesturing toward the shelf and the rest of the decorations. Do we need to have an intervention? It looks like Christmas exploded all over your apartment."

She grins brightly. "Isn't it great? I got a lot of it at a garage sale for twenty bucks. They were practically giving it away."

"Are you sure you're Jewish?"

"Yes."

I look around, dumbfounded. I'm at a loss for words.

"Oh!" She shuffles over to the tiny sofa and picks up a plush gnome—this one in a blue hat. "Did you see my Hanukkah gnome? I named him Harry."

"Please don't tell me you named all your gnomes."

"No. Just Harry." She kisses him before setting him back

down on the sofa. "He's one of the friends I brought with me from Jersey."

"Friends? Should I be concerned?"

"What for? Just don't tell my father."

"You mean your traditionally Jewish dad is not a fan of your Christmas obsession? Shocker. Or is the creepy gnome shrine?"

"They're not creepy."

I select one of the smaller porcelain statues and hold it up. It has beady eyes, bright red cheeks, and a murderous grin.

"Not creepy, you say?"

Olive twists her face. "Maybe that one is a *little* creepy."

I shake my head and set the gnome back on the shelf. Mom and Abuela are waiting to be picked up, and I'd rather not get to the fashion district too late or parking will be hell.

"Come on," I say, opening the front door. "I promise I won't breathe a word to your dad if I happen to meet him."

She snaps up her canvas tote bag, which she uses as a purse. There's a dancing taco on it which looks hand painted, along with the words *'I Could Give Up Tacos, but I'm No Quitter'* in a speech bubble.

"Oh, you won't meet him," she says, reaching for her keys. "He's in Jersey."

I roll my eyes and step outside. "I promise not to call him, then."

"What if he calls *you*?"

"Olive, can we go now?"

"Sure, sure." She touches the doorframe and kisses her

fingers before walking out. Then she locks the door, but before she starts down the stairs, I touch her arm.

"Wait. Why did you kiss your fingers? Before you closed the door?"

"Oh!" She slaps her forehead. "It's a force of habit. If you ever see a little box on a door frame, that's a mezuzah. It's like announcing to visitors, 'This is a Jewish home. Keep your guilt in check'."

"That pretty much describes my mom's house," I say. Except she has crucifixes over every door to inspire guilt.

Olive starts down the spiral staircase, and I follow her.

"My dad gave me a mezuzah as a gift before I moved out here, but it's still hanging on Aaron's front door frame. He didn't let me take it when I moved out."

"You need to go back and get it," I say.

"Nah. It's not like it's a family heirloom or anything. I can get a new one if I want to."

"But it's not Aaron's. It's yours." I don't know why this is upsetting me so much.

Before she reaches the bottom step, she turns and digs a book out of her bag, handing it to me.

"For you."

I read the title. "Love in the Time of Cholera? Are you trying to tell me something?"

"Our meet-cute, remember?" She opens the front cover and points to the writing inside. "I wrote my name and number, just in case your sister asks to see proof."

"She won't ask to see proof," I say.

Olive squints at me. "You keep saying people won't ask stuff and they always do. Trust me. Keep the book in your car. It will come up eventually."

The fashion district is packed as usual. We've been shopping for what feels like a thousand years. I check my Google Fit app, and I've already clocked more steps than Frodo Baggins when he slogged that ring through Middle Earth. How are these ladies not tired?

We reach a section of the street with nothing but bridal shops. I have no idea what Abuela could possibly want from here, but she insists on poking into every single shop.

I follow them in so they don't get mugged—this is L.A. after all. Abuela and Mom have to touch… Every. Single. Dress. Running their fingers over the fabric, checking the price tags. At one point, Abuela takes one off the rack and calls Olive over.

"*Ven, chava*. For you."

"ME?" Olive gapes at the wedding dress. "No, no grazie."

"It's gracias," I say. "Grazie's Italian."

"Oh, right. I'd eat a lot of pizza in Jersey."

Abuela sours her expression, clearly offended. "*Porque, niña? No te gusta?*"

Olive lifts her eyes up at me. "What did she say? *Niña* means baby, right? Does she think I'm… pregnant?"

"No, she doesn't think you're pregnant. *You* are the *niña* and she's being meddlesome."

Olive smiles at Abuela awkwardly.

"Abuela," I say. "*No estamos comprometidos. We're not engaged.*"

She pulls a face.

"It's a really good deal, though," says Mom. "Maybe we should get it just in case."

Abuela turns a hard stare at Mom. "*¿Recuerdas cuando te casaste?*"

Mom looks to me, then back at Abuela. How would she forget when she got married to Dad?

"*Si,*" Mom replies. "*Claro.*"

Abuela gives her a casual once-over and ticks an eyebrow. "*Eras mucho más delgada.*"

"I have an underactive thyroid!" Mom cries and storms out. Abuela shrugs and goes back to looking through the dresses.

Olive, a little startled, asks, "What just happened?"

"My grandma basically paid my mom an underhanded compliment, saying how much thinner she was on her wedding day."

Olive's jaw drops. "Are you serious?"

"I wish I wasn't. My grandmother has no filter."

She stares out for a while, jaw still hanging open, then she begins to laugh, like there's a joke only known to her.

"What's so funny?"

"Your mom should have come right back and said how much younger your grandma was on *her* wedding day."

"Uh, no. World War Three would have broken out right here in the bridal shop."

"I always think of a good comeback too late," she says. "If we ever get into an argument blunt, prepare yourself to revisit the conversation the next day."

"Duly noted."

Expressing her lack of interest in bridal shops, Olive exits the store and I happily follow. Eventually, Abuela joins us and we go on our merry way without a hint of ire between the older women. Mom and Abuela continue down the street, shopping as if nothing happened.

Mom finds a women's clothing store she wants to look at and drags Olive in with her. Meanwhile, I stay outside with Abuela, browsing the stuff for sale by the street vendors. We try on sunglasses and I buy a bag of *chicharrones* to share—extra hot sauce. She asks me questions about the restaurant and if I'm happy there, briefly touching on Abuelo and his birthday coming up. Then she winks at me and tells me she'll never forgive me if I don't go—Abuelo is turning ninety, after all—and to bring my beautiful girlfriend.

The thing is, the word for girlfriend in Spanish is *novia*, which also means bride. She wags her brows dramatically when she says it.

"Tengo un presentimiento," she says, which means she has a gut feeling.

"Puedo decir cuando alguien está enamorado, y ella esta enamorada de ti."

There's no telling Abuela she's way off base. That it's impossible for her to detect that Olive is in love with me. I suppose we're playing our part well if we're fooling Abuela.

She shakes a bony finger at me. *"Predigo que te casaras con ese mujer."*

I can't respond. How can I? Winking and nudging about noticing how my fake girlfriend seems to be in love with me is one thing. Predicting I'll marry her is quite another. Abuela is the superstitious type, and when she predicts something, she thinks it's because she has a direct telephone line to God and he's telling her all sorts of things—what to have for breakfast, if she should buy the red blouse or the blue blouse, and apparently, who I'll marry.

I'm saved from further uncomfortable questions about my love life by Mom, who's just exited the clothing store.

"Give me your credit card," she demands with her palm extended.

"Okay, when you ask like that, I get a little nervous."

"Just give me your card, Nacho." She crooks her fingers impatiently and glances over her shoulder.

"I need to know what you're going to buy first."

"Olive found some things she wants to buy. Come on, hand it over."

"*Que quiere la Olive?*" asks Abuela, not quite fluent enough in English to catch everything.

"*Se probó algunos vestidos y se ve muy hermosa,*" Mom tells her.

Abuela smacks me on the arm. "*Comprale algo a tu novia, apretado.*"

Just then, Olive runs out of the shop, adjusting the strap of her tank top. "Ignacio, you don't have to—"

"Yes, he does," says Mom, still holding out her hand.

Abuela's giving me an intense scowl.

"What did you find in there, Olive?" I ask.

"Just some clothes your mom wanted me to try. She didn't want to be the only one trying things on, so I joined her."

"Did you like the clothes?" I ask.

"Well, yeah, I liked them but—"

I shush her with my finger on her lips, then I take out

my wallet and hand my credit card to Mom. Abuela follows Mom into the store, but Olive just stares at me.

"I didn't come here so you'd buy things for me," she says. "I still owe you for the uniform pants."

"You don't owe me anything," I say. "And these women will castrate me if I don't pay. You're actually doing me a favor."

She huffs. "I feel terrible now."

"Why? Can't a man buy his girlfriend nice things?"

She looks over her shoulder into the shop and back at me. I gently tip her chin up with my thumb.

"You could give me a thank you kiss."

"Are they watching us?" she asks, fixing her wide eyes on mine.

I flick my gaze to the shop window. "I think so."

Olive bites her bottom lip and lets her gaze fall to my mouth. "I guess a little one would be appropriate. Under the circumstances."

She elevates herself on her tiptoes and I bend to meet her halfway, brushing my lips on hers in a featherlight kiss. It's over in less than a second, but a current of electric power surges through me for several moments after, shooting sparks down to my navel.

"That should do the trick," she says.

She has no idea.

For the next hour, I can't get the feel of her kiss off my lips. We circle back around, hitting all the stores on the opposite side of the street because they are *oh so different* from all the rest.

I trail a few feet behind the women in case they zip into a store on a whim without warning me. Olive falls into step with Mom and Abuela like the third musketeer—shopping bags swinging, the way she sways side to side as she walks, her absurd Christmas leggings clinging to her body. How is she not baking in this heat? And I swear, if I catch any guy rubbernecking as she passes by, I'll rearrange his face.

Finally, we stop at an open-air food court to eat. Tables are scarce so Olive and I find a four-top and hang onto all the shopping bags while Mom and Abuela decide what they want.

Olive looks around at the food vendors.

"What do you want to eat?" she asks.

I shrug. "Probably a burrito or something."

"You're going to be disappointed," she sing-songs.

"What makes you think that?"

She ticks her head to the side, giving me a playful grin. "Because you'll end up comparing it to the burritos at your restaurant and it will ruin the experience for you. Trust me. Get the sushi or something."

She has a point there.

"I don't know if I trust the sushi in a place like this. It's pretty hard to mess up beans and tortillas."

"Suit yourself."

She scrolls her phone for a minute and I take the opportunity to study her. She has a devil-may-care style—those printed leggings and Crocs—like she's oblivious to the whole world of fashion. She marches to her own beat and somehow that makes her beauty unparalleled.

"Aren't you hot?" I ask, at last getting my burning question out there.

She looks up from her phone and winks. "Thanks. I'm glad you noticed."

"I mean in temperature. Those pants."

"You're wearing pants," she says, looking at my jeans.

"And I'm feeling a little warm. It's hotter than the devil's armpit downtown."

"Maybe you should try leggings."

I scoff. "They look hotter than sausage casings."

"No, the material is thin and stretchy. They're really comfortable."

"Wouldn't a dress be more comfortable?"

"I don't really like dresses. I like something between my legs."

I swallow hard.

"I mean, I need fabric there," she amends. "You know… for the chub rub?"

"Uh, forget I brought it up."

"Here, touch it."

"Absolutely not." If there is one thing I definitely do not want to do, it's touching Olive anywhere on her body she would associate with 'chub rub'. I don't know what chub rub means, but I do know I want nothing to do with it.

"Don't be an ogre," she says, tugging on my hand and slapping it smartly right above her knee. "See? The material is breathable."

"I can feel that."

I can't *stop* feeling that.

Of its own volition, my palm traces in sweeping circles over the curves of her thigh. Somehow, her leg ends up on my lap and my fingers graze the back of her knee, trailing a course to her calf. I find myself leaning in, wanting another taste of her lips.

"I think we're being watched," I say.

Her eyes dip to my mouth. "Oh? Do you think we should… perform a little?"

"That might be a good idea."

It's not a good idea at all. It's a terrible idea.

"Okay."

I scoot my chair closer to hers and move to the edge of my seat. Seizing either side of her waist with both hands, I pull her to me, sliding her bottom across the surface of the chair until her hip presses against my leg.

"I'm thinking I'd really like to see my girlfriend in a dress," I say, my lips hovering over hers. "I'd like that very much."

"Oh, you may want it, but you're not going to get it," she says huskily.

I wrap a strand of hair around my finger and pull gently. "I tend to get what I want."

"Oh yeah? Well, get used to disappointment because… You. Can't. Have. It."

"I think I can."

"Nope. Sorry. There will be no dress wearing for you."

"You're not even going to let me see the pretty things I bought you? I don't think that's very nice."

"Maybe I'm not nice at all. Maybe I'm a man-eater."

Dayum. Where did *this* side of Olive come from?

I growl against her lips, lowering my voice an octave.

"Do you want to put me in a bad mood, Olive? Because I can get very annoyed when people aren't being… nice to me."

Her breath hitches, and I can't help noticing the labored rise and fall of her chest.

"Whatever you say, Chef Crabby Cakes."

I fix my gaze on her devilish smirk. "What did you just call me?"

"Guhhh. Chef… Crabby Cakes," she says proudly. Her cheeks flush pink and her eyes sparkle with mischief.

"Crabby Cakes? What's that supposed to mean?"

"My lips are sealed. I am a fortress of knowledge. You'd love me to reveal my ways to you, but I'll never tell."

"Hmmm," I groan. "Unfortunately for you, I have a talent for getting you to reveal your ways to me."

"Doubtful."

"You see, I know your weakness. Those lips? They won't stay sealed for long."

She nibbles on her bottom lip. I know she's just aching to kiss me.

"I happen to have some information that would be of interest to you," I rumble.

She shoots me a witchy grin. "I'm a very simple person, Chef. I don't bribe easily."

"Ah, well that's too bad," I say, nudging her nose ever so slightly with mine. She shudders under my touch. "Whatever will I do with all these beignets I bought while you ladies were in the shoe store?"

"Bei… beignets?"

Her delicate lips part, jaw hinged open in the most delectable way—and I take her mouth, invading that fortress she was so smug about. My lips glide over hers and she makes the littlest sound in her throat, like a tiny grunt of pleasure.

I move to her jaw next, rumbling into the line separating her face and neck, breathing on the shell of her ear. "Why do you call me Chef Crab Cake?"

"That's *Crabby* Cakes."

"Why?"

She takes a fistful of my shirt. "Because you're soooo crabby."

"Am I now?"

"Yes."

"And the bit about the cakes? What's up with that?"

"I just like cake a lot. Especially dulce de leche."

That was the flavor of the wedding cake. Of course she'd say that. Images of her licking the frosting off her finger flood my memory.

I take one possessive nibble of her lip and back away, leaving her flushed.

"See? I have my ways. I could get a lot more out of you, but children are present, so…"

"Ugh. Did you just play me?"

"No, not at all. If I had played you, you'd be wearing that dress by now."

Her eyes narrow. "Hmm. Well I think tomorrow it will be the snowman leggings. And gingerbread men the next time after that. And you *will* give me that beignet."

There's no doubt I will. I find myself wanting to give her all sorts of things I wouldn't normally buy—whether it's new clothes I'll never get to see or powdered sugar-covered pastries. Just seeing her face light up is worth it. She shines as bright and loud as a colored Christmas display—her smile illuminating the most boring of places. She makes me feel strangely warm inside. Not in an aroused way— although there's that, too—but in a familiar, cozy way. A chestnuts-roasting-over-an-open-fire way. Hot chocolate and marshmallows. Tamales and champurrado.

Suddenly I can picture her bundled in a scarf and bespoke Christmas hat. She'd wear those candy cane leggings while we celebrate the holidays with my family—Francesca and Mateo singing carols for us, and Dad ruining them with his booming, out-of-tune voice. Mom making Memo place the angel on the tree—and he'd inevitably tip it off center, and Nate eating all the pan dulce.

My thoughts are disrupted by the arrival of Mom and Abuela carrying trays laden with food. Olive and I jump up to help them and I've never been more grateful.

"We bought one of everything," says Mom. "Hope you're hungry."

Starved.

A balanced diet
is a cookie
in each hand.

— Barbara Johnson

Chapter Eleven

OLIVE

When a phone call lasts as long as this one, I'm gonna take a bath. It's not a video call, but I still feel a little bit saucy. Something about listening to the deep rumble of Ignacio's voice whilst covered in suds is giving me those longing feelings, sending a thrill through my veins. I should end the call and do something chaste... like go online to donate to charity. I'm sure my surplus five dollars would do some good somewhere. Scratch that.

When I checked my bank app this morning, I discovered I'm the proud owner of a checking account with a balance of fifty-four cents. How do normal people get by in Los Angeles?

I unplug the drain as quietly as possible and slush out of the bath. The bottom half of my hair is wet and I'm a soapy mess, but I dare not turn on the shower to rinse off.

"What's that sound?" asks Ignacio as I'm mid-step out of the tub. In retrospect, speaker phone wasn't the smartest idea, but what choice did I have? "Are you washing dishes?"

"Uh... no. I'm a monster and used a paper plate for dinner."

He laughs. "You're not a monster. What did you have for dinner?"

Should I tell the truth about burning my rice and getting so discouraged I plopped on my couch with a plate of bargain American cheese and saltine crackers? That's more pathetic than using a paper plate. I may not have found my calling in life, but at least I can admit I have no domestic talent.

"Oh, ya know," I say. "Charcuterie."

Charcuterie sounds much fancier than Poorman's Lunchable.

"I love a good charcuterie," says Ignacio. "How do you make yours? For me, as long as there's prosciutto and an aged manchego, I'm a happy man."

I have no idea what those things are, but in my defense, I was a sheltered child. My poor dad was widowed young and was left to raise me and my brother by himself. His idea of cooking was ordering a Goldman's Deli delivery.

I feign a sophisticated laugh. "Haha, oh yes. That."

He responds with a noncommittal harumph.

I don't even know why he called. For the last hour and a half, I've been doing most of the talking. I wonder if he took a bath, too. Or if he's talking to me from his bed wearing low slung pajama pants. Or no pants. I picture him as a boxers kind of guy.

"Soooo," he says. "Are you going out tonight?"

I snort. "Ha yeah. I have such a robust social life, you know. Anyway, it's almost ten."

"L.A. doesn't even open until after ten on a Saturday night. Or are you an early bird?"

"I am the opposite of an early bird. There was an earthquake the first week we arrived in California, and I slept right through it. I don't do mornings."

"Well, if it makes you feel any better, I can't recall any earthquakes in the last year, so it was probably small. I hardly notice them most of the time."

"A tell-tale sign of a California native," I say. "Earthquakes hardly turn heads, but if it rains, people run for shelter like it's the apocalypse."

"Sounds about right," he agrees.

I go on to tell him about my first impression of Los Angeles compared to my expectations before moving here. Even though it's not as glamorous as it seems in movies, I was still enamored by it. There's a different kind of energy here than on the East Coast. Also, the pizza isn't as good, but I haven't met a Californian yet who will admit it.

I ask him what his favorite pizza is and he gives me this highbrow answer about preferring unconventional toppings like caramelized onion, pear, gorgonzola, and micro greens, but I finally pry it out of him that a simple pepperoni and cheese is the superior pie.

I'm enjoying this call so much I don't even notice another half-hour has passed since my bath. Ignacio is so easy to talk to. From the comfort of my bed, I snuggle with my Hanukkah Harry plush gnome, wishing it was Ignacio instead. I bop his nose sticking out from under his blue, pointy hat as I give Ignacio the full run down of my favorite episode of *Psych*. He's quiet while I talk, which is why the sudden knocking on my front door scares me to smithereens.

I yelp and jump out of bed. "There's a murderer at my door," I whisper into the phone. "My locks won't save me."

He laughs, and it sounds like an echo. "It's me, Olive. Open up."

"You? You're the killer?"

"Yes. I'm going to hang up now."

I frown at my phone as it goes dark. I sure hope it's really him at the door. I don't even have a peephole to make sure.

"How do I know it's really you?" I say through the door crack.

"You'll have to take a chance and hope I don't kill you with tacos."

I unlatch the door and swing it open so fast, my hair flies back. "Did you say tacos?"

He lifts up two paper grocery bags. "If it's okay with you."

"Get your butt in here." I yank him in by the shirt and just as quickly shut the door. In hindsight, I should have helped him with the grocery bags. I'm a terrible host.

He sets the bags on my tiny kitchen table and awkwardly points in the direction of my sad excuse for a stove.

"Do you mind if I…"

"Oh! Yes. I mean, no. Make yourself at home." I pull my bathrobe tighter around my boobs. I suppose saying I'll slip into something more comfortable doesn't apply in this situation. "I'm just gonna throw on some leggings."

He nods, keeping his eyes trained on the groceries as he unloads the bags. I slip into the bathroom and change while he speaks to me through the thin wall.

"I hope it's okay to drop in on you like this. I just figured it makes more sense to talk in person if we were going to continue for another hour."

I laugh, hiking up my pants. I take a glance in the mirror and see the mascara smudge under my eye. Ugh.

"Oh, it's fine," I say, dripping makeup remover on a square of toilet paper. "My phone battery was about to die so this is perfect. I still need to tell you about my second favorite episode of *Psych*, and that one's a humdinger."

"Oh, yeah?" he calls out. "I can't wait to hear all about it."

When I'm done making myself presentable, I step out of the bathroom and am immediately arrested by the sight of this man in my kitchen, bigger than life, with a frying pan in one hand, and a bottle of olive oil in the other. I think my ovaries just exploded.

"You uh… you're cooking the tacos? From scratch?"

I thought he had brought some from the restaurant and maybe some extras from the grocery store. But no. All the ingredients are out on the counter, but he's the one looking delicious enough to eat.

"Oh, come on, Olive. I wouldn't bring you food from work. And uh…" He inclines his head to my box of saltines and cheese wrappers I hadn't thrown away. "I knew your charcuterie couldn't possibly fill you up."

I bite my bottom lip and squint one eye. "I wasn't very hungry."

"Well I hope you're hungry now, because I'm famished."

He moves around my kitchen like he's cooked in here a thousand times. He's such a natural, like those horse whisperers who can jive with a new animal they haven't met before. He's a kitchen whisperer.

"You brought your own pan?"

The cast iron skillet he's working with is definitely not mine.

"No, I picked it up at the Smart and Final. Along with some other stuff."

"I have stuff to cook with."

He glances at my pot of burnt rice and looks around my kitchen.

"Hmmm. No you don't."

He gets to work, cleaning and chopping veggies, mostly peppers and onions. He peels about a half dozen green tomatoes and roasts them with several whole garlic cloves in the cast iron skillet while the chicken breast marinates in a reddish liquid.

"Is that chili pepper in that marinade?" I ask. "It looks really spicy."

"Achiote. It's a paste made of annatto seed, and it's not

spicy at all. Cheddar cheese gets its color from annatto. Do you have a blender?"

"No. Sorry."

"That's okay. I bought a sieve."

For the next several minutes I watch in wonder as he performs magic in my little kitchen, pouring oil in a stainless steel frying pan and tossing in the marinated chicken. Smashing the roasted tomatoes into a salsa and sprinkling sea salt like fairy dust. He's like a dancer, confident in perfectly choreographed moves as if he's performing strictly from muscle memory. I've seen jazz players do the same thing. They just know their instruments so well, they can jump in and improvise music with perfect strangers and not miss a single note.

Ignacio is a true artist. Seeing him do his thing is like watching Michelangelo but with less naked bodies.

Oh, and the smells! I want to gobble up those roasted green tomatoes and garlic cloves right this second. My whole apartment is filled with a cacophony of delicious aromas.

When the marinated chicken sizzles in the pan, my senses go wild. He slides the skillet in circles and swishes the chicken around a few times before tossing it in the air, only to catch it again without spilling a morsel.

"Can you show me how to do that?" I ask, licking my lips. "The flip thing?"

He gives me a sideways smile and oh, lordy… that tiny wink!

"Actually, you know what?" I amend. "Better not. I'll just make a mess."

"No you won't. I'll make sure you don't."

He demonstrates a few times, shaking the pan front and back along the stovetop and then just… flips. Like it's no big deal.

Flip.

Flip.

Little pieces of chicken fly up and land back in the pan in a beautiful swoop.

"The secret is confidence," he says. "You can't hesitate a second. Come here."

"I just like watching," I say. "You're really good at it."

"Come here, you can do this."

He abandons the pan for a moment to take my hand, wrapping it around the handle, keeping his hand over mine. He nudges me in front of the stove, pressing his chest against my back as he curls his arm around me. His breath is hot as he speaks over the shell of my ear. I'm not ready for this. I might get burned in more ways than one.

"Now, don't lift the pan off the burner. I want you to push it forward and give it a quick pull back. Push and pull. Push and pull."

He's guiding my hand, sliding the pan over the burner back and forth. The chicken swooshes forward and sweeps over itself on the way back into the pan. None of it spills all over the place, but he's doing most of the work.

"You're doing good," he says encouragingly. "Now try it without me."

"I don't think I can do this."

"You can do it. I'll be right behind you. Just shove the handle forward then give it a quick tug."

"Ughh… like this?" I shake the pan lamely.

"A little harder," he says, nuzzling up even closer to my back. "And faster."

My face flames up. "Harder and faster?"

"Yes. Push and pull. With confidence."

I'm finding it exceedingly difficult to concentrate right now.

"You have more faith in my abilities than you should," I say. "I'm not as experienced as you."

His arm curls tighter around my waist and he dips lower to whisper against my cheek.

"I'll teach you."

Gulp.

My dad's ringtone sounds on my phone as if he knew exactly what was going through my mind and had to intercept immediately. It's super late in Jersey right now. I hope everything's okay.

"I better get that," I say, "My dad will call the national guard if I don't answer his calls."

I disengage from Ignacio's arms and pick up my phone.

"Hey Dad."

"I'll start on the tortillas," says Ignacio.

Dad barks into my ear.

"I hear a voice. You have a man over? Who is it? Aaron?"

"No, dad. I told you we broke up. Why are you calling so late? Is everything okay?"

"There's still time to fix it. He'll take you back if you ask."

Oh brother. I've gone over this with him several times.

"No, he moved on already. And I don't want to go back. I'm done."

I cover the mouthpiece to whisper to Ignacio.

"Hold off on the tortillas. I might be a minute."

Dad starts in on me.

"Who is this man in your apartment? Is he Jewish?"

"No, Dad."

"Why waste your time, then? You're not gonna marry a gentile."

"Nobody's marrying anyone. He's just a friend."

"Olive, when a guy comes over this time of night, he's not interested in being friends. Let me talk to him."

I sigh and hold out the phone to Ignacio.

"It's for you."

He points to his beautiful chest. "Me?"

I roll my eyes as he takes the phone from me.

"Hello?"

He listens intently as my dad drills him or gives his 'not my daughter' speech like he did with that poor boy who took me to prom.

"Yes sir," says Ignacio stiffly. "I'll do my best sir."

After a couple of similar exchanges, he gives the phone back to me. The line is off.

"He hung up," I say. "He didn't even say why he called."

Ignacio shrugs.

"What did he say to you?"

"He asked what my intentions are and then he said a real man would convince you to move back to Jersey."

"Ugh. Not gonna happen."

"I guess I'm not a real man, then," he quips.

"You're a fake man. Fake boyfriend anyway."

He plasters on a smile and blinks at me.

"Right. I seem to keep forgetting."

He slaps the tortillas into the cast iron skillet with a little too much gusto, takes a deep breath, and recovers.

"Taco time?"

I slide up next to him in front of the stove and watch as he flips the tortillas with his bare hands. They really are impressively large hands.

"You don't have to ask me twice," I say. "Let's eat."

Spaghetti can be eaten
most successfully
if you inhale it
like a vacuum cleaner.

– Sophia Loren

Chapter Twelve

IGNACIO

I'm at the Huntington Park restaurant today. The manager, Carlos, is giving me the tour of disrepair. In other words, we need a new sink in one of the bathrooms, install a new grease trap in the kitchen, and replace some of the chipped Spanish tiles in the dining room. Personally, I'm not a fan of the tiles. The grout is too difficult to keep clean. I have some ideas for a complete remodel. We'll have to throw some good money into this place, but I think with a bit of creativity, it will look clean and modern. Of course, we'd have to close for a month or so and that's where I get the push back from Carlos. We can't let the staff lose that much work, not to mention the revenue.

"I'll at least ask the contractor to give us a bid," I say to Carlos. "If he can do a remodel in phases, we might not have to close our doors for more than a week."

The restaurant can handle paid vacations for the staff if it's only a short amount of time. The part-timers would only lose two, three days of work, tops.

Carlos shakes his head. "I'm no chur about that, *ese*. We have our regulars, chew-no? They like to sit in their same spot, order the same ting. *Los viejos*, they don't like change, *jefe*."

Oh, Carlos. You can take the cholo out of the *barrio*, but you can't take the cholo out of the man. I'll bet under those long pants, there's a pair of white socks pulled all the way up his calves.

"Well, the Spanish tile floor is a tripping hazard, so we'd be doing the *viejos* a favor," I say.

Just then, my phone rings. It's Bernadette's ringtone.

"I gotta take this, Carlos. I'll be a minute."

Carlos does his Chicano Power fist punch with a nod and heads into the kitchen to help with the line. As the manager, it's not his job. But he started out as a cook several years ago and I think he secretly loves it. I don't blame him.

I swipe my phone screen. "Hey, Berna. What's going on?"

"Yeah, sorry to bother you, but I can't find the gift certificate option in the new POS system. I was thinking maybe count it as cash, but wasn't sure."

"What do you mean, gift certificates? We discontinued those years ago."

"Yeah, but don't we still have to honor them?"

"I mean, I guess, but we'll have to count it as a loss in the system. Is it a large amount? How many guests?"

"Just one, and you'll never guess who."

"Berna, you know I don't like guessing."

"Pancho Two. Didn't he get married and move to South America?"

An icy chill spreads through my veins. Bernadette doesn't know anything about what Pancho Two did. Only my parents and siblings.

"Pancho Two is at the restaurant? And he's trying to pay with old gift certificates?"

"What a weasel, right? Ten bucks says he never even paid for them."

If she only knew.

"Bernadette, listen to me. Keep him there as long as you can. This is important. I'm getting in my car right now."

"I'll try."

I'm out the door with my keys in hand as I speak.

"Do whatever you can. Offer him a free flan. He loves that stuff. And talk to him or something. He must not leave before I get there."

"Okay. Olive's talking to him right now."

"Olive? Why? Did she take the table?"

"No. She's just friendly with everyone and has no creep-o-meter, apparently."

Good grief. If Pancho Two even thinks about touching her…

"Rushing over now," I say and end the call.

I don't want to admit how many traffic laws I break getting to the restaurant. I skid my car up to the front door and run inside. Bernadette greets me right away.

"Where is he?"

She gives me a bewildered look. "I'm sorry. We tried to keep him here."

"He *left*?"

Freaking A. What was his game, coming in here after what he did? And he couldn't wait five minutes for me? He's up to something.

"I got his phone number, though. Or rather, Olive did."

"She didn't give *her* number to *him*, did she?"

"I don't think so. He seemed to take a liking to her, though."

I don't like the idea of Pancho Two occupying the same room as Olive, let alone talking to her. I do a quick scan of the restaurant.

"Don't see her."

"Last I saw her, she was talking to some guy."

Some guy? What guy? Something sharp lodges in my throat.

I walk past the front dining area around a wall of booths I've been meaning to knock down to create an open floor plan. As I round the corner, there's Olive, and she's talking to none other than Aaron, her cheating ex. My blood churns hot in my veins. What the blazes is he doing here? Trying to get her back? He saw me kiss her and what... has been thinking about what he's missing ever since? What a prick.

I don't know what it is, but the caveman in me takes over my steps, and I launch myself to Olive's side, wrapping her in a hug.

"I've missed you, babe."

In the corner of my eye, I see Aaron's eyes turn down and lips press in a line. He is so jealous.

I give Olive a gentle peck on the lips and meet her gaze, hoping she'll understand my silent communication.

Are you okay?

I am now.

Do you want me to kick this guy's ass?

Maybe later.

"Ignacio, this is Aaron Lipshitz. Aaron, this is my... boyfriend, Ignacio."

Aaron's lip *shitz*, alright. Everything about this guy shitz. I can tell he's sizing me up, maybe thinking of ways to bludgeon me in my sleep. But that forced smile on his face becomes prominent and he stretches out his hand.

"Heeey, nice to meet you."

I don't want to shake his clammy hands. Who knows where they've been? But Olive looks at me expectantly, and I suppose I should be the bigger man—even though I'm seconds away from kicking him out of my restaurant. I kinda wish I had one of those *'we reserve the right to turn away customers'* signs right about now. I always thought those signs were petty. Now I know why they exist.

I nod my head—because it really is nice to meet me, isn't it?—and shake the sleazemonger's hand. Just as I suspected—clammy.

"I came by to offer an—excuse my poor choice of pun—olive branch. I just want to say there are no hard feelings."

I cross my arms over my chest and straighten my back, stretching to my full height.

"No hard feelings, huh? Who do you suppose is the victim, here? You?"

He lifts his clammy hands in surrender. "Listen, I really don't want to get into the blame game. We… have a long history that I think should remain in the past. Mistakes were made on both sides. I admit it."

I seriously don't have the bandwidth for this right now. All I know is Pancho Two is back in town and the Posse is breathing down my neck. This little man has got to go.

"Right, umm… here's the thing, Alan."

"Aaron."

"That's what I said. We're a little bit busy, so unless you're going to order something, I'll have to ask you to make room for our paying customers."

Olive bends her head down and I know she's stifling a laugh.

"Oh. Okay. I actually ate before I came."

"That's a shame. Maybe a… Coke?"

Aaron is visibly uncomfortable, shifting his weight from side to side. He thinks he's all that, but he's nothing but a little lip-shitz.

"I actually wanted to invite you both to a party I'm throwing Friday night."

"Hmm, yeah, no. As you can see, I have a restaurant to run and Friday nights are packed. Sorry, bro."

"Well, what about you, Olive? You just work the lunch crowd, right?"

"Yes, that's true," she says. A rock drops in my belly. Is she actually considering this? Can't she see he's a slimeball? Then Bernadette's words ring in my mind. 'Olive has no creep-o-meter.' She's just too nice—well, unless you count that lunch in the fashion district, when she was anything *but* nice.

"Great. I'll see you at seven. Oh, and it's Comic Con themed. Cosplay your favorite fandom."

"Yeah, Aaron. There's just one problem," she says.

"Is it the costume? Because you don't have to dress up."

"Oh no, it's not that. I simply don't want to go."

That's my girl. I slide my arm around her shoulder and squeeze her close.

"The lady has spoken, Ahab. She doesn't want to go."

Aaron grimaces at me. He's quite aware I'm messing up his name on purpose. If he doesn't go soon, I'll be calling him another A word, and it might not go down well.

"Olive, if this is about not wanting to go back to the house we lived in together—"

"Nope. I'd just rather spend my Friday night on a Stair-Master than at a party with you and Eyebrows."

"Eyebrows? What are you talking about?"

I've had enough of this. He's wasted enough of my time. Meanwhile, Pancho Two is halfway across town by now, doing who knows what.

"Abel," I say.

"Aaron," he snaps through gritted teeth.

"Sure. This has all been very fun, but I'm going to go make out with my hot girlfriend now. So if you'll excuse us…"

I've never seen someone turn so red, so fast. He looks at Olive and I'm pretty sure he blew out a brain cell with the way his veins are bulging in his temple.

"I'm happy to see you've moved on so quickly," he says. "Good for you."

I feel Olive tense under my arm.

"I'm the lucky one," I say, looking down at Olive. "She's an amazing cuddler. But the spooning is my favorite."

Aaron makes a strange sound—almost like a cat dying. I honestly didn't think this would be so fun.

"Well," he says on a swallow. "If you change your mind, you know how to get there. I'm having it catered."

"Oooh, catered," I say. "That might be a game changer for us."

"Wow, definitely," says Olive. "You should have led with that, Aaron. I'll let you know if I change my mind."

"Ohhh-kay," he says tentatively, scooting toward the door. "I… will see you around."

He hustles away while Olive and I wave.

"Have fun storming the castle," she says, even though he's out of earshot. I could kiss her right now.

"Are you okay?" I ask. I know how it feels to see an ex after a nasty breakup. I want her to know I'm here for her. Fake boyfriend or not.

She takes in a breath. "Actually, I'm great."

"That's good to hear," I say. "You were amazing, by the way."

She nudges me. "You weren't so bad yourself. Ahab? I'm dying."

"I had to do something after that terrible olive branch pun."

"And did you see his face when you said we were going to go make out? You were so serious, and he was so… ehhhh."

She makes a stone face with her tongue sticking out.

She's knitting a cute little sock for my heart and holding it in her sweet hands. I don't know how to live with that.

"Olive, I need to talk to you."

Her laughter dies down. I hate that I have to dampen her joy, but dealing with Pancho Two is a time sensitive matter.

"You're fake breaking up with me," she says, a shadow casting over her features.

"No!" I take hold of her shoulders. "I'm not... fake breaking up with you."

"Whew. Because it's fine if you are, but I need a little warning. That's all."

"I promise, when it's time to end this charade, it will be mutual. I think we're both benefiting from it right now."

"You can say that again."

I give her a hug because apparently, I'm a hugger now—and I think she needs one. Once I'm enfolded in her embrace, I discover I need one, too.

"It's about that man who came into the restaurant earlier. Big belly. Bad comb-over."

She nods. "I remember. He introduced himself as Francisco Ortega, all friendly in a grooming sort of way."

So she does have a creep-o-meter. Bernadette will be glad of it.

"And then I remember something you said my first day here. You asked me what I know about Francisco Ortega. Suddenly, red lights started to go off in my head. But I kept my cool. Bernadette wasn't at all thrilled to see him, though."

"He's not a good guy, Olive."

"Yeah, I kind of gathered that."

"He was an investor in the restaurant back when my dad first opened. We call him Pancho Two because… well, you know how my nickname is Nacho?"

"Yes. Makes me super hungry." She licks her lips. Olive licking her lips is making *me* hungry—and just not for fried tortilla chips and cheese.

"The nickname for Francisco is Pancho. That's why you sometimes hear my uncles and Abuela calling my dad Pancho."

"Kind of like how William is Bill and Richard is Dick."

"Yeah. Like that. Anyway, Francisco Ortega is the other Pancho for the restaurant's namesake—Dos Panchos."

"Ahhhh. That makes more sense than what I thought."

"He did some bad things and I need to find him. Berna says you have his phone number?"

She takes her phone from her apron pocket. "He made me put it in my phone because he didn't trust me not to lose a paper note. I'll text it to you."

"You didn't give him your number, did you?"

She snorts. "Of course not."

"Good." My phone dings with her text.

"Wait a minute. What did you think Dos Panchos meant?"

She swats her hand. "Oh, you know. Those things you wear when it rains?"

"Things you wear when it rains? You mean ponchos?"

"Yeah. Why someone would name a Mexican restaurant after a rain slicker is beyond me, but who was I to ask?"

Hmm. I wonder if some of our customers also mix up the word poncho with Pancho.

"I'm going to my office now," I say. "Don't leave today without saying goodbye."

She beams. "I promise."

My gaze follows her until she's out of my sight behind the server station. She doesn't cease to amaze me. Guys like Aaron and Pancho Two underestimate her. She's smart. I need her to know that in her heart.

I go in the back, waving at the kitchen staff. Alfonso makes a joke about seeing Pancho Two, saying he put ghost peppers in his lunch. The old guy was sweating like a pig as a result.

I enter my office, preparing myself mentally to confront Pancho over the phone. I'll need to tread carefully to get him to cooperate. Maybe meet somewhere that's not the restaurant. I figure if he wanted to remain hidden, he wouldn't have come back.

He doesn't answer when I call from the landline, so I try with my cell. Straight to a computerized voicemail. I really don't know if I should leave a message. What if he gave Olive a bogus number? What if I'm walking into a trap?

I try again five more times. I'm getting really pissed and am about to call once more when my cell phone rings. It's an unknown number. My palms suddenly feel sticky. I'd say it was from shaking Aaron's hand, but it's my own sweat. I need to play my cards carefully.

"This is Ignacio," I say. Hello seems too... friendly, and I'm feeling the opposite of friendly right now.

"We know he was there," says a muffled voice. He sounds like... Optimus Prime.

"Who is this?" Duh. I know who it is. It's the guy

Churro from the freaking surfer gang. That's who it is. "Are you using a voice changer app?"

"That's not your concern."

"Sorry. What? I'm having a hard time understanding. Your Kylo Ren mask needs batteries."

"I said, that's not y—"

"Heh?"

"It doesn't—"

"Nope. You're going to have to take off the mask. It's not working."

I hear a dramatic sigh on the other end of the line and a moment later, Churro returns to his normal voice.

"Duuuude. It's not a mask."

"Much better. Is this Churro?"

"No names over the phone, bro."

Right. I'm ninety-nine percent sure Churro is not his real name, so what does it matter? Whatever.

"Anyway, as I was saying, I don't know where Pancho went."

I hear Churro taking a bite of something and chewing for a long moment. A train goes by in the background. He's crunching and crunching like he straight up forgot he's on the phone.

Finally, he says, "Did you know you can use Cheetos to start fires? They're basically just pure hydrocarbons."

"I wasn't aware of that, no."

He crunches into my ear again. "Look, bromigo. Just because I like you, I'll tell you something. The other guys in the Posse, they're not so chill. They don't like waiting. The clock is ticking, bro. Tick tock."

He takes another crunchy bite and then the line goes silent. That dirtbag hung up on me. I'd throw my phone across the room if it wasn't so expensive.

Seriously, are all the psychos out today? Is it some kind of full moon druid holiday?

I'll have to talk to my dad. He needs to know Pancho Two is back, and I'll have to tell him the Posse is back, too. I'd hoped I wouldn't have to drag him into this.

My heart pounds in my chest. I need to let off some steam before I rip someone's head off. If only Aaron were still here—his head would roll quite nicely. Just the look on his face, and the way it amused Olive, was priceless. I feel like dragging him back into the restaurant just to taunt him some more. But I suppose there's only so many insults one can throw at a man before it gets old. Best to let it go. Unless…

There *is* one thing. As long as Olive wants to go along with it, I would get massive pleasure from helping Olive steal back her mezuzah.

Life is
a combination
of magic
and pasta.

- Federico Fellini

Chapter Thirteen

OLIVE

"Who are you supposed to be? A mariachi monk?"

Ignacio's at my front door dressed in a brown robe and a straw sombrero. He's sporting this ridiculously large handlebar mustache and the most dazzling glint in his eyes.

He sweeps his robe open with a dramatic *swoosh* to reveal a beige tunic cinched at the waist with a black utility belt from which hangs a toy lightsaber.

"I'm Obi *Juan* Kenobi."

I'm cracking up. "That's so perfect."

"What are you going as? The white queen from Narnia?" He gestures to my white off-the-shoulder gown. It's a tacky wedding/prom dress I found at a thrift store. Purple tag fifty percent sale. And bonus—it has pockets.

"Not a queen," I say, putting on the wireless headphones I covered in wig hair. "A Druish princess."

I pick up my plastic space blaster to complete the look.

"From Spaceballs?"

"Ding ding ding. Mariachi Jedi wins a prize."

"I think we both do. This is the fandom pairing we never knew we needed."

"Indeed."

"I almost went as Emo Kylo Ren, but then I saw the hat." He shrugs. "I couldn't help it."

"It's the mustache that does it for me. Such a turn on."

"You look amazing. Do those headphones work?"

"Yep."

I show him the playlist set up on my Spotify app and lock up, shoving my keys, phone, and wallet into the deep pockets of my gown. When we pile into his SUV, he refuses to take off the hat, so he has to tilt the seat back to make room for the brim.

"You're sure you want to go?" he asks. "It's not too late to back out."

I'll admit, when he first suggested we attend Aaron's party, I thought he'd lost his mind. But upon further consideration, I decided who cares if he lost his mind? I'm going to make Aaron and Eyebrows regret the day they crossed me. I'll eat my weight in whatever food they serve and get my mezuzah back.

If I'm being honest, though—I just want an excuse to go out with Ignacio. Or Obi Juan, as I should call him for the rest of the night.

"I'm all dressed up and hungry," I say. "Let's do this."

We head out, taking surface streets to get to Aaron's house. The familiar streets begin to cause a lump in my tummy as we get closer. Somehow, Ignacio is keenly perceptive, and leans his hand across the console to comfort me.

"Are you okay? I can turn around."

"And miss seeing Aaron's face when he sees how awesome we are? Not a chance."

He squeezes my hand reassuringly, but in turning his head, his sombrero gets caught in the seatbelt and he swerves a little, the tires barely skimming the lane divider bumps. He rights the car without incident, but that small mistake is enough to catch the interest of a motorcycle cop. The *whoop whoop* of the siren precedes the blue and red lights. They're almost blinding in the mirrors.

Ignacio curses under his breath and pulls over. The police officer does a double take when he sees us in our costumes, but quickly recovers and requests license and registration.

What Ignacio does next both mortifies and slays me. He waves his hand sideways and says, "These are not the droids you're looking for."

My jaw hits the floorboard and I just want to disappear into thin air. The officer frowns, bending down to get a better look inside the car.

"Step out of the vehicle, sir."

Ignacio gives me a look I can't place and unlocks his seatbelt. He slides out of the car with his hands up.

The officer gives Ignacio a once over. "Where are you coming from?"

Ignacio swipes his hand again. "We're but lowly farmers from Tawl."

"Uhh, huh." The officer peeks his head in to look at me. "You guys headed to a convention, or what?"

"Mapuzo," replies Ignacio. "We have family there."

Shut up, Nacho. You're going to get us arrested.

"Mapuzo?" the officer repeats incredulously.

Ignacio nods. "In the Mid Rim Territories."

The officer leans in close to Ignacio, who, by the way, is still wearing that silly hat.

"Have you been drinking, sir?"

Please don't crack a joke about the dark side.

"No, I have not."

"It's the hat," I cry out. "He swerved because of the hat."

The officer raises a brow at Ignacio and studies him for a long moment. Then something in him relaxes and he shakes his head fighting a laugh.

"The hat?"

"It got caught on the safety belt," I say, leaning across the front seat.

The officer looks to Ignacio to confirm this and Ignacio nods coolly.

"Okay, I'll let you off with a warning, but take off the hat while driving."

"Will do."

The officer nods at me, then tips his chin at Ignacio. "Drive safe and… may the force be with you."

I wait until the officer walks back to his motorcycle before I yell at Ignacio.

"I'm going to slap you with my space buns. What were you thinking?"

He laughs as if he just cheated death. "I don't know. I hardly recognize myself anymore. It's pretty obvious the guy was a sci-fi fan—just the way he carried himself, you know? We're just lucky he's not a Trekkie."

"You're *meshuggeneh*, you know that? It means you're a crazy fool."

He grins at me and starts the engine. "Keep up the sweet talk, my dear. I'll be here all night."

We arrive at Aaron's house without further incident. Costumed guests pack the small house, spilling out onto the front and rear patios. We don't see Aaron right away, but I recognize a few people from the marketing firm. They greet me stiffly with forced politeness. Lord knows what they were told about why I no longer work with them.

Ignacio grumbles as we walk in.

"We must be cautious. You will never find a more wretched hive of scum or villainy."

"Are you going to quote space movies all night?"

He shrugs noncommittally.

There's a spread of appetizers on a table in the front room, and a server is walking around with a tray. I feel for him on a nuclear level. Here's hoping he doesn't fall into a cake.

"A little pretentious to have a server, don't you think?" Ignacio whispers in my ear.

I snort because he called it. Aaron is the most pretentious person I know. Hiring a server at a costume party in a house this size? He's trying too hard.

"It's kind of pathetic and I'm here for it," I say.

The server approaches us with his tray. "Kosher stuffed mushrooms?"

I pluck one from the tray. "Don't mind if I do."

Aaron and Eyebrows slide up to us just as I stuff the mushroom in my mouth. He's dressed as Loki but more slimy, and Eyebrows looks like a Galadriel Pinterest fail.

"Hey, you two. So glad you could make it," says Aaron. "I see you've found the snacks, Olive."

"Do you have any non-kosher mushrooms?" says Ignacio cheekily.

"Um, I don't think so."

I roll my eyes. It's so Aaron to serve kosher food just for show. I know he enjoys a ham and cheese hoagie as much as the next guy.

Eyebrows clears her throat and nudges Aaron.

"Oh, um, Ignacio, this is Pamela," Aaron says, recovering.

I press my lips together to keep me from gagging. Why did I think coming here tonight was a good idea?

"Aaron and I welcome you to our home," Eyebrows says in her usual snake voice. "And I just want to say how happy I am to see things have worked out. I hope we can be 'couple friends' and put the past behind us."

Couple friends? Pardon me while I barf. Also, she *lives* here now? I'll bet she sleeps with my quilt.

"Anyway," says Aaron. "Cash bar out back. We're going

to mingle, but have fun. We'll circle back around a little later."

"Cash bar. Looking forward to it," says Ignacio with a wave as Aaron and Eyebrows slink off.

"Well, there goes our plan to drink all of Aaron's free booze," I say.

"At least there are mushrooms."

"How are you going to eat anything with that enormous mustache?"

He shrugs and takes my hand. "Come on. Let's see what else they've got."

We weave through the crowd of cosplayers. There are two Captain Americas, a Joker, someone who painted themselves silver and is now regretting it, a disheveled Harry Potter with lipstick marks on his face, and a sexy Hermione.

Every time somebody recognizes me from the marketing firm, Ignacio puts his arm around me and says something like, "Yeah, we're friends of Aaron. Olive tried to keep him off the sauce, but there's only so much tough love you can give. Here's hoping those indecent exposure charges don't stick."

Or...

"Poor Aaron. Can you believe Pamela gave him genital herpes?"

And my personal favorite is when he shakes someone's hand, introducing himself as Aaron's male nurse. "He's a good patient. There's no shame in adult diapers."

We float around the party for a while, trying all the appetizers. Ignacio critiques them all, saying what he would do differently. The only sweet food is rugelach and even *that* is lackluster. Ignacio doesn't bother to try it.

We wander outside to the back patio where the cash bar is. Ignacio points to a bottle of Absolut Vodka and quips, "Only a sith deals in absolutes."

I snort. "Are you a closet nerd?"

"Not at all. I'm not even a fun guy. But being with you… brings out the kid in me."

"Gee thanks."

"You're welcome."

Just then, I see Aaron moving our way. Eyebrows is nowhere to be found, so I can only imagine he's about to do something slimy.

I cling to Ignacio. "Help me Obi Juan, you're my only hope."

He kisses my forehead. "I'll keep him occupied while you go on your mission impossible."

"Good idea." My hand reaches to feel for the screwdriver in my pocket. "Wish me luck."

I slip away just before Aaron reaches us. I hear Ignacio telling him something about the mushrooms not sitting well.

I mosey on over to the front door, looking over my shoulder to make sure I'm not being watched. The guests are milling about, but no one's paying attention to me. Ignacio had wanted to do this part of the mission, but he's a lot easier to notice. I never thought I'd find the perks in being virtually invisible to people, but here I am, about to heist my ex-boyfriend's house for a mezuzah.

My heart pounds from fear of getting caught by Pamela and her frightening eyebrows, but I unscrew it from the doorframe surprisingly fast and slip it into my pocket.

I go into the bathroom next, not really planning to snoop

through the medicine cabinets, but still hoping to find something incriminating. There's nothing interesting—just stuff like aspirin and band aids. I throw back the shower curtain and am sickened to find brands of personal care products for women. A devilish little voice inside me laments I didn't have the foresight to sneak in hair remover to pour into the shampoo bottles. But I wouldn't have room in my pockets anyway, and I'm not *that* vindictive.

I tell myself I'm not angry or upset at Aaron and Pamela anymore. I feel sorry for them more than anything because they're stuck with each other.

While I'm here, I use the toilet and wash my hands, then go through the primary bedroom out of habit to get to the back patio. That's when I see my quilt and my heart sinks. I'm over Aaron—I know that. But the scar is still there.

I go through the sliding doors and stay back in the shadows, away from the main part of the patio where most of the guests are hanging out. One thing I liked about this house when we first moved here was the outdoor fireplace. It's a modern upright structure with white stone masonry. Very sleek. In the short time I lived here, we only used it once, and Aaron scoffed at me for wanting to roast marshmallows. It's not in use right now, so there are no other guests on this end of the yard.

Ignacio glances my way, still in the middle of a conversation with Aaron. I give him a nod and pat my pocket to let him know I've got the loot. He nods back surreptitiously so Aaron doesn't notice and continues talking. From this distance, I only catch an errant word, but the last thing he says to Aaron reaches me loud and clear.

"You know what?" he says, slapping Aaron in the shoulder. "Thank you. I'm glad you cheated on Olive because if you hadn't, I might not have met her. And she's the best thing that has ever happened to me."

He taps Aaron on the cheek for good measure, marches over to me with purpose, throws back his hat, and tears off the mustache.

"Hello there," he says, and all of a sudden, he's kissing me. It's not so much a kiss, but rather a wanton raid of my mouth. His lips part mine like a tempest tearing through an impoverished beach town, knocking down huts and flooding the streets. He presses into me until my back hits the stone of the fireplace. I can hardly breathe, panting—kissing him in return, or at least trying to keep up. His hands skate over my bare shoulders, setting fire to my skin, and his fingers find the nape of my neck, knotting into my hair.

I'm falling apart. I've never been kissed like this in my life. As a matter of fact, if this is kissing, I'm convinced that whatever my ex-boyfriends thought they were doing in the past didn't even count as kisses at all. Ignacio takes my mouth hungrily with masterful strokes. I might die—right here against this fireplace dressed like Princess Vespa.

I clutch fistfuls of his tunic, his belt, his robes. My hands are everywhere.

"Olive," he rumbles. "You are so insanely beautiful."

All I can manage is a gurgling sound in the back of my throat. I've pretty much lost my capacity to think.

His scruff grazes my skin as he devours my neck, setting off little explosions all over my body. Heat pools in my belly, and at this point, I don't care if Aaron or anyone else at the party sees us. I don't care if this is for show or not. All

I know is I want this man, and nothing—not even donuts—will ever compare to the way he makes me feel.

He crushes into me, tilting my head at the perfect angle to devour my mouth. Stars spin behind my eyes. I may be having an out-of-body experience. He's *that* good of a kisser.

"Ignacio," I breathe into the kiss. I don't want to stop, but if this gets any hotter, I will seriously combust. And so I crack a joke I know he'll appreciate.

"Is that a lightsaber in your pocket, or are you just happy to see me?"

He smiles against my mouth. "I believe you might be referring to your blaster."

He reaches to the side of his belt and produces his toy lightsaber. "An elegant weapon for a more civilized age."

"Well then," I say. "May the schwartz be with you."

He laces his fingers through mine and tugs me away from the fireplace wall. "You wanna get outta here?"

"Yes," I groan. "More than anything."

He takes a step toward the French doors that lead into the kitchen, but I pull him in the opposite direction, away from the guests and around the side of the house where there's a gate leading to the street. As he reaches up to unlatch the gate, he stops to give me a peck on the lips.

His mouth hovers against mine and with a hot breath, he whispers. "By the way. I *am* happy to see you."

GAH!

After we sneak out, we both agree the kosher appetizers hardly made a dent in our appetite, so we end up at a burger house. I suggest the drive-through, but Ignacio is completely against eating in his car. Surprisingly, we don't turn that many heads in our costumes when we walk inside. I'm not ready to take off my space buns just yet—gotta get good mileage out of them, after all.

We're in the middle of the busy fast-food restaurant, noshing on the cheesiest, greasiest burgers in LA and are sharing a mountain of french fries. Ignacio shoves fries in his mouth so fast, I have to slap his hand away so he doesn't get into my half.

"Look at you," I say, somewhat astounded. "What happened to the health food nut I've come to know and love?"

I did *not* mean to say love. It's an expression. That's all.

"I'll let you in on a little secret," he says. "Every chef has a guilty pleasure. For Wolfgang Puck it's ice cream. Alton Brown? Cheetos."

"No!"

"It's true. A chef can create beautiful culinary master-pieces, but sometimes we just want something naughty."

I feel a blush bloom in my cheeks. I still have that mind-bending kiss on the brain and he has to go and say things like that. Doesn't everybody want something naughty from time to time? Okay—maybe I live off more naughty foods than healthy. Sue me.

"My guilty pleasure is a greasy burger and fries," he says, scooping up another fry. "And lots of ketchup."

"I feel like you just described my entire diet," I say.

His eyes pour over my face as I take a sip of my choco-late shake. I reach the point where I'm mostly sucking air through the straw and it's making that sad slurping noise. I frown at my cup.

"Do you want another one?" he offers.

Yes, I do, but I'm not going to pig out *that* much.

"If you get one for yourself, I'll take a few sips," I say.

He squints at me because, of course, I *know* he doesn't consume sugar.

"How about I get one for myself, and you can have as much as you want?" he says.

In other words, another one just for me.

"Maybe on the way out," I say. "For now, I'll steal some of your water."

It's so strange to be on this familiar plane with him—sharing a beverage out of the same cup, like we're a real couple. I've never sipped out of the same cup as Aaron or any of my previous boyfriends. This arrangement with Ignacio is supposed to be fake, and yet the lines keep blurring more and more. I guzzle some of his water and he's not even grossed out.

How can someone get grossed out about drinking from the same cup after that kiss?

That kiss! Wowza.

"Thanks for sticking up for me at the party," I say. "I need to take you everywhere to up my snark game."

"Happy to be of service."

He smiles, but it quickly fades, like something just made him a little sad. His eyes seem sort of droopy, and all I can think about is how I want to kiss the smile right back onto his face.

"We make a good team, don't we?" I say. "I'd make all your ex-girlfriends jealous and steal things from their houses if I could."

He snorts a half-laugh. "Where were you four-and-a-half years ago?"

"I can't remember that far back. It must have been incredibly boring."

"I doubt that very much. You were probably dancing through life with your sunny smile and free spirit. Wearing your Crocs and Christmas leggings."

"You're probably right. Silly Olive floating about with no real plan. No real goals."

"That's not what I meant."

"I know it's not." I shrug one shoulder. "But that's just the way I am. I can never settle on a career or any interest, really. I'm a flibbertigibbet."

"There's nothing wrong with that. As long as you're happy and spreading joy the way you do. I think that's enough—and it's a lot more than a lot of people ever do."

"It's a nice thought. It really is. But my dad wouldn't agree."

"You shouldn't let people make you feel bad for not dreaming big. Mother Teresa used to say that we can't all do great things. But we can do small things with great love."

"Small things with great love," I repeat, trying it on for size. "I can do that."

"I know you can," he says, popping a fry in his mouth.

Emboldened by his trust in me, I ask, "Do you mind me asking what happened four years ago?"

"Four and a *half*," he corrects. "I remember specifically because it was Christmas."

"Oh no. Not Christmas."

"Christmas Eve. I had the ring in my pocket. It was supposed to be perfect—like a frickin' Hallmark movie. But then she butt-dialed me right in the middle of doing the nasty with her co-worker. I heard every detail on my Bluetooth as I drove to confront her. When I arrived at her house, there was not an ounce of remorse on her face."

"I'm so sorry."

He ticks his head. "I'm over it. But when I found out what happened to you, all those feelings came flooding back. And I thought maybe this was a strange opportunity to make things right in the universe." He shakes it off. "Ridiculous, I know."

"Not ridiculous at all."

"I hate cheaters."

"Cheaters are the worst," I agree.

We sit in silence for a minute, finishing the fries. As fun as it is kissing him, I love sharing this moment with him—so comfortable around each other neither one of us has to speak. Another kiss would be nice, though.

"My grandma leaves for Arizona tomorrow," he says, breaking the silence. "My grandpa turns ninety next week, so Francesca and Edmund are driving Abuela there to celebrate."

"Wow. Ninety. That's quite an achievement."

"Yup—if being an ornery old man is an achievement. He drinks like nobody's business and eats everything with a side of lard. He swears it's the secret to youth."

"Maybe he's onto something," I say. "Is your grandma coming back to California after that?"

"No. She'll stay in Arizona for a while then go back to Mexico City for the rest of the year."

Realization dumps on top of me. I feel like I swallowed a cup of nails.

"So, I guess this means you don't need a fake girlfriend anymore?"

He blinks at me, and I wait fearfully for the words hanging on his tongue. It's over.

"Actually… and you can say no if you want to…"

My heart pounds and I want to tell him I'll never say no to him—but I dare not interrupt his thought.

He continues on. "Abuela expects me to go to Arizona for a few days—and demands I bring you with me."

High fives explode in my chest. He's not fake-dumping me. Yet.

"Oh. Well, if she demands it," I say.

"She does. Absolutely."

"Who am I to refuse the matriarch of your family?"

He bounces his head energetically. "I'm glad we agree on that."

"Great. We do… agree on that. For sure."

"And don't worry about work. We'll cover your shifts."

Oh. My shifts. Potentially a few hundred dollars.

"Uh… how many shifts are we talking about here?"

"You can make them up the following week if you really want to. Or you can take vacation pay."

"I thought vacation pay only kicks in after a year."

"Hey." He grazes a thumb over my chin. "I happen to know the boss, and I'm pretty sure he's sweet on you."

I try not to read more into that statement than was meant. Still, I can't help it when my words come out shaky.

"Sw-sw-sweet? The boss doesn't like sweets."

His eyes sparkle. "You know what? I think I'll have that shake now."

He clears up all the trash from the table, not allowing

me to do any of the work, and helps me up by the hand like a proper old-fashioned gentleman.

"You're not going to drink any of it. Are you?" I say.

"I'm just trying to butter you up because I have another favor to ask."

"Oh really? Do you need a date for a wedding? That's textbook fake girlfriend right there. Just keep me away from the cake."

His smile sparkles. "Not a wedding. A concert. And I'm not asking you as a fake girlfriend. I'm *inviting* you because I think you'll enjoy it."

Oh. Alrighty then.

I beam at him, not only because he's buying me another milkshake, but because he's inviting me somewhere. Because... he wants to spend time with me?

"Don't get *too* excited," he says. "My brother, Mateo, is playing with his sea shanty band. The city has free summer concerts in the park. And his band is not even headlining."

"That's okay. I like sea shanties. Who's headlining?"

He shrugs. "Abba tribute band or something."

"Abba?! I love Abba."

"Of course you do."

Abba and sea shanties in one day. Amazing.

"Can I ask you something?" he says.

"Anything."

"Is there anything you *don't* love?"

I don't even have to think about my answer. "Yes. Broccoli."

Delicious has
nine letters in it,
but so does
tacosssss!

– Unknown

Chapter Fourteen

IGNACIO

That dress. I can hardly keep my tongue in my mouth.

Olive is wearing the dress she found at the fashion district—the one she wouldn't let me see. It's a solid cornflower blue sundress which buttons down the front—a front which scoops up as though it was made just for her curves—and only secured on her shoulders by two delicate straps. I'm clueless about the cut of women's dresses or how to describe hemlines other than it falls a few inches above her knees and has ruffles along the bottom, show-casing her shapely—and white—legs. But the blue color of the dress only compliments her light skin, like a porcelain teacup. She calls it boho style. I think I love boho now.

When I arrived at Olive's doorstep earlier—and after I picked my jaw off the floor—I stumbled over my words to tell her how insanely beautiful she looked. She laughed and twirled, then lifted up the skirt to show me the bike shorts she was wearing underneath.

"See?" she'd said. "No chub rub."

I almost died right there. If my family wasn't waiting at the park, we would have never left her apartment. Now, walking a half-mile from the only parking spot I could find, I wish I could skip this concert and go back in time to test that chub rub for myself.

But I packed a picnic basket of artisan bread and rose-mary crackers and have an insulated bag packed with goodies such as a crisp pinot grigio, a nutty cheese, home-made hummus, grapes, and veggie sticks. Mom and Dad reserved a spot this morning and are bringing food to share as well.

"You sure know how to schlep, Ignacio," Olive says. I'm carrying most of the stuff, but she has a folding chair and an umbrella. "I packed less when I moved from Jersey."

I admit I should have dropped her off with the stuff before parking, but we're here now, and when the concert's over, I'll bring the car around for her.

"Think of it as an adventure," I say.

We get to the grassy area where a sea of blankets and beach chairs cover every inch of the park with little walking space in between. An impressive stage erected of scaffolding and moving lights sits prominently on the edge of the lawn—musical instruments already set up for the show. Currently, the enormous speakers are blasting music from The Beach Boys while parks and recreation volunteers in yellow shirts scurry around to make sure everything is ready to go.

There are some vendor tents—the rotary club selling raffle tickets for a gift basket, veterans selling bottled water and giving away paper American flags, and the boy scouts selling hot dogs and slushies. Dad texted earlier to let me know they pitched an E-Z UP tent along the right side of the stage and brought a folding table. How early did they have to get here to set that up?

As we walk past thousands of people on blankets, I spot my parents' tent almost immediately. It's pretty hard to miss with the Dos Panchos logo plastered on the top and the entire perimeter covered in papel picado.

Mom's jumping up and down, waving her arms to get our attention. Olive waves back and picks up speed like she's seen the promised land and can finally rest her poor feet. Dad is chillin' under the tent, drinking wine out of a plastic cup. There's no glass allowed in the park.

But what really catches my eye—and my nose—is the bright red meat smoker standing upright and proud just outside the tent. The folding table, instead of one of those roll-up camping tables, is a full six feet long and covered with a linen tablecloth, a galvanized utensil organizer filled with flatware, festive party plates, and a flower arrangement. Instead of an ice chest, there's a rolling cooler cart with an attached bottle opener filled with various drinks. They brought two Adirondack chairs which now flank a small, round side table. And because all that isn't quite enough, a white picket fence surrounds the entire camp.

Dad gets up when he sees Olive and calls her to look at his smoker.

"I made a brisket just for you," he says. "It's been cooking since midnight."

"Dad, what is all this? Are you moving in here?"

"I like to picnic in style," he replies.

"This stopped being a picnic a long time ago. You've been here since midnight?"

I look at my watch. It's three o'clock.

"No, silly," says Mom. We got here around… what, Francisco? Five, five-thirty?"

"Five in the *morning*?"

"All the good spots are taken by six. We had to fight *those* guys for this one." She jerks her head at the middle-aged couple in the next tent over. "We're closer to the stage."

I can just picture Mom and Dad rushing through the park at five in the morning, fighting for prime real estate at the free concert scene.

"Dad, what are you thinking? You made a brisket?"

"If your brisket is as good as your ribs," says Olive, clasping dad's hands in her own, "I would love to invite you over for Rosh Hashanah,"

"I brought hummus and cheese. I thought you were bringing cold cuts or something."

A Cheshire grin spreads across Dad's face. "How does it feel to be out-done, Nacho?"

"Is that what all this is about? Out-doing me?"

Mom rolls her eyes. "Oh, here we go. Come on, Olive. Let's go dance to Surfin' USA."

She takes Olive by the arm and the two women head over to the empty grass area reserved for dancing in front of the stage.

I turn to my dad. "Nobody's trying to out-do anybody. I brought hummus."

"I don't care what you bring."

"Obviously you do, or you wouldn't have said what you said."

"Okay, just drop it."

"Does this have to do with the experiments I make for Sunday dinners sometimes?"

"You always have to do something trendy. Why can't you just make tacos?"

"I'm not trying to compete with you, Dad, if that's what you think."

"Maybe not. But you think you're better."

I'm taken aback. "No, I don't."

"I know you don't care for the Mexican restaurants. Always making your *fusion* or whatever you call it. And the catering. You think I don't know how much you want to do anything but Mexican food?"

"I love Dos Panchos," I say.

"I see the writing on the wall, Nacho. You want to do your own thing. Fine. But at least be honest about it."

"I am honest."

"Then why didn't you tell me Pancho Two came to the restaurant the other day?"

"I... I was planning on telling you. I just got busy."

"You want to know how I found out?"

I shrug. "I'm guessing Rosa or one of the cooks."

"Pancho came to the house. We had a long talk about those surfer boys."

My blood boils.

"You let that criminal in your house? Why?"

"Because he wanted to talk."

"He's dangerous."

He swats his hand. "*Es una idiota.*"

"He stole from us. Doesn't that make you angry?"

"Of course it makes me angry. But I also don't want him sleeping with the fishes. He asked for help."

"Please don't tell me you're thinking of helping him." I lower my voice to a whisper. "The Posse is making threats."

"I know, I know. He regrets working with those punks. The reason he left the country was to escape his connections with them. But then his wife took all his money, and he had no choice other than to come back."

Unbelievable. I scrape my hands down my face. I'm just beside myself here.

"I think if his wife stole all his money, then he deserved it."

"Don't worry, Nacho. I know Dos Panchos are your restaurants now, but I'll deal with *mi tocayo* myself. In my own way."

"Yeah. I don't think I like the sound of that. What are you going to do, Dad?"

He scrapes the backs of his fingers along his jowls and thinks for a second. "I'll make him an offer he can't refuse."

"You... what?"

I want to dive deeper into this conversation—find out what he's planning and hopefully talk him out of it. But a public park is not the place for it—especially with the tent neighbors looking snoopy.

I wouldn't have the chance to continue our talk, anyway. A lady in a yellow parks and recreation T-shirt shouts into the mic, creating screeching feedback. I suppose that's one way to get a crowd's attention.

She blabbers on about the upcoming city activities, including the lobster bash, reminding everyone to buy their raffle tickets. Then, after about five minutes of city of commerce announcements, she finally introduces Mateo's sea shanty band. The High C's

I groan at the band name.

Seconds later, Mateo enters the stage with his acoustic guitar, along with a ragtag group of musicians with various instruments. I only recognize one of his band mates, Desirée, because she grew up next door to us. Her older brother was Mateo's good friend growing up. He spent a lot of time at our house hanging out with Mateo and having dinners with us. He's serving in the military now, but he comes by from time to time.

Desirée sets herself in front of a microphone with her mandolin while the fiddle player, bagpiper, a few percussionists, and a guy with a tin whistle take their places.

Okaaay, and they're all dressed like pirates, but with Mateo's long hair pulled into a ponytail, he's rockin' more of a Hamilton vibe than Jack Sparrow.

Mateo makes one long hoot into the mic, and the music hoists right into the Drunkin' Sailor song. The crowd cheers and several people flood to the dancing area.

From my viewpoint, I can still see Olive and Mom, linking elbows and skipping back and forth. Olive joyfully bouncing and dancing, her dark, wavy hair tossing behind her back—her blue dress whooshing around as she spins.

My heart thunders in my chest and I feel a rush of adrenaline flood through me. Every part of my body is light as air, just watching her. What she does to me—I can't explain it.

Before I realize I've moved, I find myself on the dance floor, joining Olive and Mom in their circle.

"Whew, I'm tired," shouts Mom over the music, and she gestures that she's going to go back to the tent with Dad. The music segues into the next song without pause, and I take Olive in my arms, spinning her around and around, doing an atrocious jig.

She laughs joyfully, throwing her head back in unbridled mirth. Her smile harnesses the very sun, and she's shining it brightly upon me with abandon.

Before I know it, she clasps hands with a lady next to us, who, in turn, clasps hands with her friend. A guy—who I hope is part of their party—joins in, taking my hand to complete a circle.

We're going round and round, doing the grapevine, kicking our legs, and Olive is just blasting pure glee from her face.

"We're doing the horah!" she shouts, laughing, leading the dance. She lifts her arms, and because we're all connected, the rest of us raise our hands, too. In we go to the center—the ladies hooting and wooting. Then the circle stretches back. By this time, more people squeeze in, then more people until the circle becomes so large, a smaller circle forms on the inside. It's a little nuts.

When the song ends, Mateo works the crowd, shouting some kind of pirate nonsense and getting people riled up.

"Ahoy landlubbers. How fares yer day?"

There's clapping and hooting. An older woman with leathery, tan skin and hardly any clothes shouts a drunken, "Yeah, baby."

"Some of ye maidens are already three sheets to the wind, I see."

That gets him a few laughs.

"We give no quarter to those of you not doing a jig. All hands on deck and sing along. We be goin' t' play a happy shanty for ye scallywags. It's called Whisky in the Jar."

I take Olive's hand as the song begins, lest we get dragged into the crowd. The horah she started was fun, but I want her all to myself now. Plus, she seems a little overheated.

We stand to the side, but still within a good view of the stage, swaying together. My arm claims her shoulder—her head fits right on my chest. I could stay like this forever. A few beach balls appear out of nowhere, and the crowd bounces them back and forth. One of them comes our way and I pop it into the air. I don't know why that's so fun, but it is. I can't remember the last time I touched a beach ball, let alone gone to the beach. Maybe I really *do* work too much.

The band plays a wildly robust set. They're actually not bad. Mateo has an incredible amount of energy to bounce around on stage the way he is, still able to sing and play guitar in this heat. All the musicians seem to be having fun up there. Desirée's gaze is trained on my brother most of the time, following his lead. It's hard to believe she's all grown up now. I feel so old.

The song they're playing is so upbeat, more and more people come up to dance. Right up front, there's an overly tanned middle-aged guy in nothing but shorts a size or two too big on him. He's swaying to the music with his hands in the air, showcasing his tattoos and nipple piercings. He's so loopy, either he doesn't notice his shorts are hanging low, or he doesn't care. That's LA for you. These free concerts bring out all the crazies.

Olive points to him and quips, "Just say no to crack."

"And Nipplegate," I reply, rubbing my thumbs and fore-fingers together. Olive dissolves into laughter, clutching her belly and covering her face.

"Staaawwwp!"

I gather her into a hug. "Wanna go eat something now?"

"Let's keep dancing."

How is she not tired yet? I'm already feeling hot and winded, but I'll continue dancing with her for as long as she wants. I'll do almost anything she wants.

We remain on the grassy area for the entire set, taking breaks from dancing to just watch Mateo and his band. After the encore, the parks and recreation lady gets back on the stage to remind everyone to buy those raffle tickets. Olive and I go from tent to tent to see what they have. I buy a few tickets to support the veterans, the local high school, and the booster club. The water district has a booth reminding us California's in a drought and to please conserve water. Olive spins their wheel and wins a key chain. In the next booth, there's a guy in a bee costume giving away a bike to drum up publicity for his bicycle store. It's a canary yellow beach cruiser with a front basket. The bicycle raffle tickets are free, so Olive and I go over and get ours.

"I hope I win," she says, clutching onto her ticket. "Although I don't have anywhere to keep a bike at my apartment."

"If you win, you can store it in my garage," I say. I put my ticket in my wallet and offer to hold on to hers, but she stuffs her ticket down her top and pats her heart.

"For luck," she says.

"My wallet is safe," I affirm.

"Oh, but is it lucky?" She wags her brows and leads the way back to my parent's glamp-ground where Dad is already serving the brisket.

Olive is all over it and sings Dad's praises with every bite. I have to admit, it's amazing. Come to think of it, I don't think I've ever had brisket before. It's so tender it melts in my mouth. I'd like to incorporate this into my menu somehow. Maybe serve it with jalapeño polenta. I'm already thinking of ideas.

Soon after, we're joined by Mateo and Desirée. They're still in their pirate garb.

"Wow, you're really committed to the act," I say.

Mateo glowers at me. "We stay in costume for the fans," he says.

I snort. "Okay, Lin Manuel Miranda."

He huffs. "For the last time, I do not look like Hamilton. I'm a captain on the high seas."

I guess I'm not the only one teasing him about it.

"Well, you're an easy target and... I'm not throwin' away my shot."

Desirée laughs. "Maybe that's why people like to come up and take pictures with you." Turning to me, she adds, "We autograph The High C's swag the fans buy."

Really? People actually buy their swag? I mean, they're fun in a drunken Irish pub kind of way, but they're not *that* good.

The thing about Mateo is that he'll jump from classic rock to sea shanties to cumbia from one week to the next. He's always collaborating with different musicians just to be able to play anything anywhere.

"Ooh, did you say swag?" Olive's face lights up. "I'll buy some swag."

Desirée waves her hand. "Oh, we'll just give you some."

"No, no," I say. "This is your business. I'll buy it."

Olive looks up at me with those cocker spaniel eyes. "You don't have to do that."

"I know. But I enjoy buying you things."

Buying her things pays off quite nicely, I've found. Like that dress she's wearing, for instance. I like to see her in it. And I like to see her face when she gets a new gift. It's like Christmas. I feel like I've discovered something about her. A childlike quality—the sheer joy in getting a present or a cheap little trinket. The gnomes she got at a garage sale. The High C's swag. That raffle ticket in her bra. My eyes dip down to her neckline instinctively and just as quickly, I tear my gaze away from her entirely and busy myself with the food. That hummus isn't going to serve itself, after all.

Olive hits it off with Desirée immediately. She's especially impressed with the mandolin. I hear her talking about how she tried to learn the ukulele once, but it didn't work out. Desirée, who plays several instruments, offers to teach her and they start in on girl talk and that's where I kind of check out.

I leave the pow wow to go buy that swag where other members of The High C's sit behind a table. I'm not sure what Olive would want, so I buy one of everything; a T-shirt, hat, stickers, an 8 X 10 glossy photo of the band, and a canvas tote bag. She'll love the tote bag. It's so Olive. The guys selling the stuff are overly appreciative and throw in an extra sticker.

After wandering around a bit, I go back to find Olive, Mom, and Desirée disco dancing to the music of the Abba tribute band. Olive has abandoned her shoes and is bouncing on the grass with bare feet. She's just jiving and swaying like the free and easy soul she is. She's the opposite of Shay, or any other girl I've gone out with in the past. It's a wonder my family believes I'm dating a woman like her. I'm beginning to think a woman like Olive is what I've needed all along.

The afternoon wears on, everyone snacking the whole time, and eventually the concert ends. People start to pack up and leave, but my parents don't budge. Dad likes to stay until the bitter end—after all the winners of the raffles are announced and the crowd disperses.

The parks and recreation team is on stage for what feels like an hour but is probably only twenty minutes. They're making announcements between every raffle draw. My tickets are all duds.

The last raffle is the bike, and Olive retrieves her ticket, holding onto it with both hands. A guy volunteer begins announcing the numbers, and Olive kisses her ticket.

The first three numbers are called. Mom boos. I guess

my parents got their tickets earlier than us, because the first three match mine and Olive's tickets, but not theirs. Then the volunteer calls out the next three numbers painfully slow. The anticipation on Olive's face is doing strange things to my heart.

"Seven. Four…"

"Ack!" Olive cries. "This is so fun."

I look at my ticket. Seven five zero. "I'm out."

The lady parks and recreation rep gets on the mic. "Can we have a drumroll, please?"

Oh, brother. Just announce it already. The Abba drummer gets on his set and trills his sticks on the drum.

The guy volunteer gets back on the mic. "And the last number is—"

The drummer hits the cymbal.

"Nine."

Olive squeals. "I won! I won!"

She's so excited, and I'm a little shocked she actually won.

"I've never won anything before. I can't believe it."

Mom claps her hands. "Go up there."

Olive hops up, shouting and waving her ticket as she hops in between people to get to the stage. She's still not wearing shoes. Someone helps her climb onto the stage, and they take pictures with the bike for the community website. Olive hugs every single person on that stage.

Mom pokes me in the back. "Are you going to join her or not?"

I get off my butt, compelled to go to Olive anyway—just because she'll need my help with the bike. When I approach the stage, she waves me up, telling the volunteer that I'm her boyfriend. They all insist I join them on stage, and then they're taking more pictures, instructing me to put my arm around Olive as we pose with the bicycle. Something stirs in my chest, provoking me to kiss her on the cheek. All the volunteers eat that up, taking more pictures.

We're finally done with all that, and I thank the guy in the bee costume, shaking his hand before hopping off the stage. I help Olive get down, wrapping my hands around her waist. She slides down my body and I'm getting a Dirty Dancing vibe from this—except I'm no Patrick Swayze and she's not as graceful as Baby. Her dress rides up to her waist as I lower her, and I've never been more thankful for bike shorts in my life. A smile spreads all the way to her ears, and her eyes sparkle as she says, "Hello, handsome."

I am wrecked.

I also have my hands all over her in front of thousands of people. So I fix her skirt and dip her back, giving her a big smack on the lips. People applaud and awww, and then two volunteers lower the bike off the stage. I take it from them as Olive blows kisses at them all. They wave back in a heartfelt way, having made an instant connection. There's just something about Olive that people find irresistibly endearing—like those puppy videos on the internet. You can't stop watching. She already has my family so in love with her, I think they'd trade me for her in a heartbeat.

I'm beginning to hate this fake girlfriend arrangement, but only the part of it that's fake.

Only the pure
in heart
can make
good soup.

− Ludwig van Beethoven

Chapter Fifteen

OLIVE

Edmund and I meet our gazes from the other side of the circle. We're the only outsiders at the Precio family farm in Arizona, and I can't help but wonder if this is some kind of test.

"What exactly are we supposed to do with the tortillas?" I ask Mateo.

I glance over at Ignacio a few spaces over from me in the

circle for help. His brothers didn't let him stand next to me, thinking we'd cheat somehow. He throws me a helpless expression, like he's in the dark, too. I'm not so sure about that.

"You use your tortilla to slap someone in the circle," explains Mateo, passing around bottles of water to everyone. "Take a swig of the water but don't swallow, and when you get tortilla slapped, try not to laugh."

"So the water just stays in our mouths?" asks Edmund.

"Exactly."

Sebastian goes to the center of the circle to stand next to Mateo.

"We'll demonstrate for you so you get an idea and then we'll start the game," he says. "Just to recap, you all take a swig of water and hold it there. Then one person slaps anyone he—or she—wants with the tortilla. If the slapped person doesn't get out, they can slap anyone they want. And it just goes around until somebody wins."

"Hang on," I say. "How does someone get out?"

"You get out if you laugh and spit your water," replies Mateo.

"I'm not sure if I like this game," says Francesca.

"If you don't want to spit," says Nate, "swallow your water instead of spit and you'll be out."

"Yeah, Francesca," adds Sebastian. "If you don't want to get spit on, get yourself out early."

Ignacio crosses his arms and glowers at his brothers. "Whose idea was this? Sebastian? This has your name all over it."

"It's a fun game they play at the frat houses. It's good, clean fun."

"Just let us demonstrate," says Sebastian. "Ready?"

Mateo adjusts his stance and takes a mouthful of water and holds his tortilla at his side for the showdown with Sebastian. Sebastian does the same, mirroring Mateo's position.

Sebastian goes first, slapping Mateo squarely across the face with his tortilla. Mateo holds in a laugh—and his water —and slaps Sebastian in turn. The two go on like that for a few rounds, and then step away, swallowing the water.

"See?" says Mateo. "Easy."

I'm sending telepathic messages to Edmund. *I have a bad feeling about this.* But he's so invested in proving himself to Francesca's brothers, he's not reading my warning eyes.

Mateo and Sebastian take their places in the circle with their water and tortillas and nod to all of us.

"I'll start," says Mateo. "Everyone, take a mouthful of water and…"

He takes in his water and begins by slapping Nate with the tortilla, who's already shaking with laughter. Nate slaps Sebastian, who slaps Ignacio. Francesca is right next to Ignacio, so he slaps her gently. I can tell Francesca doesn't want to slap anyone, but after a few seconds of indecision, she tortilla-slaps Mateo. His chest convulses and for a second I think he might lose his mouthful of water, but he keeps it in. This goes on for a few rounds—the brothers are cracking up, faces turning red, and eyes bulging out of their heads, but they're surprisingly not spitting out the water. I find it strange that no one is slapping me or Edmund. The water is getting sloshy in my mouth, and I just want to swallow it. I wonder if anyone will notice if I do. I could just puff out my cheeks and pretend they're full of water.

At last, Nate smacks Ignacio so hard, his tortilla breaks, and Ignacio's water goes flying out of his mouth.

"You're out," says Mateo. "Water break."

I guess this means we're allowed to swallow now?

Mateo kicks Ignacio out of the circle and shoos him off to sit under a tree, where there are benches and chairs. I get a shrug from Ignacio as he walks away.

"Round two," Sebastian announces. "Take your water and slap!"

This time Sebastian starts by slapping Francesca. She gets out right away by swallowing the water.

"Sorry guys," she says. "I almost choked."

Off she goes to join Ignacio. They look cozy and relaxed in the shade. Somebody please slap me so I can sit in the shade, too.

We begin again, and Mateo slaps me softly. I mean, it's hardly a slap at all. I slap Edmund, but he's determined to win this thing, so he holds it together. Sebastian is next, who slaps Nate like he's got a vendetta. Nate sprays water everywhere, busting up.

"Out," shouts Mateo.

Now there's four of us left and I'm getting a weird vibe, here.

"You want to start this time, Olive?" asks Mateo. "Try to get me out."

"Whatever you say, bro," I say, taking a swig of water.

I slap him moderately hard and he turns immediately and wallops Sebastian. Sebastian's cheeks bulge out, and he presses his lips inward as his whole body shakes. His eyes are watering, bulging off his face. After several uncomfortable moments, he breaks. Water and drool dribble down his chin as he makes a snorting sound. I can't believe he's still trying to keep it in. Mateo shakes his head and slams his hand against Sebastian's back, sending water and spit across the circle. I jump back, narrowly missing the spray, but Edmund got caught in the splash zone.

"Sorry, man." Sebastian pats Edmund on the shoulder and goes to join his siblings.

I'm not a fan of this game.

Mateo toasts his water bottle. "We're down to three. I wonder who'll win this thing."

Yeah, I wonder.

I try to make eye contact with Edmund again, but his eyes are trained on Mateo. I know how this is going down now. True to my prediction, Edmund gets Mateo good, getting him out on the first slap.

Now it's just me and Edmund, and I'm thinking this was planned from the very beginning. I look over at the siblings under the tree, and they've already broken out the beers and sodas, lounging in the shade, watching the outsiders slapping each other with tortillas. This is ridiculous.

Edmund is too polite to get me out. I don't want to get him out because I know he wants to win. We're just taking turns not getting each other out.

Slap.

Slap.

Slap.

Eventually, I swallow the water because at this point, the siblings are laughing amongst themselves, not even paying attention to us anymore.

"You can swallow your water now," I say. "They're not

even looking."

Edmund flickers his gaze to the siblings under the tree and then back at me, eyes wide. He slaps me, afraid to swallow the water.

"You know this is a trick," I say, slapping him back. "A frat boy joke. Look at Sebastian's face. They're all having fun with us."

He finally swallows. "Francesca wouldn't do that."

Slap.

"She's not in on it," I say.

Slap.

He slaps back. "Nobody will ever be good enough for their sister. And I happen to agree with them there, but Francesca chose me, so…"

He shrugs and I smack my tortilla on his face.

He laughs. "What a ridiculous game."

"I'm gonna let you win, now," I say.

"Should I pretend to clobber you?"

I glance over at the group under the tree. Ignacio looks up, somehow aware whenever my eyes are on him. He gives me a crooked smile and goes back to whatever's going on over there. Looks like someone brought out a checkers board.

"Nah," I say. "They're not even looking. Splash me with water."

"What? No."

"Just do it. Toss the contents of your bottle at me."

There's only an inch of water in my bottle because I've been secretly drinking it instead of gargling with it. I dump what's left down my shirt. Ahhh, that feels so good. It's so hot out here, even my hair is getting a sunburn.

"I'm not going to throw water at you," says Edmund.

"Please, just do it. Hurry before someone looks."

"I... I..."

"Do it, dang it, or—"

Splosh.

The contents of Edmund's bottle splatter my face, hitting me forcefully from an upward trajectory.

"Ugh! You got it up my nose."

"I didn't want to splash you in the first place."

"It's supposed to look like you spit on me. Who spits upward?"

"If I won, you would have spit on *me.*"

Stone silence falls between us as we stare at one another. And then, as if someone popped open a champagne bottle, we burst out in laughter. We couldn't get any more ridiculous if we tried. So, noticing there was still a little bit of water left in his bottle, I snag it from him and splash his face. He's left with his jaw open as I march over to the siblings and announce, "Edmund won."

Ignacio's face cracks into the most glorious, genuine smile I've ever seen on him. He's so beautiful, I want to die. But I pull up my big girl panties and give him a playful thwack with the tortilla right upside his head. The tortilla falls into pieces all over the ground, which the animals will enjoy later. I hear there are goats, but I haven't seen them yet. Nate looks up briefly but then goes back to the checkers' game. He's hovering over while Sebastian and Mateo play like their lives depend on it, and Francesca already took off somewhere with Edmund.

Ignacio doesn't miss a beat. He captures my wrist with a

confident hand and pulls me down onto his lap, arms curled around my waist, holding me there.

Fingers pressed firmly into my sides, he pins me with a roguish stare.

"I think you should pay for that," he says.

I squirm. "What are you going to do to me?"

"I haven't decided yet."

But then his fingers wiggle and pinch, sending tingling jolts through me. I squeal, both loving and hating the sensation of being tickled.

I twitch and kick my legs, but he holds me even tighter, doubling down in his efforts.

I'm screaming at this point. I am so much more ticklish than the average person, I think.

"Ask for mercy," he says.

"Never."

"Then pay your dues another way."

Gulp.

His fingers halt and loosen their hold on me, and I stop squirming. He's taking in my features with soft eyes, and a look that tells me he's surprised at himself for suggesting… well, I'm not sure what he's suggesting, but by the way he wets his lips, I have an idea.

"What did you have in mind?" I whisper, our faces so close I can smell his salty skin. If he wants a kiss, I volunteer as tribute.

He clears his throat and blinks, then slaps my hip.

"You can help me unload the car."

I hop off his lap and follow him to where he parked. The farm is so far away from civilization, we seemed to be driving forever and I really had to pee. So when we arrived,

I ran to find a bathroom. After that, with an introduction to Ignacio's grandfather and his insistence we drop everything and have lunch, Ignacio and I forgot about the luggage.

He doesn't really need help, per se. We each packed one small bag, but I also don't expect him to be my hunky bell-boy, either.

"After we settle in, I want to show you the rest of the farm," Ignacio says, leading me into the house. "Or you can take a nap if you want."

"Hold up, now." Stopping in my tracks, I slice my hand to his chest. "I know this trope. Fake relationship. One bed. The guy gets frisky." I wag my brows. "Imma gonna have to draw the line right there."

He laughs. "Olive, don't worry. It's not like that."

"Oh really? That's what the dude says in every movie and then—whoops—his clothes are on the floor."

Ignacio's holding his stomach, shaking with laughter.

"I think maybe you watch too many movies. Nothing's going to happen. My grandma's more Catholic than the Pope. My room is so far away from yours, I wouldn't be surprised if she had a moat installed."

"Are you certain about that?"

"Yes, I'm certain." He boops my nose. "She's already given me instructions."

We continue on, and he shows me to my room.

"Everything to your satisfaction, miss?"

"I'm disappointed there's no moat," I say. "But it's nice."

"I'm going to unload my stuff and take a shower," he says. "Wanna meet up in about a half-hour?"

"Sounds good."

He heads off down the hall. I watch him until he turns a corner. Yeesh. Our rooms really are far apart.

I'm not one to unpack when I'm only staying for a couple of days—I never understood the reasoning behind it. But there's a beautiful rustic wood dresser with dove carvings and painted flowers. It's too pretty not to use. So I unload my few things, reserving one drawer for pajamas and undies, and so on. Tomorrow is the Fourth of July, and incidentally, Ignacio's grandfather's ninetieth birthday. When I met him earlier today—after my bathroom run—he took me by the arm and told me all about how he was born on the fourth of July and that the fireworks are just for him. He went on to tell me some of his adventures, traveling the world until he met his wife. And then he insisted we take selfies together. I suppose it's safe to say he took a liking to me.

Anyway, I packed one of my new dresses for the party, and some other comfortable items—even a swimsuit, just in case. Once I'm unpacked, I feel like changing out of my leggings and T-shirt having gotten them all wet. I'm pretty sure there are bits of soggy tortilla in my bra.

I choose a pair of shorts and a tank top—this Arizona heat is too much for leggings, even for me. There's a full-length mirror in the corner—the freestanding kind, made of rustic wood with the same bespoke character as the dresser. I inspect my reflection, tilting my head side to side and twisting right to left. Golly, I'm white. I suppose that's what comes from wearing long pants all the time.

Making quick work of some tanning lotion, I head outside to catch a few rays while I wait for Ignacio. I spotted a beautiful cement fountain earlier. It reminded me of something you'd see in a European town square, but without water in it.

I take along my copy of *Love in the Time of Cholera*, which Ignacio fought me on when I asked him to scribble his number inside. He really does underestimate the probability of someone catching on to us. After some coaxing, however, he wrote his name and number and even added little kisses and hugs below his signature. I shall cherish it forever and ever, even when he's no longer a part of my life.

With a wistful sigh, I climb onto the rim of the fountain and stretch out my legs, angling them to get the most sun. I really do want to read this book, but I'm not feeling it, so I use it as the world's most uncomfortable pillow and lie back. The sun blasts down on me mercilessly, baking my legs like a rotisserie chicken. I'll just be here, sizzling in eleven herbs and spices, if anyone needs me. Spices only make me think of Ignacio, whose kisses are finger-licking good. Everything makes me think of Ignacio, which is why I'm sure it's a daydream when I hear a gaggle of turkeys getting louder and louder. I sit up, and sure enough, there are about a dozen large turkeys headed my way. I sit perfectly still, thinking they'll mind their business if they don't see me.

But not only do they see me, they seem to zero in on me, charging toward me with murder in their eyes.

They're enormous, fluffing up their black and brown feathers in attack mode—making weird noises with those vicious red, wrinkly necks.

I stand up on top of the fountain but they're running faster now, like they have a personal vendetta against me.

"Go away. What did I ever do to you?"

I'm screaming now because they are not slowing down. In fact, they're flapping their wings, flying up the edge of the fountain to get to me.

"Shoo! Get away from me. Aggghhh!" I cry, throwing my precious *Love in the Time of Cholera* in their direction. They flutter back enough to give me a moment to jump off the fountain and run. This gives new meaning to the term turkey trot. I feel like one of those crazy Spaniards running from bulls in Pamplona.

Now, I'm not a runner. If a murderer were to come after me with a knife, I'd weigh my options. But there's something about those beady eyes and that bumpy, flappy skin that motivate me to run for my life. These birds are savage killers. They're evil birds. They're *angry* birds. And they one hundred percent have it in for me.

"Heeeeeelp!" I cry, darting across the farm with the malicious fowl nipping at my heels. I can just see it now. Death by turkey—the bloody and untimely end to Jersey's own, Olive Isaac, non-runner, donut lover.

And then, just as I think I'm toast, Ignacio swoops in like a superhero, diverting the turkeys away from me.

"Go back to the house," he says, taking off his shirt. Okay, full pause. The man is TAKING OFF HIS SHIRT! Does he really expect me *not* to watch?

He's using his T-shirt to swat the evil turkeys back into submission, but turkeys are not like sheep. They won't just let a human round them up. I have absolutely no idea how one *does* take control over a flock of turkeys, but I'm thinking swatting the buggers with a shirt isn't gonna do the trick. Not that I'm complaining. Ignacio is a glorious specimen—all rippling muscle and rock-hard abs. The way he careens and lunges, waving those statuesque arms, flexing the hills and valleys of that strong, exquisite back.

I'm basically drooling.

Next thing I know, there's a high-pitched whistle, and a beefy rottweiler comes out of nowhere. Not gonna lie, it's a big, scary dog. For the first couple of seconds, I think we might have bigger problems on our hands than a bunch of turkeys, but I soon find out the dog is a friend. He barks and charges at the birds as Ignacio's abuelo advances onto the scene with a garden hose.

Hallelu! The cavalry is here.

"Chah, chah," he shouts, firing at the turkeys with the spray nozzle on 'ludicrous' setting. The water is coming out like bullets, and the turkeys scurry back to the pit of hell whence they came.

Abuelo and the dog keep going. At one point the hose reaches its limit and then Abuelo abandons it, still chasing the turkeys down.

Ignacio turns to me with a stormy look on his face. He's simply magnificent—that stubborn tendril falling over his twisted brow, those charcoal gray eyes etched with concern. Those lips.

He's coming my way, and my mouth turns into the Sahara Desert. His muscles look even better from this angle. His bare chest is a sight to behold. And those shoulders! Beast mode.

"You okay?" he says as he approaches me. His voice is so rumbly, it evokes lava deep in my core.

"Uhhh…"

My eyes dip to his happy trail, where a dusting of yummilicious dark hair circles his belly button, then files into a perfect line until it disappears into his jeans.

"Olive?" he repeats, touching my cheek. "Are you hurt?"

"Me? I'm fine. Just a little…"

I lick my lips. Yes, lick my lips. It's hot as Hades, there's a sexy, shirtless man in front of me, and he's tenderly stroking my face. I'm licking these lips, baby, and I have no shame.

Then he wraps his arms around me and pulls me to his chest, stroking my hair. I can hear his heartbeat—strong and steady, and elevated just a little. I don't know what to do with my hands. Would it be weird if I sneak them up his torso to cop a feel of that six-pack?

Slowly, his body begins to tremor, and I feel a rumble coming from his chest. The sound amplifies in my ear as he begins to chuckle, then giggle, then propels into a full-blown laugh.

I lean back to look at his face. "What's so funny?"

"I wish I'd caught that on camera. What did you do to cause a turkey stampede?"

"Nothing. I was minding my business, and they just attacked out of nowhere."

He keeps laughing and I should be righteously peeved about it, but his laughter is contagious, so I shove his perfect chest to fight it.

"It's not funny. I could have died."

"Come here." He drags me into him again. I could get used to this. "You weren't going to die. Just maimed a little."

"Whaaaat?"

"Just kidding. Let's go inside. I want you to meet my brother, Memo. He just arrived with my parents and Bernadette."

I cook with wine.
Sometimes I even
add it
to the food.

\- W.C. Fields

Chapter Sixteen

IGNACIO

The farmhouse is officially at capacity. If there were a hotel within an hour from here, I'd tolerate the drive each day just so I wouldn't have to share a room with Mateo and Tío Enrique tonight. Mateo talks in his sleep and Tío Enrique snores—I'm talking Formula One race car noises coming from the back of his throat. I'm not looking forward to it.

Even with a full house, Abuela made sure Olive gets her

own room, saying that she wants her to feel all the comforts of the farm. Then she went on to say the next time we visit, Olive won't be sleeping alone, *wink wink*, because we'd be married.

The way Abuela's invested in our relationship, I'll be fake dating Olive forever. If I'm being honest with myself, I don't want it to end.

Or maybe I do want it to end—at least the fake part.

She's invading every inch of my life, and yet I still can't get enough of her. I find myself unable to take my eyes off her, dreaming about her, wanting her. I look for excuses to touch her every chance I get. To kiss those sweet lips and feel her pressed against me. And the few times I have kissed her, pretending it was all for show, I almost passed out from pure bliss. And the way she gives back, her little moans, the exquisite dance of her lips on my mouth, fingers digging into my ba—

"¡Nacho!" Abuela throws a raw pinto bean at me. "*Qué haces?*"

"Wha—what does it look like I'm doing? I'm cleaning beans."

"Spanish," Mom warns.

Abuela snorts.

I take a breath. "*Abuela, te estoy ayudando a limpiar los frijoles.*"

"No!" she snaps. "*Que haces adentro con nosotras viejas cuando tu novia está solita?*"

Right. Of course I know Olive is alone. I can see her through the window, swinging on the rope swing on the old cottonwood tree. It's the whole reason I chose this exact spot to help Abuela and Mom sort the beans. Also, my fingers are burning to touch Olive, and I'm afraid to be alone with her. So, I decided these fingers are put to better use in the kitchen, where they are most comfortable.

I look to my brother, Memo, for support. He's stuffing his face full of strawberries at the moment after a car ride with my parents he described as the longest day of his life. Apparently, they stopped every few miles to let the dog out to do her business and took twice as long to get here.

"Lulu has a small bladder," Dad had said, kissing the dog on the nose. I'm just grateful that January's assistant has Brownie for the next week.

"I should stay here to make sure Memo doesn't eat all the strawberries," I say.

"Don't drag me into this," says Memo. "And good luck taking away my aggregate fruit, brother."

I roll my eyes at Memo's propensity for technical accuracy. He'll talk your ear off about how strawberries aren't berries, but bananas are. An hour later, you still won't really care, but he'll expect you to call it an aggregate fruit in his presence forevermore.

"We don't need you in here," says Mom. "Go."

It's futile to argue with the women in my family, and I might as well escape the *genus fragaria* lecture while I can. So I wash my hands and reach in my pocket for the Altoids tin, popping one on my mouth.

I love this time of day in the summer. The golden hour. The hottest part of the day is behind us, and there's a certain magic in the Arizona mountain air before the sun falls behind the horizon.

After a loud and rowdy dinner with the whole family, Francesca and Bernadette stole Olive to do girl things. I have no idea what that could be. Now that the day is winding down, everyone is preparing for the early morning surprise we have for Abuelo, but trying to act nonchalant about it. Dad hired Mariachis who are coming all the way from Flagstaff at five in the morning, and my brothers drove into Seligman to buy a cake.

The crunch of my footsteps alerts Olive to my presence before I reach her. She's swinging gaily, kicking off the trunk of the tree. Smiling at me, she leans back so her hair falls almost to the ground and the rope twists on itself, spinning her around.

I stuff my hands in my pockets, just enjoying the sight of her having fun.

"Are you done with your work?" she asks, letting the rope spin in the opposite direction.

"They kicked me out of the kitchen," I say. "Care for some company?"

She skids her feet on the dirt to stop the swing. "I would love your company."

Taking her hand, I help her off the swing, then let it drop away.

Keep your hands to yourself, man. You can do this.

We begin to stroll past the house when Abuela cries out through the window, *"Tómense de la mano, jóvenes."*

Olive laughs. "What did she say?"

"She wants us to hold hands."

She flashes one of her kittenish grins. "Okey dokey."

I reach for her, and she takes my hand, falling into step with me. Her palm fits in mine as if a sculptor had formed them out of the same slab of clay. I have at least six or seven inches on her and yet her strides match mine perfectly.

We wander the grounds, taking a little path lined with stones which leads to a grotto. As we get further from the house, the trail becomes more uneven, the surrounding terrain more wild. I forgot how peaceful it is out here. The stress of eight restaurants finally catching up to me has been burning me out. I have managers in place for seven of them. I think it's time to appoint one for the flagship location where I spend most of my time.

But I can't do anything until I know there are no more threats or danger.

"Penny for your thoughts." Olive glances up to me, her face so effervescent in the glow of the setting sun.

"Oh, I was just thinking of the restaurant."

"Really? All this beauty and your mind is at work? Yeesh. Your dad was right."

"Wha—? When did you talk to my dad?"

"At the concert in the park. You were super salty about your ice melting all over the cheese and stormed off, cursing. Your mom laughed and said something about the apple not falling far from the tree."

"I'm not at all like my dad."

"If you say so. But your dad got all huffy and said *he's* not a workaholic like Nacho, and your mom laughed even harder, saying how your dad never took a day off for twenty years."

"Oh crap. I'm turning into my dad."

We go over the ridge, down the trail to where the grotto is. It's a sturdy stone structure with talavera tile bordering the archway under which a four-foot statue is sheltered. The colors of Guadalupe's robes have chipped and faded over time, but I can tell by the fresh flowers and pristine state of the grotto it's been well cared for.

"Abuelo built this for Abuela when he bought the farm," I say, pointing to an engraved plaque on the pedestal.

Olive reads it out loud slowly, chopping her way through the Spanish pronunciation.

"*Pa-ra mi her-mosa esposa… que sabe que nece… sito que ore mucho por mí.* What does it mean?"

"Um, it basically says this is for his beautiful wife, who knows she needs to pray extra hard for the likes of him."

She laughs. "That's really sweet. You know, when you told me your grandparents live separately most of the time, I thought it was because they didn't get along. But seeing them together, I can tell it's the opposite. They really love each other."

"Yeah, they do. Their rooms are on opposite sides of the house, but they do."

"Hmmm. Rooms on the opposite side of the house? Kind of like yours and mine."

"Well, our rooms are at least in the same zip code," I say. "Abuelo likes to be close to the animals in case he hears something at night. So he built a room on the other side of the garage. Far away from the rest of the rooms. Abuela doesn't like it. She says it's too drafty in the winter and too hot in the summer, so she stays in her own room. And even though Abuelo employs full-time ranch hands, he still likes to be close to the action."

"He's a spitfire," says Olive. "The way he swooped in and saved me from the turkeys… he's got a lot of energy for his age."

"Two cups of coffee in the morning, two shots of tequila in the evening. That's Abuelo."

Olive smiles and inspects the statue appreciatively, ticking her head to the side.

"Ha. Look at that. Her toenails are painted pink."

I lean in to inspect. Sure enough. All ten of Mary's toenails have been covered in pink, sparkly nail polish.

"So they are. Who could have done that? Maybe Francesca or Bernadette when they were little. But that would have been too long ago for the paint to stay."

Olive hums. "I don't know. Have you ever tried to remove glitter nail polish? That stuff would survive whatever killed the dinosaurs."

"You may be right. There was still glitter in the carpet when my parents tore it out of the craft room three years ago."

"Your parents have a craft room?"

"My mom likes to make weird stuff, and we don't have the heart to tell her how bad it is." I dig in my pocket for the Altoids tin. "Mint?"

She takes one and pops it in her mouth.

"I'd like to make weird stuff with your mom."

"I'm sure that can be arranged. Come on. We should head back before we lose daylight."

We continue on the path that eventually circles around back to the house. I'm holding her hand again and we're walking as slowly as possible, neither one of us wanting this to end. A coyote howls in the distance, and Olive crushes herself closer to my side.

"I'll bet the stars are bright out here at night," she says dreamily.

"They are. You'll see them later, although we should probably get to bed in an hour or two."

"Are we really waking up at five?"

"Four thirty. We surprise Abuelo at five."

The tradition is to sing Mañanitas to someone on their birthday at the crack of dawn, waking them up in their bed with sweets and music. Mariachis are optional, but it's a milestone birthday. It's not every day you turn ninety.

Olive slumps. "Ugh. Have I told you I'm not a morning person?"

"Several times."

"I've been known to sleep through my alarm."

"Then set two alarms."

"I sleep through all alarms."

"Okay. I'll ask Bernadette to wake you up. It's a lot of fun. We'll sing happy birthday, Abuelo will yell at us all, then we'll go into the kitchen for pan dulce and Mexican hot chocolate."

"You? Drinking hot chocolate?"

"On special occasions, yes."

"Okay. It's worth getting up to see that."

We stroll at a leisurely pace until we reach a fork in the path. If we continue on, the trail leads down a slope to the house. But if we veer to the right, there's a small terrace overlooking the property. It's not attached to anything, which I always thought was strange. If you take the trail that way, it just kind of ends with an abrupt drop off. I guess it was easier to build a balcony with a cement railing than something like stairs.

We instinctively curve to the right, feeling this spell between us and milking it until we have no other excuse to stay out here. There's something different in the air—the soft breeze caressing us with a strange alchemy. We stop at the balustrade and take in the view. Olive sucks in a breath, and with it, a little bit of the tranquility this place affords. The romantic aspect doesn't escape me. Even I feel it—the gentle weight of it.

A lock of hair falls onto Olive's face and I sweep it away —my fingers aching to touch her. I want this woman. I don't know how much longer I'll be able to resist her.

"I… I'm looking into hiring a full-time manager. All the other locations are self-sufficient—"

"Your mind is still on work? Look at this place."

"I'm only telling you this because you asked me earlier. And I wanted you to know that I'm not carrying my work with me, but that I'm going to delegate more stuff and take more time off. Being here, away from the restaurant, it's making me realize there's more to life than staring at the walls of a restaurant for twelve hours a day."

I still want to open my own concept, but I'm determined not to work myself into the ground to do it.

"Really? That's great. Who do you have in mind?"

"I don't know. Rosa won't do it. We've asked her to manage one of the other locations many times, but she likes being a server."

"How about Roberto? He's a hard worker and everybody respects him."

"Roberto is great at what he does, but I don't know if he's management material. I need someone who can keep all the yoyos in line and still keep up with the books."

"All I know is he's a smart guy and people love him.

And he's mathy. He helped me with my close-out one time when I was confused."

"Okay, I'll consider it when the time comes."

Note to self: To obliterate a romantic mood, bring up work topics. Guaranteed to kill any amorous notions you might be entertaining.

I'm still feeling that ache low in my belly, though. At this point in the day, I've already digested the tacos we had for dinner, so it can't be that. And I know this feeling—the sweet tingling pain of being so near to a woman you know you shouldn't touch. If you touch her, you'll lose yourself in her.

Definitely not tacos.

My body draws close to Olive, like she's the center of gravity. I'm facing her, leaning into her as her elbows rest on the balustrade. She feels the shift in the air, too. Turning her head over her shoulder, her gaze meets mine, her nose barely brushing against my lips. I'm done pretending, prancing around with this charade.

I hook a finger under her chin and guide her to face me, and then, with her shoulders under my hands, I incline my head down. Her eyes glimmer, drugged with desire, and I hold them with a level gaze.

"I'm going to kiss you now," I rumble. "Is that okay?"

She nods, swallowing hard. "Are… people watching?"

"Gaaaad, I hope not."

With an undeviating resolve, I dip my head and caress her lips in a slow, sweet kiss. Her mouth is warm, soft, inviting. This isn't a kiss to ravage her—it's not a means to an end. It's a promise. A promise to cherish and adore her. To treasure her. To love her.

I feel her arms slide around my waist, loving me in return. I cup her face with my hands, tilting her head just right to explore her mouth. She's so responsive to my touch, embracing me tightly and lulling me with every stroke of her lips. A wave of nirvana cascades over me, so euphoric in nature, I imagine this is what it feels like to be weightless in space—without the danger of decompression or asphyxiation, of course. But she does take my breath away, so it's not that far off by comparison.

Taking my time, I nip her bottom lip and move to the corner of her mouth, then the other. I want to know every inch of her face with reverent touches of lips on skin. She lets out a shuddering breath, her chest rising and falling.

"Ignacio," she gasps. "You need to stop."

I pause, halting my mouth just above her jaw.

"Why?"

"Because it feels real."

"It is real, *cariño*. At least I hope it is."

She wheezes, gulping for air. "You do?"

"Yes," I rumble, lowering my voice. "Do you?"

Her eyes dart to mine, and she licks her lips with an audible gulp. "Yes, please."

Warmth spreads across my chest, and nothing but pure joy floods my senses.

We're laughing and kissing, mouths falling over one another, tripping, and spiraling out of control. She smiles and giggles, tilting her head back as I reach to capture her mouth. We're grinning like it's so hilarious and wonderful to want this to be a real thing between us, and in that smiling and mouths crashing, our teeth clank together, but only causing moderate pain. I wrap my arms around her and pick her up, kissing her as she hovers over me, legs dangling. Then I set her down gently and graze my lips over hers with the softest touch.

"We're really doing this," she says, almost stupefied. "We're not… fake dating anymore."

"Baby, this hasn't been fake for a long time. Not for me."

Maybe I couldn't admit it before, but if I had to pin a time to when it began to be real for me, I believe I would date it back to the moment I stepped into her apartment the first time and caught a glimpse of who Olive really was. All those gnomes and Christmas decorations.

"Not for me either," she admits. "And that scared me a little."

"Does it still scare you?"

"No. Not at all."

I stroke her cheek, dragging a thumb across her bottom lip. I could adore her all day, but the night is falling fast.

I steal one last kiss before we have to go back to the house, taking in my fill of her, willing it to last as long as possible. When we part, her lips are plump and rosy. I need a moment or two before leaving this slice of paradise. We touch foreheads and catch our breath for a minute, soaking in this new reality. We haven't defined terms yet, but that can wait. For now, we're just enjoying it.

I dip my gaze down to the ground to get my bearings, and that's when something dark catches my attention. I blink to make sure my eyes are adjusted to the low light, thinking it's just a shadow. But as my focus becomes clearer, I'm aware it's definitely something else.

"Olive? I don't want you to be alarmed, so please don't move a muscle."

She freezes. "What's that supposed to mean? Of course, when you say it like that, I'm going to be alarmed."

"Just… hold still. It's not a big deal. Probably harmless."

"Okay, now you're just plain scaring me."

I hold up my hands. "There's a scorpion on your foot."

"A whaaat?"

"Please, just remain calm and don't make any sudden moves."

"I'm calm. I'm so calm. I am a pillar of calmness."

I reach into my back pocket for my Altoids and open the tin. There are about six or seven mints left.

"I need you to eat three of these."

"How is minty fresh breath going to help with a dang scorpion on my foot?"

"How big do scorpions get? It looks small from here."

"Maybe it's a baby scorpion, and he's lost his way."

"I'm going to trap it in this tin. Put three mints in your mouth and I'll take the rest."

I pop four mints and chew them to bits. Olive takes her three, but prefers to suck on them.

"Okay. It's probably just a baby scorpion. Take a calm, minty breath and don't even think about it."

She squeezes her eyes shut. "Okayeeee."

I slowly take to one knee, carefully hovering over Olive's sandaled foot so as not to alert the scorpion. I'm surprised she didn't feel it crawl on her, actually. I have to be swift about this. I don't know a lot about scorpions, but I don't want to take a chance it might sting Olive's foot if it feels threatened.

With measured, steady movements, I bring the tin closer and closer, and then with a quick sweep, I capture the little bugger, snapping the tin shut. Part of his feet get stuck on the outside, but the tin mostly closes all the way.

"Got him!"

Olive un-squeezes her eyes and looks down at me.

"Ewww. He's halfway out."

"It's okay. He's trapped in there. Look."

I hold up the tin to show her the scorpion isn't going anywhere, and she squeals, her hands flying to her mouth. Now I just need to figure out what I'm going to do with the thing.

I'm still on the ground, weighing my options between killing this arachnid or setting it free, when a robust cheer comes from the house. Olive and I turn to look at what could have caused such a racket, and realize it's my entire family cheering for us, jumping up and down, and heading our way.

"Um, Ignacio?" Olive says. "You're down on one knee."

Oh, for goodness' sake.

"Were they watching us this whole time?"

She shrugs.

Every one of them are hooting and hollering, ambling toward us—Mom reaches us first and gathers Olive in a hug as I rise to my feet.

"Oh, I'm so happy. I prayed this would happen."

"Congrats, man," says Nate, slapping my back.

Sebastian and Mateo echo his congratulations and turn to Olive, welcoming her to the family. Francesca and Edmund exchange a look, but then Francesca plasters on a smile and hugs me.

"This is big news. Wow! Another wedding."

She elbows Edmund, jolting a smile out of him. "*Mozel*

Tov," he says, rubbing the spot on his arm where my sister jabbed her bony elbow.

Olive and I are shaking our heads, trying to tell them it's not what it seems, but the Precio family is too noisy in general, let alone when they think I just proposed to my girlfriend. Dad and Tío Enrique are shouting *"Felicidades,"* while Bernadette quietly mouths, "Congratulations," from outside the mob of people surrounding Olive and me. Memo manages to reach a long arm over my other brothers to pat me on the head.

"Gratulationes," he says in Latin.

I'm so caught up in the craziness of it all, I almost say thank you, but no. Just no. Meanwhile, I still have the scorpion to deal with.

"Ring! Let's see the ring," Mom exclaims.

"There's no ring," I cry.

She points at my Altoid tin. "But…"

"Yo tengo el anillo." Abuela holds a box above her head as she ambles up the path from the house. Abuelo is right behind her, rolling his eyes. My brothers and uncles rush to help her, but she's so determined to get to Olive and me, their efforts are futile.

"Mijito. Guardé este anillo para el mayor de mis nietos, pero Memo no lo necesitará."

She passes the box to me, urging me to open it.

"What's all this?" Olive says tentatively.

"She says she's saved this ring for her oldest grandchild, but since Memo won't need it, I'm the next in line."

Abuela opens the box and Olive gasps. Inside, there's a dazzling topaz ring.

"Ya no le cabe a mis dedos de salchicha," Abuela says with a

wink.

"She says it no longer fits her sausage fingers," shouts Mateo from behind Dad.

"Yeah, I gathered that," says Olive.

Abuela pushes the ring at her. "Take."

"Uh, no thanks?" Olive says with a forced smile.

"*Abuela*," I say. "*Ha habido un error. No hay...*" I look around for help. "How do you say engagement?"

"*Compromiso*," Dad supplies.

"Right." I say. "*Compromiso*."

Abuela narrows her eyes at me and takes the ring out of the box herself, pressing it into my hand.

¿Cómo puede ser un compromiso sin anillo? Andalé. Ponlo en su dedo, muchacho."

"Yeah, Nacho," says Nate. "Put it on."

"Put the ring on," bellows Mateo. "Do it."

Memo grunts, "Do it," with his Emperor Palpatine impersonation.

Tío Enrique pipes in. "*¡Pónle lo!*"

Pretty soon my whole family is shouting at me, and rumbling. Francesca is the only one raising her voice in my favor.

"Don't pressure him," she cries, but she's drowned out by everyone else.

Sebastian starts chanting, "Put. It. On. Put. It. On."

Mateo jumps on that, just because he enjoys a chant, I think.

Olive's looking at me bewildered.

The noise level is getting out of hand, even for my family—which is saying a lot.

Then, on top of the hullabaloo, a sharp whistle cuts

through the noise, and everyone turns to see Abuelo removing his fingers from his mouth.

"*¡Callense!*"

He doesn't even bother to wade through the sea of bodies to reach me. He just flicks his hand and shakes his head.

"*No lo presionen, barbosos.*"

And as he hobbles back to the house, he murmurs, "I don't have time *para estas tonterias.*"

Abuela dismisses him with a wave of her hand and glares at me expectantly. I look at Olive, attempting to read her features. I lean to her until we're touching cheek to cheek.

"Your call."

"Go ahead," she whispers. "I have a feeling they'll never leave us alone if we don't play along."

"More play acting?" I whisper in return.

She chuckles. "What's the harm in one more ruse?"

"I'll fix this," I say.

Her eyes slice to mine playfully. "I've heard that before."

Man, I love this woman. I kiss her on the forehead and pass the Altoids tin to Nate so I can have use of two hands. Fixing my gaze on Olive's, I slide the ring on her finger and my heart flip-flops. She's looking at me with slushy eyes now, and I just want to wrap her up and keep her under my arm. But I content myself with a quiet kiss on her lips, which is met with a round of applause from my shame-lessly obtrusive family.

Then, out of the clatter and fanfare, Nate exclaims at the top of his lungs, "Why is there a dead scorpion in the Altoids?"

The early bird
gets the worm.
I'll sleep in
and have tacos.

— Unknown

Chapter Seventeen

IGNACIO

"Has anyone seen Olive?" I ask.

My whole family—also Edmund—is gathered outside. The mariachis have just arrived, and it's almost time to wake up Abuelo. Abuela is hushing everyone, but surprisingly, the people in my family who are usually the noisiest, are standing half asleep like zombies.

"I woke her up a half-hour ago," says Bernadette. "She talked to me and everything."

Great.

Olive wasn't kidding around when she said she sleeps through several alarms.

"I guess I'll go take a crack at it," I say.

I head into the house to find her, hoping I'll catch her walking down the hallway. Maybe she's lost? Hopefully not being attacked by anymore farm critters. I'm not ruling out that possibility, though. What will it be next? Goats eating her Christmas leggings?

After not seeing her anywhere, I knock softly on her door. She doesn't answer. I check the bathrooms. They're all empty. Reluctantly, I return to her room and knock again. Now I'm starting to get worried.

Carefully and cautiously, I open the door a crack and poke my nose in with my eyes closed.

"Olive? You in there?"

When there's no response, I open my eyes and peek in some more. The lights are off, and I hear soft snores coming from inside.

She's still sleeping?

"Olive," I say a little louder. "Time to go."

She mumbles something and rustles in the bed. I wonder if I should just let her sleep, but she seemed excited about experiencing Mañanitas last night, even after the mistaken engagement fiasco. And I don't want her to feel bad for missing out.

"I'm going to turn on the light, now," I warn her, flicking on the switch. She squeaks and covers her face with the blankets. I approach the bed and wrench the blanket out of her fingers, yanking it down. I realize as I'm in the middle of pulling down her covers, that I may not be prepared for what I see underneath. How am I supposed to know if she sleeps in the buff?

Fortunately, she's in a sleeper shorts set—with Rudolph the Red-Nosed Reindeer print. I chuckle inwardly. She would have pajamas like that.

"Olive, you're going to be late," I say. "Get up."

"Naaaaoooo," she groans. Even in this state, she's adorable. My heart swells.

I tug on her hand to help her up, but she pulls me toward her with surprising force. I topple over her sideways, and my shoulder has got to be digging into her tender places, but she doesn't complain. She just wiggles so she's lying on her side and wraps her arms around me like I'm one giant teddy bear.

"G'night," she mumbles.

"No, Olive. Not good night. Good morning. Everyone is waiting outside."

"Uh-huh."

I peel her arm off my body and scoot away, but she slings her arms back with renewed pluckiness, and flops her leg over my thigh.

"Mine," she rumbles, snuggling into my back.

"Yes," I rasp, feeling all too comfortable with this arrangement. "Yours."

A small voice inside my head tells me to stay with her in this bed. To roll over and put my hands all over her. To forget about Mañanitas, making some lame excuse. But then I imagine Abuela's angry face and remember that my family is expecting me to return with my new fiancée ready to go sing 'Las Mañanitas' to Abuelo. And that's enough to get me moving.

I slide my hand over hers and bring it to my lips. The ring on her finger miraculously fits her perfectly, and I twist it side to side with my thumb. I could get used to this.

"Come on, beautiful. Up we go."

With all the might I possess, I tear myself away from her and roll off the bed. She groans in protest, patting the bed where my body had just been.

Heaven help me.

I grab onto her ankles and swing her so her feet are hanging off the bed. Then I pull her up by the arms to a standing position. She's in my arms, all floppy and sleepy, and I'm doing everything I can to keep her upright. Her body is pressed against mine as I hold on to her and I'm just chanting unsexy things in my head.

Filing taxes.

Traffic on the 405.

The Kardashians.

"Sweet dreams are made of cheese," Olive softly sings, and I notice she's holding up her own weight now. "Huuu-ungreeee."

I slowly let go and step back a few inches.

"There's pan dulce and hot chocolate," I say. "How fast can you get ready?"

She blinks up at me, awareness catching up to her. "What time is it?"

"Five."

"Five?! Why didn't anyone wake me up?"

She scurries around the room frantically.

"Bernadette woke you up, and you talked to her. And you had three alarms set."

She stops her flittering and freezes with knees bent and arms out. She looks like a surfer who's thinking really hard.

"I don't remember any of that."

She jumps back into action, this time with a purpose. Opening drawers, she flings clothes over her shoulders, letting it rain shirts and bottoms and… unmentionables.

"If I wait for you outside, do you promise not to go back to sleep?"

She turns to look at me. "I'll try."

"Okay, I'll be right outside this door." I go to open the door. "Two words. Hot chocolate."

"Got it. Give me thirty seconds."

Clicking the door shut behind me, I check my phone. It's after five now, and my family won't wait forever. I consider texting Sebastian to give them a heads up, but true to her word, Olive is dressed and ready in thirty seconds flat.

"Wow. I should motivate you with hot chocolate all the time," I say, taking in her slapdash appearance. Even with her messy hair in a hoodie, she sets my heart racing.

"I can be quick when I want to. I didn't brush my teeth, though."

I wrap my arms around her and lead her down the hallway. "I don't think anybody did."

When we reach the rest of the party, they're already walking around the corner of the house and we have to jog to catch up.

Mateo snorts when he sees us. "Finally. We almost forgot you existed."

"That's funny, because I forget you exist all the time," I say.

"Shhhh." Francesca smacks me in the arm.

"Ouch!"

"Quiet."

Dad has Lulu perched on one arm. That poor little dog is trembling with her button eyes dodging around from person to person.

"Dad, don't you think the Mariachi music will freak her out?" I say.

He scratches her behind her pointy ears. "Oh, my baby *preciosa. Mi perrita tan linda, probrecita.*"

Francesca shakes her head and whispers to me, "They're inseparable."

Nate is carrying his iPad, which is illuminated with the faces of Enrique, January, Dante, and two of my uncles smiling back at me on a Zoom call. Dante looks exhausted. I'm a little bummed he couldn't come, but he says the Fourth of July is one of the busiest towing days of the year. He has to be in LA to make sure everything runs smoothly with his business.

Enrique and January, however, have that honeymoon glow. It's sunny wherever they are. Probably somewhere in Europe.

We reach the far end of the house, where Abuelo has his room. There's an entrance from the outside which he always keeps unlocked, but Mom wants to make sure.

"Does anybody have the key?" she stage whispers.

"I have the key," replies Dad, in an even louder stage whisper. They are the worst at sneaking up on people. Unless Abuelo's a heavy sleeper, I'm sure he's heard us by now.

"*Empezamos?*" asks the leader of the mariachi band.

Abuela nods and waves her hands like she's about to conduct an orchestra, but mom hisses to wait.

"Check the lock first."

Dad huffs and jiggles the doorknob.

"It's not locked."

Mom shoos him to go in. "Okay, then go!"

Dad opens the door, letting Abuela be the first one inside. The mariachis exchange looks, confused if it's time to play yet.

Dad growls at them. "*¡Oralé. ¡Qué poca madre! Tocan.*"

The musicians spring right into 'Las Mañanitas', horns blasting, fiddles screeching just slightly out of tune. We all begin to file into Abuelo's room, Zoom callers and all. Then Abuela pushes us all out, screaming.

"*No está. Este hijo del averno.*"

"What do you mean, he's not here?" cries Dad. "*No puedo creer.* Somebody check the bathroom."

Tío Enrique rushes into the room and comes right back out.

"*No está en el baño.*"

"Try the kitchen," says Francesca. "Maybe he got hungry."

Everyone is chattering, voicing their theories about where Abuelo could have gone, meanwhile the musicians are still playing.

Dad swats his arms across. "*¡Basta ya!*"

They stop at different intervals like a sad, deflated balloon, and we're all staring at one another not sure what we should do next.

"So, I'm guessing your grandpa left somewhere?" Olive whispers to me.

"I have no idea. His truck's here. Sebastian's searching the house."

"Who's that?" She points at a pair of headlights coming up the road. "A neighbor?"

"There are no neighbors out here. Not for miles."

The lights get closer and closer, and the sound of *banda* music blasting from the car becomes increasingly louder. Abuela marches furiously to the middle of the gravel driveway and plants her fists on her hips. As a person trying to stay on her good side for weeks, I'm a little terrified, even though her fury isn't directed at me, thank goodness. Abuela's wrath is a sight to behold. A terrifying, put-the-fear-of-God-into-you sight.

The car comes to a stop right in front of her, the headlights beaming light on her Wonder Woman power stance so that from my vantage point, it looks like a horror movie poster.

With the car still running, Abuelo stumbles out and slaps his hand on the roof, saying his goodbyes to a rowdy bunch of old men. They blubber their drunken responses, and the car backs up, still blasting the *banda* music—if you can call it music. It's basically just horns blasting to off-tempo drums, and maybe an accordion.

When Abuelo notices Abuela and the rest of us watching him, he hiccups, and that's when Abuela takes off one of her new Crocs and chucks it smartly across his face. He blinks as it bounces off his head and watches where it falls.

Abuela spares no words as she rips him a new one.

"*Donde andabas? Con quien estabas? ¡Viene no mas como llegas! !Borracho nada menos!*"

She's on a roll, yelping a string of expletives like nobody's business, and throws her other shoe at him. For some reason, the lead musician considers this his cue, and directs the other mariachis to pitch once more into 'Las Mañanitas'.

Memo and Dad go to help Abuelo walk upright before he falls flat on his face. Mom's trying and failing to calm Abuela down. Nate is still holding up his iPad with the ongoing Zoom call, and I get a glimpse of Enrique laughing his head off. Mateo, also finding this extremely hilarious, sings along with the mariachis, encouraging Sebastian and Tío Enrique to join in. And Bernadette emerges from the kitchen with the box of pan dulce. Suddenly, it's a true Precio party—with someone drunk, someone on the warpath, everybody eating, obnoxiously deafening music, and a cacophony of disorderly chatter. Francesca just shrugs and smiles sweetly at her boyfriend, who has a petrified expression on his face.

Olive nuzzles into me, wrapping an arm around my waist.

"I'm glad you got me up for this. You were right. It *is* fun."

Eventually we move the party inside—the mariachi never ceasing as we drink the hot chocolate, dipping our pan dulce in it, and basically get a sugar rush. I don't feel very well afterward. Before Nate shuts down the Zoom call, I tell Enrique to call me later today. I'm not one to interrupt his honeymoon with work stuff, but I have a couple of questions about the spreadsheets he made for the restaurant. I would have asked him last week, but the guy is ridiculously difficult to get a hold of. Besides, how long of a honeymoon does he need?

Abuelo passes out almost immediately after Dad and Memo help him into bed, and Abuela's pretty much gotten over it after she got all her feelings off her chest, cursing at Abuelo all the way into the bedroom. We were all relieved to learn Abuelo took an Uber home, and was not at a nudie bar as Abuela had assumed, but at a friend's house, playing poker all night to celebrate his birthday.

Everyone is slaphappy by the time the musicians leave. Olive and I are slumped on the couch, discussing if we should stay up at this point or go back to sleep, when Abuela comes over to sit right next to us.

"*Cuando van a tener la boda*?" she asks point blank.

Olive looks up at me for the translation and I sigh, flopping my head back on the sofa.

"She's asking us to set a date," I say. "For the wedding."

Olive blushes. "Oh! *No mucho. Es… no mucho tiempo*."

"You just told her it will happen in not much time. At least I think that's what you said."

"My Spanish too choppy?"

"A little."

Abuela claps her hands. "*¿Por qué no se casan hoy? Es un día festivo y tenemos un sacerdote en la familia*."

Memo, who I thought was sleeping on the recliner, perks up when he hears her talking about him—the priest in the family.

"They can't get married today, Abuela. They need to go through classes first and the banns need to be read…"

Abuela raises one silver brow. "*Puedes concederles una dispensa especial*."

"That's not how dispensations work. The bishop would have to get involved, and there would have to be dire circumstances. They don't just pass these things out, even if the woman is—"

His eyes flash to Olive, darting from her face to her belly.

"Oh, for goodness' sake, we don't want a rush job," I cry.

Olive finally realizes what we're talking about and pulls a face. "Why does everybody think I'm preggo?"

"Nobody thinks you're preggo," I say.

"You don't look… preggo," says Memo.

Abuela throws her hands in the air. *"Pero ya tememos el pastel."*

Memo shakes his head and pretends to go back to sleep.

"Sorry, Abuela," I say. "No wedding today."

She gives me the silent treatment for the next hour.

I decide to stay awake and cook breakfast for the family. Those sweets aren't sitting right in my stomach and I need some protein.

With a family this size, it's easier to make a skillet meal than make individual eggs thirteen different ways. So I'm whisking the eggs while the tortillas and onions are in the pan getting crispy. Tomatoes are chopped and ready to go in any second, now. Olive slides up next to me, watching the process.

"What are you making?"

"Sopitas con huevos," I say, stealing a kiss on the nose. "It's the perfect hangover breakfast."

The only one hungover is Abuelo, and he's sleeping, but I think a sugar hangover counts.

"It smells scrummy. Can you show me how to make it?"

"All right. Finish whisking the eggs while I sautée the tomatoes." I pass the stainless steel mixing bowl to her and toss the tomatoes in the pan with the tortillas and onions, letting them soften. After a minute, I stand aside so she can add the eggs to the pan.

"Okay, now pour the eggs over everything else. We want to coat the tortillas. Sort of like a Mexican French toast."

She pours the mixture in the pan while I stir.

"Ooooh. This is like matzo brei."

"Isn't matzo a cracker?"

"Yeah, it's so good."

"So I'm guessing the cracker replaces the tortilla."

"Yup. But there's no tomato. And no onions. Oh, and it's great with applesauce."

"So in other words, nothing like *sopitas con huevos*?

"The egg is the same," she reasons. "It's really best cooked in schmaltz."

"Do I dare ask?"

"Rendered chicken fat."

"Good to know so I can never use it," I say.

It's so domestic—working side by side in the kitchen. Going through the motions of making breakfast with Olive is causing strange flip flops in my chest. I want this. I want this every single day.

I glance over my shoulder to see if anyone is looking. Through the opening to the living room, all I can see is half of Mateo, and he's snoring on the couch.

I pluck the bowl out of Olive's hands and toss it into the sink with a clank. I hope the noise doesn't alert anyone, because in two seconds flat, my hands are on Olive's hips and I'm backing her into the counter.

"You're so hot when you cook," I rumble against her mouth. My arms skate around her waist and I crush her into me, claiming her mouth with a greedy kiss. I take her lips hungrily, this insatiable need clawing at my core. I kiss her thoroughly and abundantly, giving her my heart and soul while selfishly stealing her sweet kisses like a thief.

Her body is so soft and pliant against my chest. It's driving me insane.

Eager little fingers climb under my T-shirt, all grabby and pinchy. She's totally feeling me up.

"Gahh, Olive. What you do to me," I groan, brushing my lips down her neck.

She arches against me, panting softly. "More."

Her hands slide around my waist, kneading my skin like I'm pizza dough and she's craving stuffed crust with all the toppings.

My pulse drums, blood racing as I cup her chin to angle her just so—the perfect angle to devour her mouth. My teeth tug at her bottom lip, coaxing them open. She sucks in a breath, coming undone.

"More?" I rumble. "More what?"

"All of it," she says thickly. "All of… this."

"This?" I say, breathing hotly against her mouth. I graze my fingers down her shoulders, turning slow circles on the bare flesh just to the left of the thin strap of her shirt.

She shudders. "Guh, that's… nice."

"You like that?"

"Uh huh."

My mouth moves down the column of her neck until I

reach her collarbone. Pressing her into the counter, I kiss a trail across her shoulder, hooking a finger under that maddeningly thin strap. I slip it down, just an inch. Just enough to give my lips free rein of her delicious shoulder.

She makes a noise in the back of her throat. I love her little sounds. I love the way she feels under my hands. I love her scent. Warm, sweet spice, like gingerbread and... burnt tortillas?

Burnt tortillas!

"My *huevos!*"

"Your whaaat?"

"Eggs. Eggs." I throw myself at the stove, shutting off the flame. Smoke gusts from the pan, charred fumes billowing all over the kitchen. I fan a towel to clear the air, but not soon enough to keep the smoke alarm from sounding. Olive swooshes her hands back and forth.

"I'm so sorry I ruined breakfast. I told you I was a bad cook."

I laugh as the fire alarm stops beeping. Someone will barge into the kitchen any second now, so I steal a quiet kiss.

"You're not a bad cook," I say. "You're just a really hot kisser."

We spend a lazy day doing virtually nothing. It's glorious. Sebastian brought his Nintendo and several of us play Jackbox Games the entire afternoon, laughing our heads off when it's obvious Dad or one of the uncles answers a question from the prompts. Abuelo even plays a round once he emerges from his room. The games require a smartphone or other device to play along, so he borrows Nate's iPad and racks up quite a few points.

At dinner, Olive is introduced to the culinary master-piece which is corn on the cob—Mexican style. Francesca is guiding her (AKA forcefully instructing her) how to prepare the corn *her* way. In other words, double the calories.

"Mayo *and* butter?" I say. "Francesca, that's overdoing it."

She cuts me a hard look. "Don't judge me."

Olive slathers on the butter and mayonnaise as instructed by my grease-loving sister, and cakes on a metric ton of parmesan cheese, also at the urging of Francesca.

"What are you two doing? It only needs a sprinkle."

"Sprinkles are for losers," says Francesca. "I say go big or go home."

"Sounds about right to me," Olive agrees.

Great. My own sister has turned my girlfriend against me.

Real girlfriend. Fake fiancée. What is my life coming to?

"Now for the best part." Francesca holds up the bottle of Tajín like she's a game show model.

"What's that?" asks Olive.

"Only the most amazing condiment that ever did condiment."

I roll my eyes. "That makes absolutely no sense."

"Nobody asked you, brother."

"It looks spicy," says Olive. "I'll pass on that."

"No," Francesca cries. "Is it even Mexican corn without Tajín? I submit that no, it is not."

She shakes half the bottle all over her corn and passes it to Olive.

"Eh, I think I'll stick with the non-spicy version."

"Olive. Are you a Mexi-can or a Mexi-can't?"

"I... Neither."

Francesca shakes her head. "Girl, you are marrying into this family. You may find our ways strange and mysterious, but I know you can adapt. I have faith in you."

"Is this some kind of test? Like the tortilla slap?"

Francesca and I exchange a look. "That was Sebastian's idea," I say. "And it was just to mess with Edmund. They're always messing with Edmund."

"I've been friends with Edmund since we were in first grade together," says Francesca. "They've always picked on him."

"That's because he's an easy target," I say. What I don't say, is how us brothers will always give Edmund a hard time as long as we worry he'll break her heart.

Francesca places a hand on Olive's arm. "Everybody likes you, don't worry."

Olive bites her lip. "Well… maybe I'll try it on one bite. Just tell me on a scale of one to inferno of eternal flames, how hot is it?"

"It's actually more tangy than hot," I say. "Sort of like lemon pepper. If you hate it, I'll finish your corn and you can get a fresh one."

She agrees, and Francesca adds the Tajín to Olive's corn. Olive tentatively takes a bite and her eyes go wide.

"Oh mylanta. This is amazing." She grabs the bottle and shakes it all over, taking another bite. "Wow. So good."

Francesca crosses her arms smugly. "My work here is done."

Meanwhile, Olive devours her corn. She ends up gobbling up two ears, which doesn't ruin her appetite for the main course much. We have our traditional Fourth of July carne asada tacos and Abuela's pinto beans. Olive declares it the best meal of her life, but Mom says it's only because she's newly engaged. "Everything tastes better when you're engaged."

Except when you're faking it. When you're lying to your whole family, the tacos taste like deceit.

I'm exhausted by the time the sun goes down. It's been a long day and Abuelo had a great time. I'm ready to turn in.

But my brothers have other plans. Nate had bought a boatload of fireworks on a surfing trip in Mexico, unbeknownst to me. He drags the boxes from his car with Mateo's and Sebastian's help, and they set up all the rockets in an open gravel lot.

"You can't blow stuff up," I snap at them. "You'll start a fire. Do you even know what you're doing?"

"Dude," says Nate. "It's safe. Abuelo's all for it."

"Abuelo's running on tequila fumes and birthday cake. I wouldn't exactly trust his judgment right now."

He gets out a mini blowtorch. "I got this."

"Is that… my crème brûlée torch?"

He wags his brows.

Que la madre. How is everyone onboard with fireworks except me? Even my parents are setting up chairs with Bernadette and my grandparents to watch from a distance. Tío Enrique couldn't be more excited and has his own set of opinions about how to set up everything. Tío Enrique on firework duty scares me most of all.

I'm trying to be the voice of reason, I really am. Sometimes I feel like I was switched at birth.

"Did you forget this is a farm? Fireworks scare animals," I assert. But does Nate listen to me? Nope. I might as well be invisible. Sebastian and Mateo are having an animated discussion about which order they should set off the rockets, while Memo watches amused.

"Memo, you're the oldest. Make them stop."

He laughs. "You should see the ones we used to shoot off from the roof of the monastery in Rome. Frater Bartolomeo almost blew his finger off."

Fabulous. Just fabulous.

Norbertines are nuts. Most of the time, they're all *benedictus dominus deus*, but when it's just the guys on a Tuesday afternoon, they're playing extreme basketball and driving pickup trucks sideways up hills. It's like belonging to a frat house, but instead of hazing, they take a vow of chastity.

Now my brothers have recruited Olive to help set up the boxes in neat rows. Nate tells her they're called 'cakes' and that's all the inducement she needs to joyfully hop at the opportunity to help.

I'm standing away from them all, watching from behind the circle of pyromaniacs. I may not approve, but I can't help but smile as I follow Olive's every movement with my eyes. How she listens intently to Nate's instructions and carries them out with that endearing charm of hers. How she laughs and jokes with my brothers, working alongside them—as insane as they are.

"You chose well." Francesca pops over, startling me a little. "I'm happy for you."

I sigh. "Yep."

"I will admit, you surprised us all."

I snort. "Tell me about it."

She kicks her foot around in a circle, crunching gravel under the soles of her shoes. This is one of her tells when she has something on her mind.

"Just spit it out, *Panchita*. What is it?"

"Well… I was just wondering if it was going to be a *long* engagement."

"I don't know." I try not to snap at her. I'm just a little on edge right now. I'm falling hard for Olive, but asking her to wear my grandmother's ring is a lot. "Years maybe."

"Years?!"

"Yeah. Years and years. Why?"

"Um, no reason. I just thought since you've only been dating for a few months…"

"So what? Edmund's been farting around for two years. What's *his* deal? Is he gonna poop or get off the pot?"

I regret the words even as they are leaving my lips.

"Ewww. Don't say that. Don't ever, ever, *ever* say that. Just… don't."

Oops. My bad.

"Sorry. I'll chalk that one up there with *'who's da man'* and *'booyah'*, okay?"

"Fair enough."

She gets quiet, watching the scene unfold. Most of the boxes—or cakes as Nate calls them—are set up now. Nate turns on his—*my*—crème brûlée torch and goes to light one of the rockets and everyone scatters. Olive hides behind

Mateo's back, and Sebastian ducks with his hands over his head. Tío Enrique laughs, calling them all chickens until the screeching cuts through the air ending in a bright pop.

"*Híjole de su madre,*" he exclaims, hopping backwards.

After the explosion dies down, and the fright is over, my brothers and Edmund hoot and make whooping noises like banshees. Those back in the cheap seats (my parents, grandparents, and Bernadette) gasp in awe, cheering from the safety of the lawn chairs.

Mateo goes to set up the next one and I'm thinking, with the amount of fireworks Nate brought, we'll be here all night.

Francesca kicks a pebble and sighs dramatically.

"Okay, if you really must know…"

Are we still talking about this?

"No," I say. "You don't have to tell me anything. I didn't mean to get in your business. You do you."

"The thing is," she continues. "We've been secretly engaged for a while now."

I snap around so quickly I'm going to feel the whiplash once the shock wears off.

"Whattt?"

"Edmund and I have been wanting to tell everyone, but then Enrique got engaged. We didn't want to be like '*hey, look at us. We're engaged, too. Yay!*'—so we decided to wait until after the wedding. And we thought, what better time to make an announcement than the Fourth of July?"

"You're engaged. For real this time?"

"Yes, for real this time. Sheesh!"

Okay, so her engagement to that movie star only lasted a day, and she admitted to the family that it was only going to be in name only—some kind of Hollywood publicity stunt—but I guess that's one of the reasons why none of us have fully welcomed Edmund. I admit we *are* a little too hard on him.

"How long?"

"About a year."

I scrub my hand down my face. "And you've been waiting this whole time?"

"It's been really hard. Edmund is going out of his mind."

He better be. Nobody's going to touch my little sister until the ink is dry on that marriage certificate.

"You need to make the announcement, Francesca. Do it tonight."

"No! I don't want to steal your limelight."

"You're an actress. Stealing the limelight is in your job description."

"Nacho, this is *your* special time. It wouldn't be fair to ask you to share it with me."

Perfect. Now I'm lying to my family and keeping Francesca from her happiness.

"You wouldn't be stealing anything from me. I'm not engaged."

"Wait. What? We saw you propose to her. You were on one knee."

"I was capturing a scorpion from her foot."

She blinks at me. "Oooh. I was wondering what the deal was with that Altoids tin."

"Everyone just jumped to conclusions. And you know there's no arguing with Abuela."

"I do know that all too well."

"You should have that ring," I suggest.

"No! I have one."

She slips her fingers under her collar and pulls out a chain with a ring attached.

"Is that a ruby?" It's hard to see in the dark.

"Yes. I didn't want a diamond—because of unethical mining practices. So you should hold onto Abuela's ring until you propose to Olive for real."

"Francesca..." I have to come clean, but admitting I outright lied doesn't come easy to me. "We were pretending. All of it. The engagement, the dating story. It was all fake."

"What do mean, fake? Like, she's nacho girlfriend?"

"Very funny, and... it's complicated. We were trying to make her cheating ex-boyfriend jealous. Then Abuela and Dad saw us... ahem *pretending*... and then it snowballed from there."

I twist my features, ready for my super good-girl sister to lecture me, but she's laughing instead. Doubling over, belly clutching, ugly snort laughing.

"I knew it," she blurts. "Edmund owes me ten bucks."

"You knew it? Wha... how?"

"Oh come on. You reached for the same black cashmere glove and wrote your phone numbers in used books? Suuuure, John Cusac. Loved the movie, by the way. You were great in it."

"I knew I shouldn't have left Olive in charge of the meet-cute."

Admittedly, I didn't even know what a meet-cute was before Olive. In retrospect, I could have handled it better.

Francesca wipes tears from her eyes. "She's adorable, Ignacio. I really was rooting for you."

"You and Edmund had a bet going. How is that rooting for me?"

"I see the way you look at her with your tongue hanging out and those puppy eyes. And when you're not looking at her, she's watching you all dreamy and gooey. It's not as fake as you think."

I know that's true at least.

"I need to find a way to break the news to Abuela, don't I?"

She shrugs. "Maybe tomorrow. In the meantime, I'm going to go collect my ten bucks."

She starts to skip away.

"Hey, *Panchita.* Keep it between you two, okay?"

She zips her lips and takes off.

Nate lights one of his cakes. Streaks of fire coil upward and crackle into a spectacular display of blazing sparks so bright, they illuminate our faces, almost as blinding as daylight. Speckles of vivid orange, yellow, and blue cascade across the night sky like weeping willows made of glittering gemstones, just raining down sparkles. One after another, deafening bangs transform into sunbursts of color leaving behind smoke and the smell of campfire.

From where I stand, I can just make out the side of Olive's face—an enormous radiant smile spread across her features as flashes of color dance across her cheeks.

I breathe in the sight of her and I can see for the first time in my life, that nothing and everything makes sense. This beautiful chaos that is life is a whirling, shimmering firework. All I've been doing is burning out, while Olive glows and shines. She's the human equivalent of pop rocks.

My phone buzzes in my pocket, drawing me back to the real world like cat hair into a vacuum.

I've been waiting all day and he decides to call *now*? It's already the next day in Europe. What gives, Enrique?

I answer the call as I walk away from the firework noise, although it's impossible to escape it.

"You dork. What have you been doing that takes you forever to call back? Wait. Don't answer that. I don't want to know."

"Mr. Precio?" The voice on the other end of the line is definitely not Enrique.

"Um, that depends on which Mr. Precio you're looking for," I say tentatively.

"Ignacio Precio?"

Crap.

"Yeah, that's me."

If this is a telemarketer, I'm going to have a serious beef with my mobile carrier.

"This is Officer Fletcher from the Los Angeles Police Department. There's been a fire."

To eat is a necessity,
but to eat intelligently
is an art.

– François de la
Rochefoucauld

Chapter Eighteen

IGNACIO

"Someone went outta their way to make it look like fireworks, *ese*." Carlos points his chin at the charred remains of the Huntington Park Dos Panchos restaurant. "But I had my homie come out to sheck it out. Este *vato* is like an exspert in arson, chew-no?"

Eh, I don't want to know how his friend became such an expert in arson, so I don't ask.

"We'll have to see what the fire department says, Carlos.

Thanks for calling a friend, but there are professionals investigating it now."

After I got the call, I drove all night to get back to LA and spent hours at the police station, pouring over every detail about the Point Break Posse with Officer Fletcher. I haven't slept for over twenty-six hours, and I feel sick to my stomach. Olive wanted to drive back with me, but I had a feeling she'd be no help in keeping me awake, so I insisted she drive back with Francesca and Edmund.

I know the fire has to do with Pancho Two and the Posse, but Officer Fletcher told me their hands are tied until after the investigation. Apparently the notorious surfer gang is incredibly evasive.

"Whatever you say, *jefe*. But my homie says to look out for the burn pattern discrepancy. He's like, real smart. Got his certificate and evry-ting."

"That's nice. Anyway, my brother, Nate, is filing the insurance claim, so don't worry about payroll."

"Did you see the lastest Danny Trejo movie? Foo walking away from the explosion all calm an' chee? My homie did that."

"Your homie did what?"

"The explosions, man."

"Wait. So your homie… is a film pyrotechnician?"

"Dat's what I said, *jefe*. Exspert."

That's actually kind of cool, but not relevant at all.

Since Carlos came to the scene in my stead, he's able to show me where the firefighters think it started. He goes over all the details with me, pointing out areas of interest within the charred remains of the building.

"Thank God no one was here at the time," I say, shaking

my head at the black soot. Yellow tape surrounds the property as it's still under investigation, but I get a pretty good idea of the point of origin.

"My guess is whoever did it, they knew we were going to close early for the Fourth of July. No witnesses."

"And the camera footage?"

He shakes his head. "Nothing. They tripped the system or something. I'm talking ninja level, *jefe*."

Carlos and I discuss logistics, agreeing to meet at my office later to discuss the losses for the insurance claim and our plan moving forward. I make some calls and hire a security company for twenty-four-hour surveillance at all other restaurant locations and try Pancho Two's number for the thousandth time to no avail.

When I get home, I pass out as soon as my head hits the pillow and sleep heavily for hours. I only stir back into consciousness when I hear my ringtone, dazed and out of sorts. For a minute, I forget about the fire, not even sure what day it is, and let it ring unanswered. But when I check my phone, I see six missed calls from Olive, a couple from Dad, and an unknown number. I should really call Dad first. If anyone can reach Pancho Two, it's him.

But I need to hear Olive's voice right now. I want her with me—somewhere far from here. I'm seriously thinking about selling the restaurants for once. Take off to the Midwest or Spain. Settling down with Olive and leaving all this mess behind. But that would be selfish of me. I have hundreds of employees to think about. And even if I unload Dos Panchos, there's no telling what the Posse might do. They could come after my parents or siblings.

I'm calling Olive before I'm even fully awake. Lately,

I've discovered that dialing her number is the first thing I want to do when I pick up my phone. It's like a shot of dopamine.

"Hey there," she says, answering immediately. "You okay? I was worried."

"I am now," I say. "I miss you."

She laughs. "Already?"

"You got a problem with that?"

"Only because I miss you more. What did you find out about the fire?"

"I don't want to talk about the fire. When are you coming home?"

"I am home, and by the way—your sister and Edmund are hilarious. Edmund is scared to death of you and your brothers, but he's actually a lot of fun."

Fine. Edmund is fun. He's good for my sister. I see that now. But I don't care about that right now. All I care about is seeing Olive's face.

"Come over," I demand. "I want you. I want to spoon all afternoon."

"Oooh. Would you like me to bring over some dinner? I make a mean frozen pizza. I'll try not to burn it."

"Dinner? What time is it?" I'm so out of it, I didn't check the time on my phone before I called.

"It's a quarter to seven," she says. "I'm starved."

"Quarter to seven? Crap!"

I overslept. The summer sun still filters brightly into my room, making it seem earlier than it is. Carlos is supposed to meet me at my office in fifteen minutes. I hobble out of bed looking for my shoes.

"Is a quarter to seven a bad time for spooning?" she quips. "I could maybe fit you in at eight-fifteen."

"No. I need to see you. Meet me at the restaurant. I have a meeting in fifteen, but I can get it over with in three minutes."

I'll show Carlos how to get around on my computer and let him have at it. Thank goodness Enrique had the foresight to digitize everything for all the restaurants and put it on the cloud. I'm confident Carlos can find what he needs. Then I can discuss it with him later—when I have a clearer head.

"Are you sure?" Olive asks. "You have a lot going on right now. I can see you tomorrow."

"I can't wait until tomorrow, Olive. I need to talk to you, and then I need to do other things to you. Preferably *now*."

"*Rrrowr*, tiger. So demanding."

"Get used to it, woman," I tease.

I can hear her shuddering breath over the phone line. If I could only touch her right this second, she'd internally combust in two point five seconds.

"I um… better get ready then," she rasps.

"Fifteen minutes, Olive."

I pull into the restaurant parking lot exactly fourteen minutes later—which isn't bad, considering I decided on a shower after doing the sniff test, brushed and flossed my teeth to a shine, and shaved. When I park my car, I see her standing near the front entrance. She's radiant in the pink-orange glow of the setting sun, her wild hair flapping in the breeze, and the brilliant smile spread over her angelic face.

As our gazes lock, my heart thunders in my chest.

Suddenly it's all clear to me. She is my future—and I want to run as fast as I can to begin my new life with her. Or at least take long, swift strides. With a laser focused intent to sweep her into my arms and kiss her to kingdom come, I go to her, almost gliding on air. My gaze trained only on her. I don't notice the men until they're in my path, crowding around me.

"And here I was thinking, you'd left me for another man," says the dark-haired one with a really nice-looking dress shirt. He's Churro. I'd remember that snaggletooth grin anywhere. "I have to admit, I was getting a little bit jealous."

He slings his arm over my shoulder, and the other two guys close in. I know the big guy as Roach. He's jamming something into my lower back. I'm ninety-eight percent sure it's not one of those massagers from Costco, so I don't even think about struggling. My eyes slice to Olive, willing her not to come this way. She seems confused, but not alarmed. From her point of view, it must look like I'm just chatting with a few guys. And I want to keep it that way. For her protection, the less she knows, the better.

"I was just out of town for the holiday," I say. "Barbe-quing… fireworks."

"How patriotic. Too bad fireworks can be so dangerous."

I cut him a look. "Like setting a building on fire?"

He probably used Cheetos as kindle.

"Oooh, yes. I heard about that. What a shame." He clicks his tongue. "It would be a travesty if something like that should happen again."

"Listen, I don't know where Pancho Ortega is. He won't answer my calls."

Churro slaps my shoulder and gives me a hard squeeze. "I have no more use for Pancho Ortega."

"Then what do you want?"

He points his chin across the parking lot where there's a classic, blue Volkswagen bus. Roach and the other guy take that as a cue and poke me to move it, Churro's arm still slung around my shoulder like we're the best of amigos.

"I just want to talk, that's all."

They lead me inside the bus, Churro and Roach slipping in with me. Seconds before they slam the door shut, my gaze shifts to Olive again. She runs inside the restaurant.

"Where are we going?" I hiss.

"Ah, that is a surprise, bromigo."

A mere month ago I would have imagined myself brave enough to say, "If you're going to kill me, do it now." But that's the thing about imaginations. When faced with a real-life situation such as this, all you can think about is your family and the woman you love, and you'll do anything to live for them.

Naturally, the fear still plays on my features like a bad drive-in movie, and that gives Churro ammunition to intimidate me even more.

"Relax, dude. You're not going to end up in a ditch somewhere."

He chortles and is joined by Roach and the other guy who's driving, blubbering with maniacal laughter.

"If I wanted to kill you, I would have done so already."

He laughs again and slaps my knee.

Eh, nope. That line isn't even funny in old mobster movies. I can just picture Joe Pesci or Robert DeNiro delivering that line with a Brooklyn-Italian accent instead of sounding like that turtle in *Finding Nemo*.

My phone goes off in my pocket, doing the double duty of sounding the ringtone *and* buzzing incessantly.

"I wonder who that could be," says Churro. "Could it be that babe waiting for you outside the restaurant? Well done, amigo."

I swallow hard. They saw Olive.

Churro jerks his chin for Roach to search my pockets. Roach finds my phone and hands it to Churro just as the ringing ends. Churro looks at the screen.

"Who's... Olive?"

"Just a stupid waitress."

He raises a brow. "Whoa! Doin' it with the waitress. I like your style."

"It's not like that. She's... annoying." I toss my hand to the side, trying to act casual about it. "We're probably gonna fire her soon."

I am really bad at lies, but I have to come up with something. I can't have Olive connected to me in any way. If anything goes down tonight and I don't make it, I don't want them going after her.

Churro narrows his eyes at me. "Why wait?"

Sucking in a breath through my nose, I hold it inside, hitching up one shoulder as I purse my lips.

"We gave her a warning."

He leans in and whispers in my ear. "If I want to terminate someone... I do it."

The phone rings again. Churro swipes the screen and hands it to me. "She's a little bloodhound, isn't she?"

The call is live, and even before I accept the phone from Churro, I hear Olive's voice.

"Hello? Ignacio?"

"Ignacio speaking," I say.

"Is… everything okay? Say the code word if you're being kidnapped. Oh wait, we don't have a code word. Am I on speaker phone? If so, hey anyone who's listening—I'm just joking. Ha ha."

Oh good heavens.

"Yes, I have to cancel our meeting today. I wanted to tell you in person, but we're going to have to let you go."

"Whaaaat?"

"Please gather all your personal belongings and leave the premises immediately."

Olive is quiet for a moment, and I hope she gets the hint. She's smart, no doubt about it. But she's also sensitive.

"So, does this mean spooning is off the table?"

"All the silverware is off the table," I say.

"Hmmm. I'll have to get back to you tomorrow with my reply. You know I need time to come up with something clever to say."

I'm trying hard not to laugh. "That won't be necessary."

"Can I at least get a letter of recommendation?"

"No can do. And I think it's better if you leave quietly without causing a fuss."

In other words, don't get involved.

"So, should I put your number on job applications in that little spot where they ask—"

"I don't care what you put on job applications, just please don't ever call me again."

I hang up before she gets any crazy ideas.

Churro raises a brow with surprise approval.

"Not bad."

He plucks my phone out of my fingers and slips it in his pocket. The rest of the van ride is more or less unremarkable, except for the little detail of being here against my will.

We reach our destination, which is in the middle of an industrial park. When we get out of the bus, Churro leads me to a nondescript warehouse.

I want to say, "Is this where you dump the bodies?" but instead I settle on, "What is this place?"

"The beginning of a beautiful partnership."

Okay, maybe not a dumping ground for his victims, but not Disneyland, either.

We go inside through a large roll-up door, and I don't know what I expected, but it wasn't this.

"It's just an empty warehouse," I say.

"Not exactly," says Churro. "Check this out. You are going to love this."

I am?

He takes me to through to a separate section of the warehouse only separated by a heavy plastic curtain. On the other side of the curtain, the temperature is a good fifty degrees cooler, and on highly stacked shelves are boxes of what appear to be cuts of meat.

Churro spins around with his arms out. "Eh? Eh? What do you think?"

"I think it looks like you're well stocked for a barbecue."

He points at me and grins. "I knew I liked this guy."

"I still don't understand why you brought me here."

"We're your new meat supplier."

"I don't need a new meat supplier."

"What does that have to do with anything?"

He laughs and pulls a box from the shelf with ease, tossing it to me. It weighs almost nothing.

"It's empty," I say.

"Of course it's empty. I don't want to deal with raw meat. Besides, Roach is a vegan."

He gestures to Roach, who is the burliest surfer I've ever seen. There's a guy somewhere beneath all that muscle I just know it.

"On paper, we'll be supplying seven hundred pounds per week for each restaurant you own."

"Seven hundred pounds? We don't go through that much meat in a week. We'll get audited."

"How do you think Pancho got away with it all those years without you even knowing?"

I close my eyes and take a breath. "A second set of books?"

"You catch on quick, Nacho. And just for cooperating with us, there will be some leftovers for you."

"Not everyone is for sale, Churro."

"Nacho, chill out. It's just business."

"And if I respectfully decline?"

"Then I'm afraid we can't be friends, and if we can't be friends, I can't offer you my protection."

"This was never my deal. It was all Pancho."

He swats his hand down and blows a raspberry. "Psht. Pancho's dead to me."

My blood turns to ice. "I can't believe I'm saying this, but please don't kill Pancho Ortega. He's just a weasel, nothing else."

He laughs. "Kill him? Why would I kill my own uncle?"

"Your uncle?"

I did not make that connection.

"My mom would have my hide. I just mean he's dead to me, not *dead* dead. Like, I don't care about him one way or another. It's just an expression, dude."

"Ah, got it. So when I say, 'You kill me,' it just means I think you're funny for even asking me to launder money for you, and we'll all laugh about it when we never see each other again."

"Ha ha. No. If you're not a friend of the Posse, you're an enemy of the Posse." He throws his hands up. "I don't make the rules, bro."

"It kinda looks like you do make the rules, Churro. Sorry, but I think we're done here."

"We are NOT done here!" He shouts, running to the nearest metal shelving unit and crashing it to the floor. Boy, *that* escalated quickly. Veins are popping out of his neck. "I'm done waiting."

"Well, I'm not your guy," I shout back. "Find someone else. Or get a real job like the rest of us."

He screams. Like really screams, and starts throwing chairs—he's basically a giant toddler having a temper tantrum.

I raise my hands, palms out, to try to calm him down lest he try to throw me next.

"Okay, okay, Churro. I'll tell you what. Pancho stole from us both. A lot of money. I'm not any happier with him than you are. But this is *his* mess. I will help you find him, and you can make him pay you back, or whatever, and I promise I'll walk away with no hard feelings. I'll drop the investigation on the fire and count all that money as lost. No harm, no foul, and we go our separate ways."

Churro stares at me for a moment, then looks between Roach and the other guy. I wonder where the other members are. From what I understand, there are at least a dozen surfers in The Point Break Posse, but it seems like Churro and Roach are the major players.

Just then, we hear a whack and then a cracking sound coming from outside. We all turn around and see something sticking out of the windshield of the bus. If I didn't know better, I'd think it looked a lot like…

"My ride!" cries Churro. "What the actual f—"

All you need is love.
But a little chocolate
now and then
doesn't hurt.

— Charles M. Schulz

Chapter Nineteen

OLIVE

I wait at the front entrance of the restaurant for Ignacio simply because I didn't want to walk through the kitchen in these heels. When I see him pulling into the parking lot, my breath catches somewhere in my esophagus. This man literally takes my breath away. Even from this distance, I can see the exact moment his chest rises—like a wave swelling his upper body into one giant smile. I smile right back, overcome with emotion.

But then three men approach him. At first, I thought they might be regular customers or buddies of his. But then they pile into a Volkswagen bus, taking him with them. I can only guess that these were the people he was supposed to meet, but something in Ignacio's expression sets off warning bells. Why would he ask to meet me here if his plan was to just leave?

The thing that throws me off is the casual way he went with them. When you get kidnapped in Jersey, thugs will throw you in an unmarked cargo van—or that's what I've seen on TV shows. In California, it seems, kidnappers accost you with a beach-mobile with surfboards on the roof rack.

I shouldn't jump to conclusions, but what else should I think? So I call Ignacio on his cell phone. He doesn't pick up on my first try. The second time I call, however, he answers, seemingly calm.

I realize, here, that even if he were being taken against his will, there would be no way for him to tell me. Should I worry? Is he okay? Who knows?

And then he fires me.

Fires me!

My first reaction hurts. After all we've been through! But then I quickly recover. This has to be his code phrase, like 'The eagle has landed', or 'The turd is in the punch bowl'.

If 'You're fired' isn't a code phrase, then I'll have a few choice code words for him when he gets back. But I doubt it. Something is amiss.

Under the circumstances, I'm calm and collected.

Heading inside the restaurant, I run into Rosa, who stops me in my path.

"Are you here to work? We're slammed."

"Uh, no. I was supposed to meet Ignacio."

She sighs. "We've got the Huntington Park customers coming here now. Carlos is waiting in Nacho's office."

"Who's Carlos?"

"Manager at Huntington Park. Are you sure you can't jump in? You'll get double pay. Of course you'll have to change out of that dress."

Gosh, I feel bad for Rosa, but I just can't. My boyfriend could be in danger.

"I'm so sorry but I have to find Ignacio. He just left with some surfer guys."

Rosa blinks with a confused expression. "Surfer guys? Okay, well, I need to get back to my tables. Can you tell Carlos that Nacho's running late? Or whatever's going on with that man. I can't keep up."

She hurries off and disappears into the crowd of patrons.

When I go into the kitchen, the cooks are bustling like I've never seen before. Most of the lunch cooks have left for the day, but a couple of the guys I know are still here. I get an appreciative whistle from one of them. I'm too focused on not slipping in these heels to acknowledge them properly.

The door to Ignacio's office is open, and there's a man inside, sitting across from Ignacio's desk.

"Carlos?" I ask, closing the door behind me.

He looks at me up and down (because who wears a

cocktail dress at a restaurant like this?), then glances back to the closed door.

"Yeah?" he says tentatively.

Now, I should probably mention that this guy is a hundred times more frightening than the surfers who took off with Ignacio. He wears a brown bandana around his shaved head, a white, sleeveless undershirt revealing tan skin completely covered in tattoos, and has a tough-looking goatee. He even has tattoos on his face—a face with a permanent scowl. I don't think he's scowling at *me* for any particular reason. I just think that's his resting face.

"I… I'm Olive," I say. "Ignacio's—"

"Ah! You're Nacho's old lady. Nice to mee-chu."

"Um, nice to meet you too. Listen, Ignacio said he had a meeting with someone at seven?"

"That would be chores truly."

"So he was supposed to meet you? Not three surfer-looking guys?"

"Surfer-looking guys? No."

"Well, as soon as Ignacio got here, he left with them in a V.W. bus."

"Way way way way wait. Back up. Nacho was here? Just now?"

"Yep."

"And he left with three surfer dudes?"

"Uh huh."

He snaps something out in Spanish I don't understand. Probably something curse-wordish.

"I knew something was going down, *esa*, but wasn't chure what."

"Going down? What do you mean by that?"

"The fire. I saw some guys hangin' around the restaurant about three days ago. They be acting all suspicious but I dinnit think twice, chew know? But if these *locos* are who I think they are… *órale*, Nacho's in deep *caca*."

"Deep… who do you think they are?"

"The Point Break Posse. Only the meanest surfer gang in Los Angeles."

"Surfer gang? That's really a thing?"

He shrugs, bobbing his head side to side. "Well, not really. I never heard of any other surfer gangs actually. But that doesn't mean they ain't around."

Surfer gangs. Arson. This is so nuts.

"We gotta do something," I say. "Call the police."

"Lady, I'm tight with the cops. I'll call my homies down at the precinct. You call Nacho's old man."

"Wait. Ignacio said something about a man… Francisco Ortega. Does this have anything to do with him?"

"Pancho Two? That fool? He's bad news, but I dunno about any connection with the Posse."

I reach into my tote bag for my phone. "I have his number."

Carlos raises a brow, which disappears into his bandana. "Better call Nacho's dad first. I'm going outside to make my calls. Then we can figure out what's going on with Pancho Two."

"Right. Thank you."

Carlos leaves me alone in the office, and I open my dialer only to realize I don't have anyone's number. Well, except for Pancho Two. I've got that. But Nacho's family? Nope.

Realizing it's a long shot, I go around to his side of the

desk to boot up his computer but spot an iPad. Contacts are on iPads, right?

There's a Post-It Note taped to the computer monitor with the iPad password in bold sharpie. I suppose that's for Rosa, or whoever else might need to get info for the restaurant system.

Once I'm in, I click on folders, searching for anything that looks not restaurant related. Honestly, gleaning important info from someone's device looks a lot easier in spy movies.

And then I notice a green icon, showing a notification. Clicking on it, I discover it's an app for finding lost devices —and people. I'm totally channeling my inner 007, navigating this app like a boss. It's not long before I find a blinking cursor on a map labeled 'My iPhone'. It has to be Ignacio.

Yes!

Clutching the iPad in my arms, I run out of the office in search of Carlos, but I bump right into Rosa, almost knocking heads.

"What's going on?" she asks frantically. "Carlos just bolted out of here. He said to tell you he had to rush out to take care of something with Señor Fransisco—Pancho One. Is everything okay? He looked spooked."

"Did he say where they were going?"

"No. Olive, what happened?"

I shake my head, not knowing where to start, and seriously pressed for time. Every minute counts.

"Okay, don't freak out but... Ignacio's been kidnapped by a surfer gang. I have his location right here." I hold up the iPad. "I need you to do me a favor. Call Carlos and tell him where I'm going. I'll ping you my location as soon as I get there."

"Wait, what? Are you serious? Kidnapped? Why?"

"I don't know. But I need to find him."

"Olive, what are you thinking? Call the police."

"Rosa, Carlos already called the police. That's why I need you to tell him my location."

"Let me get this straight. Nacho's been kidnapped, and you're going to stroll in there and… what? Rescue him? What exactly is your plan, *hija*?"

"My plan is to wait outside until the police arrive. And what if it's not a kidnapping? What if he went willingly?"

Even as the words leave my mouth, I know it's false hope. I'm ninety percent sure he was taken by force. Quietly and without struggle, but force just the same.

Rosa shakes her head. "I don't like this."

"I'll tell you what. If Ignacio has a find my phone app on this iPad, chances are there's one on his computer. Do a search for him and let Carlos know. But I have to get going now."

I wobble out of the restaurant and throw my shoes in the back seat as soon as I reach my car. With the iPad Wi-Fi switched to my phone's hotspot, I follow the map to find my man.

It's so strange. Other than a quickening in my pulse, I'm not a complete wreck. I feel like one of those badass women in action movies. If only I had the car to go with it. My putt-putt economy car barely makes the speed limit. Oh well.

The cursor on the map hasn't moved in a while, and I find the Volkswagen bus parked in front of an industrial warehouse. Making sure I stop my car out of sight, I ping my location to Rosa and wait. And wait. Aaaand wait.

After what seems like forever, I call Rosa. Maybe she's not getting my texts.

"Roger roger, birdwatcher, Operation Nacho Cheese is underway. Did you send the location to agent C? I have the scene under surveillance. Over."

"What the… Olive?"

"Shhh. It's Agent O. Don't blow my cover. Over."

"*Niña*, Carlos gave the address to *la policía*. They're coming soon. Are you hiding?"

"Affirmative. I'm in stakeout mode. My cover is not blown."

"*Ay Dios mio*. Get out of there."

"No! My boyfriend is inside. Afraid. Bargaining for his life. I'm not leaving until I know he's safe."

"Okay, okay. Just keep away from the danger, *por favor*."

"Roger that. I will stay put until backup arrives."

True to my word, I don't budge from the safety of my car. I'm just close enough to the warehouse that I can see if there's activity going in or out. It's pretty much quiet, and I'm starting to worry if the police are coming or not. What if they don't believe Carlos?

Suddenly, there's shouting and a clanging sound coming from inside the building. My heart catches in my throat.

Ignacio!

I can't wait another minute. I dial 911 and wail, "Heeeelp!" into the phone, leaving it on the passenger seat of my car for the first responders to locate me via GPS. Then I look for something—anything—to protect myself should someone find me. I just need to get close enough to hear what's going on inside that warehouse.

Checking the back seat, my eye catches on the gnomes Tom gave me. I quickly empty the contents of my tote bag and load it with the small gnomes first, then the big, heavy one.

I creep up to the building, all covert and sneaky. Adrenaline courses through my veins, my heart pounding in my chest. The Mission Impossible theme song plays in my head. I'm invisible—just like the mezuzah heist at Aaron's party.

I plaster my body against the wall, scooting closer to the roll-up door inch by inch. And then I hear Ignacio's voice, barely a mumble. He's saying something about Pancho.

By instinct, I peek around the corner, and that's when I see the man behind Ignacio, and he's got a rope. I have to do something. A distraction maybe, just to buy some time to break Ignacio out of there or else the police might arrive too late.

I reach into my bag and pull out one of the small gnomes. He's a cute little guy the size of a baseball, with rosy cheeks and a green pointy hat.

"Don't fail me, my friend," I whisper, kissing him on the nose. Then I throw him as hard as I can at the bus, cracking the windshield.

Wow. That didn't do much at all. The little gnome is just wedged into the windshield, butt first. With those rosy cheeks and the lopsided grin on his face, he looks like he's taking a dump on the dashboard.

There are a few more little gnomes left in my bag, but I

might have to throw the big one in order to distract the bad guys enough for Ignacio to escape.

I take the heavy gnome out of my bag, but just then, footsteps approach, and I hear one of the guys order the other one to investigate.

I try to make myself blend in with the wall as he comes outside, praying he doesn't see me. But he stops right outside the door, less than a foot away from me. If he turns around, we'll be face to face. So I act fast. Lifting the cement gnome in the air, I crash it down over the man's head with all my might—and he goes tumbling down.

Holy guacamole. I can't believe that worked. The guy is out cold.

Unfortunately, I'm not prepared for an encore, and when the two other surfers come rushing out, they don't get as close as the big guy.

They're too far away to sneak up on. So I throw my large bearded friend, hoping the short time I spent on the girls' softball team pays off.

I aim for their heads, but my gnome is incredibly heavy and crashes on the ground next to their feet.

The two men whip around, ready to kill.

The light-haired man charges at me and grabs me by the arm, yanking me out into the open. And that's when I see him. My Ignacio—with his jaw dropped all the way to Australia.

"Olive!"

The darker-haired surfer—I think he's the leader—barks out a laugh.

"Dude. I knew it." Then he saunters over to me and squeezes my face in one hand. "You're more than a waitress, aren't you?" He whistles, assessing me from head to foot. "Not bad, bromigo. Kudos to you, my man."

"Leave her alone," snaps Ignacio.

The dark-haired surfer stomps over to Ignacio. "I'm disappointed in you, Nacho. I really thought this was the beginning of a beautiful friendship. I don't know how your lady love found us, but now I'll have to go find out."

He jerks his head at the other guy, just as the big one is coming to.

"Put them in the cooler," he orders, then goes over to check on the guy I hit with the gnome.

The light-haired man yanks me by the arm and shoves me into a cold room, pushing Ignacio in behind me."

"Stay cool," he quips, and slides a heavy door, shutting us inside with a clank of a lever.

We're trapped inside a giant refrigerator.

Destiny may ride
with us today,
but there is no reason
for it to interfere
with lunch.

          – *Peter the Great*

"Olive, are you okay? What are you doing here?"

The beautiful woman I love blinks up at me and frowns.

"I was worried."

"So you just decided to throw gnomes around?"

She winces and darts her eyes around. "Yes?"

I pull her into a hug. "What am I going to do with you? And where are your shoes?"

She shivers in my arms.

"Sorry I botched up your rescue. I seem to ruin everything."

I kiss the top of her head.

"You do. You ruined me—and I'm so glad of it."

She smiles, tears forming in her eyes.

"You ruined me, too."

She looks around. "What is this place?"

"It's a meat cooler. Without the meat."

Laughing, she says, "I guess we're the meat. It's so cold. We're just going to have to strip down to keep each other warm with our body heat. Oh well."

"I don't think it will come to that. Here."

I take off my shirt and wrap it around her bare shoulders. She looks stunning in this dress, but I'd rather she not turn blue.

"Whoa, what's all that?" She's pointing to the wires taped to my chest.

"Well, Olive, I'm bugged."

Her jaw drops. "Bugged? Do you need me to tackle you into a cake?"

"Maybe later," I say, drawing her into me. "When we're… alone."

"Are you going to tell me what's going on?"

"I will. I promise. For now, we should wait for the D.E.A. to arrive."

"Carlos called the police," she says. "And your dad, apparently. But they should have been here by now."

"How did you find me?"

She squeezes her arms tighter around my waist. "Your *'Find my Phone'* app and my spy instincts."

"You're the most amazing woman I've ever known," I say. "What do you say about keeping that ring on your finger?"

She doesn't have time to answer because of the sounds of gunshots and shouting from outside. We both lie flat on the floor, even though we're probably safe in here. The floor is hard and cold. If I had more clothes to spread out on the floor for Olive, I would.

Ten minutes pass before the door to the meat cooler opens. I cover Olive's body with mine, bracing myself for the worst. But the man standing in the doorway is my dad, and right behind him are Carlos and Pancho Two.

The people who
give you their food
give you
their heart.

— Cesar Chavez

Chapter Twenty-One

IGNACIO

"We're just glad you're safe now," says Mom.

My parents called an emergency family meeting after last night's fiasco. I suppose this meeting is all about keeping the lines of communication open in the family—no matter what the subject is. I glance at Olive, who's sitting on the sofa next to me, holding my hand. We're both feeling the guilt.

Apparently, there were four sets of responders yesterday. The D.E.A. was listening to my wiretap, ready to move in once I gathered enough evidence to convict The Posse. Carlos had called friends of his on the police force, and they had my location thanks to Olive's spy prowess. Dad had forged a deal with Pancho Two, who was willing to make a plea bargain for intel on the capture of The Point Break Posse, so their contacts came to raid the warehouse, too. And Olive had called 911 in her panicked state, sending the police, the fire department, and an ambulance.

The D.E.A. caught the guy who drove the V.W. bus yesterday. He was found running from the scene. Later they raided the Posse clubhouse, arresting several other members.

Churro and Roach got away, but we're told they won't evade arrest for long.

After too much questioning, I finally got to rest, taking Olive back to my house to spoon all night. No seggsy cake time—just cuddling.

Now, we're all gathered in my parents' living room, discussing familial transparency. Even Edmund is here.

"From now on," says Dad. "We're all going to tell each other everything. No more secrets. And if any of you is involved in any kind of danger, or even financial trouble, we bring it to the family."

I know my dad isn't doing it on purpose, but he's projecting some major Don Corleone vibes. He's even sporting the beginnings of a mustache.

Everyone agrees to this new pact, even though I see the shifting eyes between Francesca and Edmund.

Mom claps her hands together.

"Great. Now we have a wedding to look forward to."

I clear my throat. "Actually, I have an announcement."

All heads turn to me.

"There will be no wedding. At least, not mine."

I glance over at Francesca and wink. She nods her head and exchanges a look with Edmund.

I go on. "Olive and I… we're not engaged. In fact, we've been faking our relationship for weeks. The first time I met her was at Enrique's wedding."

Mom gasps, and Dad says a few words in Spanish I wish I could unhear.

"You're not serious," says Mom. "Why would you do that?"

"It's my fault," says Olive. "We were just trying to make my ex-boyfriend jealous, and then you saw us… fake kiss-ing… and so did Abuela. I swear I didn't mean to let it go this far."

"I'm the one who lied about it," I say. "I dragged Olive into this. Don't blame her."

Mom waves her fingers at our entwined hands. "But… look at you two. And we want to keep Olive."

I wrap my arm around Olive's shoulders. "I'm keeping Olive. Maybe I'll share her every once in a while."

"So, are you fake dating or not?" asks Mateo. My other brothers are equally confused, adding to the questions thrown at me.

"Not anymore," I say, beaming at my beautiful—not fake—girlfriend. "She's stuck with me."

"But," adds Olive. "I think I should give this back."

She wiggles the ring off her finger and hands it to my

mom. Mom gives her a quizzical look, but then narrows her eyes at me.

"What did you mean when you said, 'at least not mine'?"

I glance over at Francesca, who smiles gratefully and stands up with Edmund, holding hands. She pulls the chain around her neck, revealing the ruby ring that was hiding under her blouse.

"We have an announcement."

Mom screams. My brothers shout and laugh. Dad gets up and wraps his arms around Francesca and Edmund.

"It's about time, you gringo wussy. We've all been waiting."

"You have?" says Edmund. "We've been waiting for the right time to tell you."

All my brothers crowd around Francesca and Edmund, offering their congratulations, just like they did a few days ago to Olive and me. Hugs are exchanged all around, and Mom is already pressing them to set a date.

Olive and I watch the bustle, happy for my sister and relaxing into this new reality for our own relationship. It's new, but I have a feeling it's forever.

Once the excitement dies down a little, and Mom wanders into the kitchen to serve some celebratory ice cream, I take her to the side and apologize, especially to her, for the deception.

"You're the last person I want to lie to," I say. "I want you to know that."

She pats me on the cheek. "I know more than you realize. Just make sure you always tell the truth to that woman. She sees the sun and moon in you."

"It's just a reflection of herself in my eyes, that's all."

Mom winks at me with a big grin.

"And Mom? Can you hold on to Abuela's ring for me? I have a feeling I'll need it sooner than later."

THE END

A party
without a cake
is really
just a meeting.

          – Julia Child

Epilogue
IGNACIO

"Happy Hanukkah."

I'm surprising Olive tonight by coming home an hour early to help her get everything ready for tonight. Dad's bringing the brisket, and several of my siblings will be here later. Olive's dad is in town for the holidays, so we're celebrating all eight nights with him. We offered him our spare bedroom, but when January gave him a suite at the Madison Hotel, he dropped our invitation like a hot potato knish. Apparently he's being treated like a king at the Madison.

As I walk through the front door, I'm excited to give Olive her present for tonight. I found leggings with Hanukkah gnomes on a repeat pattern. She'll love them.

No sooner do I close the door behind me, the smoke hits me in the face. The fire alarm is going off, and I can hardly breathe.

"Olive? What are you burning now?" I swat my hands through the smoke to get through the fumes.

"Nothing," she calls from the kitchen. "Everything's under control."

I reach the kitchen to find Olive in a frilly apron, using a magazine to fan the smoke away from the stove.

I set down the present and grab some junk mail and climb on a chair to fan at the smoke detector on our high ceiling.

As soon as we quiet the alarm, I go to see what Olive is attempting to cook. All I see are charred, black hockey pucks—and a whole bucketload of oil in the pan.

"Mmmm," I say. "Looks delish."

She squints one eye. "Maybe if we scrape off the outside…"

"You mean it's not supposed to be lumps of coal?"

"As a matter of fact, Chef Crabby Cakes, coal is for your stocking."

I curl my arms around her from behind and yank her into me. "Because I've been a bad boy?"

She wiggles in my arms, and I dig my teeth into the

sweet flesh of her neck. "How much time do we have until your dad gets here?"

She jabs me with her elbow. "You're supposed to pick him up."

"Hmmm, at least an hour, then." I tug at her apron strings.

She giggles and spins around to face me. "I wanted to surprise you with latkes. Why are you home so early?"

"Maybe I missed my wife." I tug her flush against me and nibble her ear. "Upstairs, woman."

"Guuuh, guests will be here soon."

"Not for a while," I rumble, trailing kisses along her jaw. My lips press onto the corner of her mouth, coaxing her.

She throws her head back. I've almost got her. Then her eyes dart to the counter where I left her present.

"Ooooh! What's that?"

I wrapped it in blue and silver paper, which is how we differentiate it as *not* a Christmas gift. We have more than our fair share of those. The tree is already surrounded with piles and piles of red and green boxes.

"That?" I feign ignorance. "How did that get there?"

Olive bounces up and down, still wrapped in my arms. "Can I open it now?"

"Um aren't we supposed to wait until after dinner?"

"Ignacio, would you rather I open all my Christmas presents? Because I totally will."

"Okay, okay." I pass the boyfrent to her, not that I can keep it from her. "Here."

She snatches the box from my hands and annihilates the wrapping paper. Shreds of blue and silver fly through the air in a frenzy.

When she gets to the box, she rips it open, tearing through the tissue inside.

"Haaaa!" she gasps, tossing the box on the floor with one hand while holding up the clothing with the other. "Hanukkah Harry leggings! I love them."

She throws herself at me and smacks a thousand kisses all over my face. I wish I had another gift for her so she'd kiss me like that all night long. Then again, she doesn't need much persuasion on a regular day.

"Okay, now your turn," she says, clasping her hands together.

"My turn?"

I told her she doesn't have to get presents for me, but she loves it so much, I humor her. Yesterday it was a pair of socks.

She runs out of the kitchen to the living room where we keep the tree, so I follow her. Climbing over the plethora of other presents, she fishes out a present from the back, and pops up with a huge grin on her face.

"What are you up to, gorgeous? I know that look."

"What look?"

"That look. You have something up your sleeve. Is this a gag gift?"

Olive's mouth wags open like she's offended—which she's not. Nothing offends her.

"Can't I give my husband a gift for the Festival of Lights?"

I glance down at the sloppily wrapped gift. She wrapped it in red and green paper. It's something soft—like a T-shirt or something, judging by the bumpy shape. And it appears she used a whole roll of scotch tape to secure the paper.

"Are you trying to drive me mad?"

She knows I like to meticulously remove the tape and save the paper. This paper is barely intact, which is partly why she used so much tape.

She shrugs. "I'm not the best gift wrapper. I miscalculated the measurement and fell short, so I had to cut some other scraps and piece them together like Frankenstein's monster.

She licks her lips, glancing from the present to me, back to the present.

"Nacho! I can't stand it anymore. Open it."

I grin, ripping one little corner excruciatingly slow… "This is killing you, isn't it?"

"Ignacio!" She digs her fingers into the paper and yanks. Really, this woman has no self- control.

"Come upstairs and I'll give you more stuff to rip off," I tease.

She smacks my chest and continues to unwrap my gift for me. Next thing I know, I'm holding up a tiny red and green onesie.

"Is this another elf costume for your garden gnomes?"

She jumps up and down, clapping her hands. "Yes! It's for my little gnome. Do you like it?"

I turn it over in my hands. "Besides the fact that it's not a Hanukkah gift? Nor is it for me? Yeah. I think it's great."

"You really think so?"

I press a gentle kiss on her lips. I love anything that makes her happy. "Yes, my love. Which lucky gnome gets to wear this costume?"

She points to her belly. "This one."

I furrow my brow. "You ate a gnome?"

She bites her lower lip and twists excitedly. "Something like that."

Stealing the costume from me, she drapes it over the front of her body and pulls my hand to touch her belly. Her face is absolutely radiant.

Waves of awareness rush through me. "You… you're having a…"

She nods, grinning and tearing up. "A little gnome."

Joy floods my heart. "Olive!"

I don't have any other words. This is definitely better than socks.

I gather her in my arms and hold her to my chest. I want to keep her here forever. Safe and sound.

"Are you happy?" she asks.

"The happiest," I reply. "I'm over the moon."

She lifts her chin to meet my gaze and winks. "Yay. Since you're in a good mood, you can make a new batch of latkes while I take a bath."

"Nah. I think my services are put to better use washing your back. And all the other parts you can't reach."

"You do need to practice pampering me." She taps a finger on her temple.

"Yes! I absolutely do."

"Okay," she says coquettishly. "See that small gold present? That's lavender oil. Me and my tired feet will be waiting."

She saunters out of the room, tossing her apron on the floor.

"Hang on." I move to chase her, but then backtrack for

the gold present. "You bought a Christmas gift? For yourself?"

She continues up the stairs, swaying her hips on purpose.

"You want to unwrap it, or what?"

Why do I get the feeling she's not talking about the little gold present?

"I do," I say thickly. "Very much."

"Better call off our guests, then."

I have my phone out before she takes another step up the stairs.

Happy holidays to us, and to us a good night.

THANK YOU

You, dear reader, are amazing.

Thank you for spending time with Ignacio and Olive. I hope you fell in love with them as I did.

If you want more Precio Brothers, be sure to pick up book one in the series: **The Hate Zone**.

Also, don't miss book three in the Precio Brothers series, where we get to know Mateo and his best friend's little sister in **Just Amigos**.

Fear Of Missing Out can be a real bummer, right? Not to worry. I got you covered. Visit me at gigiblume.com

Also, get all the deets on future releases, first-look cover reveals, freebies, romcom book recs, current bookish news, and questionable inspirational quotes in my Sunday email blast.

Oh, and get a free book as a thank you gift, just for subscribing. Cool, huh?

https://BookHip.com/CKMQST

Social media more your thing? Follow me in all the places. (Hint: Instagram is my favorite)

Facebook: @gigiblume

Instagram: @gigiblume

TikTok: @gigiblumeauthor

ROMCOMS IN THE GIGIVERSE

BACKSTAGE ROMANCE

Confessions of a Hollywood Matchmaker

Love and Loathing

Secrets of a Hollywood Matchmaker

Driving Miss Darcy

The Friend Act

PRECIO BROTHERS

Messy Love

The Hate Zone

Nacho Boyfriend

Just Amigos

ACKNOWLEDGMENTS

Shout out to Katie Bailey for being my cheerleader and butt-kicker. You saved this book. Thank you! And to Summer Dowell who, with the help of her own tiny surfer gang, suggested the name Point Break Posse.

Thanks to my author besties, who are incredibly supportive and make me laugh every day. I love you all.

Special kudos to Jenn for the tortilla slap idea. I just had to put that in the book. Your reels are always so much fun.

And, it's fitting I should offer my gratitude to my husband for listening to my ramblings while bouncing ideas off him, answering my incessant questions about the restaurant business, and for offering me terrible advice on what I should *really* write about. Sorry, dude. Not gonna happen. XOXO